D0098223

THE HEALER

Also by Donna Freitas:

The Unplugged Series
Unplugged
The Body Market
The Mind Virus

The Survival Kit
The Possibilities of Sainthood

THE HEALER

DONNA FREITAS

HARPER TEEN
An Imprint of HarperCollinsPublishers

HarperTeen is an imprint of HarperCollins Publishers.

The Healer

Copyright © 2018 by Donna Freitas

All rights reserved. Printed in the United States of America.

No part of this book may be used or reproduced in any manner whatsoever without

written permission except in the case of brief quotations embodied in critical

articles and reviews. For information address HarperCollins Children's Books, a

division of HarperCollins Publishers, 195 Broadway, New York, NY 10007.

www.epicreads.com

ISBN 978-0-06-266211-8

Typography by Michelle Taormina

18 19 20 21 22 PC/LSCH 10 9 8 7 6 5 4 3 2 1

❖

First Edition

To my father and his family, who came from the Azores, and who fed me sweet bread on Sundays as a child and malasadas on feast days

And to all my friends who, like me, prefer to dwell in the liminal spaces

PROLOGUE

When you love someone, you will do anything for them. You will travel to the ends of the earth and bargain away your soul to sorcerers if it might give you just one more day together. You will crawl on your knees until they are scraped and bloodied. You will give away your money, your possessions, your dignity. You will throw yourself upon the mercy of doctors, of witches, of criminals.

You will trade your life for theirs in a heartbeat. You will if you know this is the bargain before you, if someone lays it out plainly, like the price tag on a trinket you might buy at the store.

Your life. For theirs.

Simple.

I know this now. I know so many other things I didn't back then. Helplessness and hopelessness. Desperation. Love beyond all other loves. Love so big and vast that words fail. It would have been an easy decision.

My life. For theirs.

The problem comes when you've no idea that in choosing your own life, you've given theirs away.

PART ONE

Now & Then

ONE

People say I am a saint.

They sell T-shirts with my image. They come to me with gifts and offerings. A vase full of flowers. A beautiful dress. A flat-screen TV that sits unwatched because I am not allowed the luxury of television. They mean well, but sometimes I hate them. Sometimes, when some earnest soul comes to wash my feet because this is all the person has to give, I want to lash out. I want to kick them in the jaw with my brown bony foot. I don't, of course. But I think about it.

"Hello, Marlena," Gertie says, reverently, from the doorway of her shop.

I am strolling by on the street, parting the seas of people like Moses. No one dares get too close.

Gertie wrings her hands, eyeing me.

I stop before her, and she takes a step back out of respect. I wish she wouldn't. The breeze carries the briny scent of seaweed baking in the sun, of the clean cold ocean, of fish being pulled in by the boats.

The tail of a kite with my name stitched across it flutters in the open window of Gertie's store. She has it on sale for $34.99. Gertie hesitates, then offers, "I think maybe these are the last days of summer, yeah?"

I tear my gaze from the kite, from the seven-day candle she has burning on the sill emblazoned with a photograph of me when I was seven. In it, I'm wearing a white shift, much like the one I have on now, which will be much like the one I wear tomorrow. My mother insists these cotton sheaths are simple ways of reminding others of who I am, of my purity, of the great gift bestowed upon me at birth. Lately I'm tempted to lie down in the dirt and roll around like a dog. Then I would arrive home filthy and cackling to my scandalized mother, hair wild, a devil child.

My long sleeves cling to my skin in the humidity. "Do you think so?" I say to Gertie, mostly to be polite, but her comment about the end of summer has my brain churning like a waterspout.

She nods. Stares like I am a ghost, or a wraith come to carry her away to some fearful place. "Sometimes I think this heat wave is never leaving us. But they're saying that once it does, summer is over."

I nod. "I'm sure you're right. See you later, Gertie."

I hurry down the street, past the other shops selling their framed photographs of the most famous moments of my life, little china babies that are supposedly me, tiny bottles of water I purportedly blessed but didn't. In the window of the Almeidas' bakery is a stone statue of me, nearly as tall as I am. It is covered in colorful slips of paper, prayers that the sick have left behind in the hope that petitioning this replica of me is as good as petitioning the real thing. As I walk, the hem of my dress gets taken up by the hot breeze, baring my knees. The tourists stare and whisper. They pull out their phones to snap pictures. I raise an arm, bury my face in the crook of my elbow. They step back when I get close, like Gertie did, as if I might be contagious. I remind myself they are only doing this out of respect.

So much respect, everywhere I turn.

I am sick of this, sick with it, sick from it.

What happens when the Healer gets sick? Who will cure her?

I reach the edge of Main Street and turn down the hill, cross the street toward the beach. A car stops to let me pass, the driver's eyes widening when he recognizes me. His hands are gripping the steering wheel like it's the only tether holding him to earth.

I keep on going until I get to the rickety wooden ramp that leads down to the sand, ignoring the stares of nearby families, children playing with pails and shovels, splashing happily in tide pools. I do my best to ignore the other boys and girls my age, the way they look at me, girls in bikinis showing off so much tanned skin, boys touching their arms, even their flat stomachs. I try not to be jealous. I try not to think of the boy named Finn who I wish would touch my stomach and make the skin all over my body flush. I try to not care about how strange I must look in my thin cotton dress, like some child from another time and place, a girl escaped from an asylum.

One by one, I take the slippers from my feet and toss them aside. My legs move me forward with purpose, right to the ocean's edge. I hesitate there, wondering how long it will be before the rumors reach my mother's ears, knowing that I don't have much time, so I shouldn't waste any. The waves coming into the shore sizzle as they stretch toward my bare toes, and I inhale the pungent scent of seaweed. My hair flies in the wind, its knots and tangles visible in my shadow.

I've longed for the heat wave to be over, I've wished for it, even prayed for it, but suddenly I take it all back, wanting this stretch of humidity to go on and on, willing away the icy winter cold that will surely come to our New England town within a few months and not leave us until the first warm days of spring.

A little girl stares at me from the place where she sits, building a dribble castle across her legs. "Are you an angel?" she asks.

I watch the way the castle slides down her knees. Then I shake my head.

"No," I tell her.

I'm tired of being the angel.

This is the thought that pushes me forward again, that compels my feet until I am ankle-deep, then knee-deep, then waist-deep in the waves, white dress and all. When the ocean swirls up around my chest, I dive under.

A too short while later, I pick my way across the sand, everything dripping, dress and hair and skin, shoes in hand. I go the back way toward home to avoid the eyes greedy for gossip, the people hoping for a photo. This is not the image of me they expect or want, my white dress turned nearly transparent by the sea and clinging to the curves of my body, curves my mother wishes she could pray away. I used to try to pray them away, too. It's far better when a healer has the stick-straight figure of an innocent girl. When the girl starts to look like a young woman, some people fear she is a witch. I pull the soaking dress away from my skin, but it only puckers back against me. I look around but thankfully I see no one else to disappoint.

The town, the tourists, they all want the angel Marlena.

The Healer Marlena, virginal and pure and divine.

And I have behaved badly today.

The guilt cuts across me in the wind and I hang my head, wrap my arms around my middle. The town's survival depends on my existence, my continued ability to heal the old lady who cannot walk, the young boy who seems trapped inside his mind. The broken heart of a man who has lost his wife and the deadened eyes of the woman who cannot see. The sick and the grief-stricken come to me and I lay my hands on them, my precious, God-touched, miracle-making hands. The contact between my skin and theirs,

9

my flesh and theirs, somehow sets them free. People come from all over to be at one of my audiences. They fly, they drive, they hitch-hike. Some even walk, the most devout making the last mile on their knees, arriving scraped and bloodied, pebbles embedded in their skin. Just for a glimpse. Just to be near me.

Hundreds of years ago, men and women claimed visions, special gifts that allowed them to heal, to have intimate knowledge of the divine, of God, to live suspended in ecstasy. They were called mystics. I've read everything I can get my hands on about them. Most wrote about their experiences in poetry, in prose, reaching for anything and everything to describe what they saw, how they felt, who they were. Hildegard of Bingen is my favorite. She was a real doctor, studying the way that plants and herbs could heal the sick. Her visions led her to write, like everyone else, but also to compose music. And make art. She drew and painted her visions.

I, too, am an artist.

But I am more like Julian of Norwich. She enclosed herself in the walls of a church and lived there in a tiny stone cell. Isolated, in prayer. People would pilgrimage to speak to her through a sliver in the stone, to ask for her intercession, for her help. Being near Julian was like being near God. She was an anchorite, drawing down God from the heavens to the earthen floor and pinning him there. Her life's purpose was to hold the world steady with her body and soul.

A car turns the corner up ahead and slows as it approaches. It's

Mrs. Jacobs. A knowing smile spreads across her lips. Mrs. Jacobs is one of my doubters. She thinks I am a fake.

I raise my arm. A cascade of water drips from my sleeve as I wave. I can't stop trying to win over Mrs. Jacobs.

She drives off without waving back.

What will she say to others? What rumors will she spread?

My mother is always reminding me how it only takes one misstep to ruin a girl with a reputation like mine. I must be above reproach, holier-than-thou in being and word. I used to agree, used to be so obedient. Happy to shut myself away from the things of this world like Julian did. Grateful to be chosen.

My shoulders curve forward as I trudge up the hill, sand chafing my calves.

When I was a child, I used to love the stature that comes with my gift, that people brought me shiny toys to thank me, that when I got up on the stage at the United Holiest Church, the audience would hush. I could do no wrong. I could scream. I could writhe and faint. I could cry out with joy and laughter. People expect this from me. Apparently, the power to heal lies in frenzy.

Now that I am older, I am more subdued.

My mother has taken to complaining about this.

"Marlena Imaculada Oliveira," she'll say, using my full name so I know we are talking business. "People don't come to our church to see you standing there, like a child afraid to enter the water." Then she'll sigh and look at me with those familiar black eyes, eyes identical to mine. "You could at least raise your arms and call out to God now and then. You used to be so good at this. You used to love this work."

"Yes, Mama," I respond. "I know."

I still do love it. The visions, I will always love. The colors and emotions that flood my body along with them. But lately my gift feels tainted. A weight I carry, an anchor chaining me to the sea-floor.

This thought nearly makes me laugh.

I really am an anchor, like Julian.

I, too, draw down miracles from the heavens. But unlike Julian I also draw tourists from all around to spend their money in the shops. Through my gift and the sacrifices that go with it, I anchor the town and everyone in it. That is my job, has always been my life's purpose. It's all I've ever known.

But I want to know more. I want to know *other* things.

The heat of the sun bears down on me, the salt from the sea turning the cotton of my dress stiff and rough. The house where I live with my mother appears ahead, perched on a bluff above the sparkling ocean. As I pass the sea grass and the cattails that border our yard, I stretch my arms wide and high and turn my face toward the sky. Soak up the world around me. Let the world lift me up.

I am unmoored.

TWO

It is three years ago. I am fifteen and there is a boy my age in the front row of the church.

He is the first person I see when I step out onto the stage. His eyes are the pale gray color of glass worn smooth by the sea, his long legs bent at sharp angles in the chair that is too small for him. The outline of his shoulders shows through the fabric of his T-shirt. His mouth forms a small smile. A mocking one.

My skin burns hot. It prickles under the heavy dress I'm wearing. I will show him who I am and then we'll see if he still wears a grin. I am not someone to be ridiculed. My gift is a thing of beauty. Worthy of reverence.

I lift my chin. Take a step forward. Walk until I am parked in front of him on the stage, looking down at his shiny black hair. I want him to see me. To study the girl who is about to perform miracles.

The boy tilts his head upward, watches me with a stare that is unwavering. Like he can see straight through the fabric covering my body. Like he might want to do just this if only I'd let him.

How dare he? I think.

Then, *What would it be like, if I let him?*

His eyes travel across me, head to toe. I feel them like fingertips on skin. I swallow. The flush rolls over my cheeks. What does he think when he looks at me? Why can't I stop looking back at him?

But I can and I will and I do.

I turn slightly, move in a different direction, take in the crowd gathered for my Saturday audience. The church is packed. People kneel in the aisles, stand crushed together in the back like fish. All of them are here for me, to see me, to experience the healing power of my hands. My mother stands off to the right side of the room. She catches my eye and nods.

My entire body tingles with static. I am a lightning bolt readying to brighten the world. To strike at the sea. The storm of emotion in the room rises upward, pressing outward, filling every corner and hidden space.

I move through it.

Walking into the audience is like wading into the ocean. Waves roll across the room and over my body, my skin a sponge. Hope, then despair. More hope, fear, dismay, relief, joy. Hope again. Disappointment. Resolve. Bitterness. Sorrow. Love. Pain. Rage. More hope. Five minutes pass, ten, fifteen. I am soaked with emotion. I take it in without falter. Each feeling is a long strand of seaweed, swirling around my limbs, wrapping around my knees and my thighs. Clinging. Covering me.

People get up from their seats and swell toward me, some of them shouting.

"Marlena!"

"*¡Aquí, aquí!*"

"I need you!"

I lean forward. Raise my arms to them. "I am here!"

A line forms in the center aisle. Each week, there is a waiting list for healings, a list I am supposed to stick to. My mother informs me who is at the top and seats them in a special section. A woman holding a baby moves through the masses to the end of the platform. The staff helps to make room for her. I walk to the edge and crouch down. The wide skirt of my dress billows around me, suspends my body on an exquisite silken raft. I can already feel my gift gathering strength.

The woman lowers her eyes. She is shaking, the tiny baby wrapped in blue shaking with her.

I reach out and touch her cheek. "Please. Don't be afraid."

She returns her eyes to me. "*Mijo,* Miguel, *es . . .*" She doesn't finish. Tears roll down her face, wetting my fingers.

"It's okay," I tell her. "I know what to do."

The mother holds the baby out to me and I take him in my arms. I adjust my position so I am cross-legged underneath my dress. I cradle him, I whisper to him, I press the soft skin of his forehead to my own. I kiss his tiny nose and each one of his fingertips. He squirms and whimpers. His suffering makes my eyes sting with tears. It is a rusty color, a putrid halo edged around his little form.

The crowd hushes, watching, hovering, a curious school of fish.

The wave of my gift is gentle, rippling from my heart like a soft swell on a day when the ocean is glass. It moves easily through the shore of the infant's sickness. I can see everything inside him, straight to the sandy bottom of his blue-green soul. I close my eyes until his soul is all I know, until I am standing inside it, until all of its secrets are also my secrets. My gift presses right through his suffering, until everything about this baby in my arms is as blue-green and calm as the beautiful glass-ocean.

When I open my eyes and look into his, they are wide and looking back at me, his face no longer scrunched in pain. "You are precious, aren't you?" I say to him, before handing the tranquil bundle back to his mother. Her tears have dried and she is watching me with an uncertain expression.

"He's going to be fine," I tell her, because he is.

I rise up from my crouch, arranging my dress, and await the next petitioner, and the next and then the next. One after the other, they come to me, and the process repeats. I go and go and go until I am near collapse, until I am dry as a riverbed in drought, until my mother announces to everyone that my audience is over. My brain barely registers her words because it has grown murky, shot through with the ink of exhaustion. But a satisfied current of peace buoys me. The posture of my body is proud and sure.

As I ready to leave the room, I know the eyes of the boy in the front row are still on me, that his eyes have been on me for hours because somehow I could feel them underneath everything else. I wish I could see if his mockery has transformed into awe. I wish I could know his name. I wish I could talk to him. I wish I could have the conversation with him that I keep imagining, which goes something like *Hello, my name is Marlena*, and he responds, *Hi, I'm Guillaume*, because for some reason I decide he is French, and then says to me, *I have so many questions—would you like to go for coffee?* I wish I could banish these wishes, because healers are meant to walk among the people but not be of them. My only purpose is to protect my gift. To live for it and only it. To let it be enough for me. Like Julian. Like Hildegard. Like all the mystics and saints.

The backstage door is open and I sweep through it in a streak of expensive white satin, disappearing from the church and all those watchful eyes. His eyes.

I am safe.

THREE

I sneak inside the house, hoping my mother is out, or taking a nap. She likes taking naps on the hot, humid days of this heat wave. Our house is enormous, an old coastal New England beauty, graying and weathered, with views to the ocean on three sides. In every room with the windows open you can hear the waves crashing against the rocks. Even with the windows closed you can hear them if the water is rough enough. I will never tire of hearing the ocean.

I tiptoe into the kitchen, leaving a trail of sand behind me.

It's quiet.

"Hello?" I call out.

There is no response.

My mother isn't here. Fatima, our maid, must be out for the afternoon, too.

I let out a long breath.

While the house is all traditional New England on the

outside—long wooden clapboards, rustic and worn from the salty sea air and the harsh winter storms—the inside is newly renovated with every comfort a person could want. The kitchen is state-of-the-art, spotless, stainless-steel appliances gleaming alongside white countertops and cabinets, the exact kitchen my mother picked out of a design magazine. The floors in the house are heated. Plush couches and chairs with their perfectly puffed and color-coordinated pillows sit there invitingly in the living room, an arrangement also plucked straight from one of my mother's magazines. The entire first floor is open, so we can see the ocean out of every window whether we are in the kitchen or lounging reading a book. Gauzy white curtains flutter in the hot breeze. Fresh flowers dot the tables, arrangements delivered weekly from the best florist in town.

My mother spares no expense. She loves to spend our money. My money.

I fill a glass with water and guzzle it down, gasping for breath when it's empty. Then I fill it again and drink this one slowly. My cheeks still feel warm with the sun.

We used to live in a tiny cottage built by the hands of my grandfather, Manuel Oliveira, the next town over. My mother grew up in that house, cramped by the endless clutter of my grandmother, who filled the space with glass figurines and other knickknacks, displayed on shelves also built by my grandfather. There was a chicken coop in the yard, and they raised pigs and fished.

My grandparents and Mama immigrated from a tiny archipelago of islands called the Azores when she was six, determined to make a new and better life. On a map, the archipelago is midway between the west coast of Portugal and Morocco, but the islands are so far from land they may as well be their own country. My mother was born on São Miguel, the biggest one. It is an ancient place, small and isolated, where people live simply off the food they catch from the sea and the land, their days divided by the sacred rituals of the liturgical calendar and the rhythms of the sea. It is a religious place, where it is as likely as not that the entire population will be gathered in the streets parading a statue of Jesus across the island, holding candles and singing in harmony. A place where a healer like me could easily emerge, where people are as ready and willing to believe in miracles as they believe the sun will rise every morning after the moon disappears from the sky.

When my mother and I lived in her childhood house, she did her best to keep the rooms tidy, the one bedroom, the living room with the kitchen along the back wall, the narrow bathroom at the other end. I slept on a bed next to hers and played on the worn shag carpet near the kitchen, my mother stepping around me as she cooked. Steaming soups stocked with bitter greens and beans, spicy sausages cradled in bright roasted sweet peppers, great domed sweet breads steaming and fresh from the oven. My grandmother's glass figurines sat there on the shelves, dusty ballerinas twisting and turning, spinning their tulle tutus for an audience of two, perched in between the elaborate portraits of Mary and Jesus that my grandmother hand carried from Portugal. I used to love to play with the great cookie tin of buttons my grandmother left behind when she died, spreading them on the floor in lines and circles, counting them, admiring their colors and shine.

I was happy in that house. It was perfect for my child-sized self, small and cozy. I loved feeding the chickens. I gave them names. Charlotte. Jason. Alvina. Josépha. I would go and hide under the bed when my mother would wring their necks before we would eat them for dinner. She would talk to me about her life with my grandparents while I sat on the floor of the kitchen, surrounded by the buttons of my grandmother, sorting the pink ones from the rest like raisins from a box of cereal. Mama would wash the kale that would go into the soup for lunch, telling stories about the pigs they'd raised, about the toys my grandfather made for her in his carpentry workshop in the basement, about my grandmother's talent for cooking. Eventually she'd pull the big bitter leaves out of the icy water, soaked and dripping, to dry in a colander that sat on the counter. I would arrange and rearrange the buttons, forming them into a coil like the pearly pink insides of a snail.

This was before I became famous, before the roadside stands hawking candles with my face painted on the glass, the T-shirts and coffee mugs and wooden signs to hang above mantels and altars. Before the news of my gift spread far beyond our town and my mother moved us to a new and bigger house, this giant house where we live now, and she became obsessed with my growing renown and all that it could offer us.

Somewhere during those early years, I'd become my mother's hope, her own salvation, the perfect child healer, as devout as Julian of Norwich. I let my gift mold everything that I was, let my mother mold everything about me, happy that my gift seemed to ease the pain of her past. That it pulled us up and out of the hardship of poverty and gave my mother riches she thought she would never see. In return, she loved me with all that she was and I was never lonely. But lately, the more I begin to love the world, the more my mother begins to hate me.

I put the empty glass in the sink and head upstairs to my room. It's on a different floor than my mother's. She likes her privacy, and the grandiosity of having an entire wing to herself. She used to invite me to sleep in her bed, but the last time she did was years ago.

There is a step that creaks loudly and I avoid it out of habit and keep on going. I grab some underwear from a drawer and head into the bathroom to strip off my dress, the fabric coarse and itchy with sand, and get in the shower. Soon I am washed clean, my hair free of its knots and tangles, of my forbidden swim. I dry off, put on a new white sheath, and wander down the hall to a room at the far end of the house.

The gift room.

It's where we store the offerings we can't use or that I'm not supposed to use, until the appointed day each month when Goodwill comes to pick them up. You'd be surprised how quickly this room fills, sometimes the gifts stacked nearly to the ceiling, teetering like a misshapen wedding cake.

There's one gift in particular that draws me. My mother scoffed at it, was shocked that someone would think it appropriate. Ever since it arrived in its big box carried by the UPS man I've been thinking about it, and wishing we didn't have to give it away.

I move past the unopened boxes filled with iPads and game consoles, lamps and blenders and other household objects, until I get to the clothing. People send us piles and piles of clothing, some of it fit for a girl ten years my junior. I search until I find what I'm looking for buried under a stack of dresses I would have liked when I was eight. I carry the garment bag to my room and lay it across the bed. The woman who sent this was from New York City. She worked for some fashion magazine. I healed her young son. Somehow she saw beyond Marlena the Healer to the teenage girl underneath when she chose this gift. I appreciated this. My mother did not.

I unzip the bag and my heart flutters. Skinny jeans and fashionable tank tops are laid out before me, the kinds I've seen girls in town wearing when they're walking with their boyfriends. There are bright summer dresses with spaghetti straps and a couple of tiny skirts and tops, everything so different from the clothing I always wear.

White gauzy nightgowns hang in a narrow row one after the

other on the left side of my closet. On the right side are wedding gowns. For each audience, I'm dressed like a bride. The audience comes expecting a pageant, and they *ooh* and *aah* when I sweep onstage in a big, beautiful gown. The white is supposed to emphasize my saintliness, my purity. But the paintings I've created from my visions are a riot of color on the wall of my room, interrupting so much blankness, the daily blandness of my attire. They are a rebellion without being a rebellion that gets me in trouble with my mother.

I run my hand across the items in the garment bag. A short, blue slip of a dress catches my eye, perfect for a hot day. I pluck it from the hanger and set it on the bed. Then I pull my white sheath off and throw it on the floor. I stand there in my underwear, hovering over the pretty blue silk, the same blue as the sky today. I slide the new dress over my head, shimmying it down my body. There is a long mirror on the wall and I check out my reflection.

Even with my hair still wet from the shower, I look almost normal.

No. I look almost sexy.

Like I, too, have the kind of legs that boys would admire, just like they admire the girls on the beach who flaunt their bodies in tiny bikinis. I think about Finn, the boy who refuses to leave my heart and my mind, wonder if he would admire me in this, and tug the hem a little higher up my thighs. The dress shows off my smooth olive skin, and the subtle curves of my chest and hips. Would it make him notice me in the way I want him to? Would he love me in this? I don't know.

But I love me in it.

And my mother would hate me in it. This makes me love it even more.

FOUR

I am seventeen. It is last summer.

We are getting ready for my Saturday audience and my mother is helping me into the wedding dress she's picked out for this afternoon. She's working through the tiny pearl buttons that take forever to close, and I am staring at my reflection. I am wondering if I am pretty. If other people find me pretty. If other people *my age* find me pretty or if they just think I'm some freak show. I don't want to be a freak show. I want to be attractive to others, to the boys I can't stop noticing of late, as though they've been invisible all these years and suddenly appeared out of nowhere, like the hidden things of the sea after a hurricane spills them onto shore.

I've learned to stop asking my mother questions about boys and my appearance because they upset her. We used to be on the same page about who I was, who I am. But the minute I started asking questions my mother grew obsessed with stamping them out, with forbidding me the thoughts that she didn't like. She sees them as threats to our life, to my life, to my reputation as a healer.

But I am a hermit crab grown too big for its shell. And today I am feeling stifled.

I catch my mother's eye in the mirror. "So, Mama, when I fall in love, do you think my healing powers will evaporate? Do you think the visions will stop?"

My mother halts the work of buttoning. Her face grows pained.

"Marlena," she whispers. "Don't say things like that. You should never tempt God."

I lower my eyes. "Okay, Mama," I say softly. "I'm sorry."

And I am sorry. I don't want to do or say anything to make my visions go away. They are as real to me as the floor under my feet. During a vision I am never more certain of why I am here on this earth, never more me, and never more not me. Most of the time I want to protect my gift, hold it close so no one else can use it. But in the real world people try and take this tender part of me to capitalize on it, even my own mother, and I am tired. People twist it so it's no longer something I recognize, no longer beautiful or mine. They turn my healings into something to sell for profit and they sell me for profit with it. I don't want to be sold and branded and merchandized. I don't like what my life is becoming.

I've started to wonder, too, whether the life of a healer really does mean I have to cloister myself like Julian of Norwich. Does it really require me to be homeschooled and removed from other people my age? Do I need to live apart from the rest of the world, with only my mother for company? Isn't there another way to do this? To be who I am?

My mother goes back to buttoning.

"But you *do* want me to fall in love one day, don't you?" I ask.

We stare at each other in the mirror.

My mother lifts the traditional Portuguese veil that she will pin in my hair from the top of the dresser, the kind of veil you might see placed over the head of a statue of a saint or on the women who march in the parades of São Miguel. I don't always wear it, but I guess today my mother wants to make a point by ensuring I do. It is a delicate thing, nearly weightless, hand sewn by my grandmother. It does not go over my face but stands up a bit from the top of my head because of the white pearl comb to which it is attached, fixed just so that it cascades down my hair. A treasured heirloom made for me before I was born, as though my grandmother knew that her daughter would give birth to a girl whose hands would make miracles. Or maybe she simply thought that someday I would wear it at my First Communion, or even my wedding.

My mother disappears behind me in the reflection as she fixes the veil. "Marlena, stop being selfish. You can't have everything. Look around you." She pauses, I suppose to allow me to take a moment and focus on the beauty of the room, with its stunning ocean views and accompanying ocean sounds, its tasteful, understated decor.

"Your gift has given you more than most people dream of having."

It has given *you* more, I think, but manage not to say.

My very first healing, I healed my mother. At least, this is what I've been told.

It was right after the accident that killed my father and my mother's parents. Her entire family and everyone my mother loved gone in an instant. She was pregnant with me, and the trauma of the accident forced her into labor. The doctors delivered me, tried to save my mother, but couldn't. They waited for her breathing to fade, and a kind nurse set me onto my mother's chest so she could feel her baby once before death. As the story goes, I placed my hands flat against my mother's skin. Within seconds her breaths quickened, her lids slid open, her limbs stirred, and her hands found my little body. The nurse called the doctors.

My mother was completely well within hours. No one could explain what had happened, though the nurse was convinced that whatever it was, it had to do with me. My mother took me home to the now empty cottage she'd shared with her parents and my father, the little house my grandfather built and where I would spend my first years of life. It was a while before my mother understood, before she really believed it was me who'd fetched her from the brink of death. She'd always been a person of faith, but it took several more healings—a few kind neighbors who'd come to check on my mother after the accident, who held me, and who'd been sick or hurt at the time—before my mother began to wonder if she'd given birth to a saint. If her baby might be a miracle worker. She began to offer my gift to others with more confidence, and that gift began to offer my mother a new sense of purpose after so much tragic death.

For so many of my healings, I was too young to comprehend what I was doing, what was being done to me, taken from me. My mother has photo albums from that time. There are pictures of people—an old man, a young mother, a boy my age—laying their hands on my downy baby's head, eyes closed, willing whatever divine power might reside in my little brain and body to pass into their own. Sometimes my tiny fist curls around one of their fingers. Sometimes I am crying, wailing loudly, mouth wide, gums bared. My mother is always standing nearby, or she is holding me out to the miracle seekers like she might be giving me away.

"Your gift saved me," my mother always says. Though as I get older she says it less and less.

I am grateful that my gift could give my mother's broken heart relief.

But do I ever get to stop saving her?

It is after my audience.

Colorful bits of paper clutter my room. They cover every surface in a fractured mosaic of greens and blues, some pale, some bright, some saturated with yellow, like sunlight beaming over the sea. I step right, my bare toes kicking scraps of aqua and navy confetti into the air, making a soft shush as they slide across the floor. I am chasing after a picture that I hold in my mind, a vision from one of my healings. It is like trying to catch a fish with bare hands as it swims through dark water. My fingers are coated in sticky shellac as I work, piecing the image together. I tear the pieces of paper smaller and smaller, until they are just right.

I call the healing down from the sky, pull it up from the floor of the ocean. My hands are frantic trying to capture it before it can dart away, like a shy crab burrowing deep into the sand and disappearing from human eyes forever. I can't let that happen. My whole being yearns to express it, to bring it into existence. The sun descends bit by bit, then disappears from the window as it slides toward the horizon. My mother was right earlier today. I was being selfish. I already have everything I need. My gift alone has given me more than most people dream about.

By the time I am done with this collage of my vision, my face is soaked with tears.

I have never been happier.

My mother pokes her head into my room that evening.

I've fallen asleep on the bare wooden planks of the floor. I open my eyes when I hear her. "Mama?"

"Oh Marlena!" She is looking down at my newest artwork in the dusky shadows. "My miracle girl. This one is more beautiful even than the last."

"That was from the man with the thick white hair," I whisper, my throat thick with sleep. "The man with the rare blood disorder. He had a yellow shirt?"

My mother nods. "I remember." She walks over to me. "Why collage this time, and not paint?"

"I don't know. It just seemed right."

A silence grows between us as the two of us take in the collage that lies between my narrow bed and the chair by the windows where I like to read. Layers of greens and blues radiate outward, big intersecting circles. It is what I first saw when I touched the man's hands. My mother seems moved by it, and I am moved by this. "I'm so sorry, Mama, about before," I tell her. "I don't know why I was asking all those questions. I love you so much. You were right about everything. About me."

"I know, *querida*," she says, her voice smooth and forgiving. "I know you love me." *I know I was right, am right,* we both hear her say without her actually saying it. But when she turns to me I don't see love in her eyes. There is a hardness. A shrewdness.

I look away.

FIVE

I shimmy out of the slinky blue dress and trade it for the skinny jeans and a tank top. At the bottom of the garment bag are several pairs of shoes, including strappy, high heeled sandals covered in metal studs. I buckle them on and stare at myself again.

I really do look normal. Like maybe I could go out and be just Marlena, average teenager, with regular dreams of having a boyfriend and enjoying the beach at the end of a hot summer. Maybe even going for ice cream down on the pier, or a milkshake at Nana's, or for a burger at the diner that is always packed when I walk by but where I've never eaten. I wonder what would happen if I quit being Marlena the Healer.

Can a miracle worker just quit her job? Can a living saint hand in her resignation?

On my way downstairs I hold the shoes in my hand. They would make such a racket against the wood and I have learned to move silently. This is the best way to avoid calling the attention of my mother. I round the corner into the big open space of the first floor and hear a sharp intake of breath.

Fatima, our maid, jumps up from the couch. "Marlena! I thought no one was home!" Her oval face and dark eyes are startled, her black hair hanging long and loose, when usually it is up in a tight bun.

I am frozen, contraband shoes in hand and contraband outfit on my body. There is no hiding any of it. "So did I."

We stare at each other in silence, two criminal offenders taking each other in. I am dressed in forbidden clothing but Fatima was lounging in the living room on the furniture, her shoes off. Fatima's eyes keep darting to my shoulders, which are bared in the tank top. My shoulders are never bared.

"I won't tell if you won't," I offer.

At first Fatima's face is blank. Then she erupts into loud laughter.

I bite my lip. I've never seen Fatima laugh like this. But then I find myself giggling along with her.

She tries to catch her breath. "It's a deal, Marlena. It's a deal."

I smile. Fatima smiles back.

Normally, we barely interact, only speak to each other when necessary. Those are the rules of the house, of my life, and everyone around me knows this. The Healer is meant to be left alone, to not be touched or approached unnecessarily. This is explained in the programs given out at my audiences so the seekers know what to do and what not to. I am the one who decides to go to them, to touch them, and not the other way around.

I am learning that I like breaking rules, and breaking them with someone else, like Fatima. Marlena the Rule Breaker. That sounds so much different than Marlena the Healer, Marlena the Virgin Miracle Worker. Marlena the Living Saint.

"What were you doing?" I ask Fatima, since we are already engaged in behavior that isn't normal for us. "Were you taking in the view?" Before Fatima shot up off the couch she'd been staring toward the great picture windows, the ocean bobbing with white-caps behind it, the sky hazy with humidity.

Fatima is Portuguese like we are. She and my mother could be sisters, with their matching dark features and rich olive skin. She is a talented cook, and sometimes I think she is even better than my mother at baking the sweet breads and little custard-filled pastéis de Belém that we eat on feast days.

"No, actually, not the view," Fatima says, but doesn't elaborate.

"Then what?"

Her face wears an expression I can't read and the laughter is gone. She nods in the direction of the wall between the two big windows that look onto the sea. On that wall is a painting. One of mine.

"Oh," I say.

She glances at me. Then, maybe because the two of us are

already in uncharted territory, she explains. "I was thinking about what that image says about you." She turns her attention back to it and the room grows quiet as we stand there, taking it in.

The painting is a self-portrait.

I made it when I was twelve. It is of a great ship, nearly an ark. On it are the little houses and shops that make up our town. People crowd its decks, some peering worriedly over the stern. Behind the ship is a violent storm, but the boat is pointed away from heavy gray clouds, driving rain, fierce waves. It will head fast and sure into the bright sun and the warm blue sea. In the painting, I am the figure-head attached to the prow of the ship. My hair flows long and wavy around the wooden upper decks, my foot wound by the thick metal chain attached to the iron anchor that reaches below to the bottom of the ocean.

I've long thought that being a healer is akin to protecting a ship's occupants from storm and sea, from pirates and invaders, for being responsible for everyone's safety, for guiding its people into calmer waters and better days, my job to anchor everything and everyone to this earthen floor like Julian of Norwich anchored her church to God. One day, I turned this vision of myself into a painting. Maybe it sounds arrogant. But it's who I've always been.

The painting has been hanging on the living room wall only since the beginning of summer. My mother put it there to make a statement. To remind me of who I am. Or who she wants me to remain.

"What does it say about me, Fatima?"

She turns to me. "That you feel responsible for the well-being of the world. That you are an otherworldly being, with otherworldly powers."

My cheeks prickle with heat hearing Fatima say this. Shame creeps up the bare skin of my arms. The painting doesn't just make me sound arrogant, it makes me the embodiment of it.

"But," Fatima goes on, "the girl I see before me is something different." She sounds pleased.

Some of the shame recedes. "What is she then?"

"I don't know yet."

"Me neither," I say quickly.

Fatima's smile is slow to appear but it gets wider and wider. "That's okay, Marlena. You don't need to know yet. You're young and you have your whole life ahead of you."

"Do I? What kind of life?"

My colliding questions make Fatima laugh. "You'll just have to wait and see." Then she shakes her head. "No, let me rephrase that. You'll just have to go looking and find out." She slips her shoes back onto her feet and picks up the duster she left on one of the side tables. "Remember, you didn't see me and I didn't see you," she calls over her shoulder and disappears down the hall.

I stand there, staring after her. Our conversation was so strange, so out of the blue, but somehow it made me happy. Gave me a shot of hope. Of curiosity.

I have to go looking to find out what my life could be, Fatima thinks.

Well, okay. Challenge accepted.

I run back upstairs, grab the house phone along the way, and call José, my driver. I have a driver because I'm not allowed to go anywhere outside of town without a chaperone. Also, there's the part about how even though I'm eighteen I don't know how to drive.

"José," I say, when I hear the familiar *sí* on the other end of the line. "Can you come pick me up?"

There is a long sigh. "*Señorita*, your mother will not be happy you've gone out."

"So what if she's not happy?" I say. Then, "What about *my* happiness?"

"Marlena, you're going to get me in trouble. *You* are going to get into trouble."

I step into the bathroom and dab on the makeup I'm only supposed to use when I have a healing audience. "Please, Josélito? For me? I have to do something. Today. *Now*."

There comes another long sigh. A string of colorful swears in Spanish.

I smile. José cannot resist me for long. Unlike Fatima, José has never tiptoed around me. He's one of the few people who treat me like a real person. I don't want to get him in trouble, but at the moment, I'm more concerned with my own needs.

"You are going to get me fired, *amorcita*."

"My mother will never fire you," I tell him. I go into my bedroom and grab one of my gauzy white dresses and shove it into a bag for later. "I wouldn't let her if she tried."

"Your mother will do what she wants, when she wants to," José says.

"I'll refuse to heal," I throw out.

"Oh, Marlenita." His voice is heavy, sagging like the center of a raft with too much cargo. "She would never allow *that*," he says. The sound of the car starting comes through the phone, followed by silence.

SIX

José drives along the coast. The spray of the ocean leaps into the sky as waves crash against the rocks. A path winds by the side of the road and people are out taking walks, jogging, running. Occasionally a couple admires the view, hand in hand. I've never walked down this path, but I'd like to. I suppose José would stop the car and accompany me if I asked, but as much as I love José, he's not the person with whom I imagine sharing this experience. Our destination isn't too far away, but it takes us well beyond the distance my mother would approve.

When I'm not staring out the window, I'm staring at my legs. My jeans. My bare arms and shoulders. I put a finger to my lips and it comes away dark red. So many transgressions in a single day. First my swim. Now this.

"José?" I call up to the front of the car.

He glances in the rearview mirror. "*Sí, Marlenita?*"

"Has my mother noticed we're gone? Has she texted or called?"

There is a long sigh—José is the master of the long sigh. "Not yet, *guapa*. Not yet."

I don't have a phone, so when my mother can't find me she has to call José. There are a lot of things I don't have or do that most people have and do. Television. Computers. A phone. I've always been homeschooled, which basically means I sit by myself all day reading books. I used to think this made me like Julian and Hildegard, Catherine of Siena and Teresa of Ávila, since women mystics studied alone in their cloistered, sheltered lives, their educations solely from books. But now it just makes me want to scream. It's yet another thing I've missed out on, that separates me from everyone else.

"What's different this year from other ones, that suddenly you want to go to school?" my mother said in July when I begged her to let me go this fall. "You've always been so happy to stay home with me. Besides, now is not a good time. You have a reputation to protect."

I wiggle my toes, admiring the heeled sandals on my feet.

What reputation do these give me? Can a pair of skinny jeans and a tank top that shows off just a hint of cleavage really affect my image? Might it feel a little bit good to stop protecting it for a while?

"José?"

He harrumphs. *"Sí, guapa?"*

"Can I borrow your phone? Please?"

This time he doesn't resist, reaches back to pass the phone to me. I take the crumpled business card from my purse, type the number into the keypad, and wait for it to ring. Someone picks up right away.

"Hello?"

I take a deep breath. "Dr. Holbrook." My voice cracks. For a second I think I might pass out. I take another deep breath. "It's me. Marlena Oliveira. Finally calling you."

There is a long pause, long enough for me to wonder if I called the wrong number. But then she speaks. "Marlena!" She sounds happy. "What an unexpected surprise! What can I do for you?"

My heart pounds in my chest. "I'm actually on my way to see you. To your office, I mean. It's kind of a spontaneous trip." I close my eyes, suddenly feeling stupid. "I guess I should have called sooner. Before I left. I'm sorry. I wasn't thinking. You're probably very busy."

"No, no," she responds. "I'm glad you're coming. I can be at the office in ten minutes. I live just down the road. Does that sound good?"

My heart pounds harder. "That sounds perfect."

"See you soon, Marlena," she says, then hangs up.

I hand the phone back to José. She made that seem so easy.

"Everything okay, *guapa?*" José calls back.

"Yes."

He holds my gaze in the rearview mirror, before his eyes return to the road.

After a few more minutes the Center for the Mind & Brain Sciences appears ahead and I press my face against the window. It is a beautiful glass box on the edge of the sea that calls the sun and the ocean to its windows. It is bright in the hazy heat of the day.

"We're here," José says, turning into the drive and pulling to a stop.

I loop my arm through the straps of my bag and scramble out of the car. "Bye, José," I call, one foot already on the asphalt.

"Marlenita!" José sounds nervous. "I'll be here waiting. No more than an hour or we'll both be in trouble with your mother. *Por favor.*"

"Sure," I reply, hoping that I can live up to his expectation. I really don't want José to get in trouble. He sighs like he doesn't believe me, but the *whoosh* of it is cut off when I slam the car door.

I practically run to the entrance, my legs strange and stiff in these jeans. I want to get inside before I change my mind.

"May I help you?" a pretty young woman asks, looking up from a thick textbook. She's sitting at the front desk, dressed in jeans and a T-shirt. Dressed like me.

Or is it that I'm dressed like her?

Even our skin is the same color, our eyes and our hair. Maybe she is Portuguese, too. Maybe she eats toasted sweet bread on Sunday afternoons and *malasadas* during the summer as a special treat and endless amounts of kale soup during winter. Maybe soon we'll find we have so much in common we'll become best friends.

"Um," I try, speechless.

Recognition dawns in her eyes. "You must be Marlena! Angie called and told me you were on your way. I'm Lexi."

"Do you like *malasadas*?" I blurt.

"I don't know." She gets a funny look on her face, but her voice is still sunny and cheerful. "I don't even know what that is."

"It's kind of like a doughnut."

Her smile helps me to stop feeling like such an idiot. "Well, I love doughnuts, so I'm sure I'd like one if I tried it."

"Okay. It's, um, nice to meet you. Lexi."

She laughs. "Sure. Let me show you where you can wait for Angie." Lexi leads me to a spacious room with a plaque outside with Dr. Holbrook's name on it. She smiles again and tells me to have a seat. I do as I'm told. "I have to keep studying," she says apologetically, but I am relieved when she disappears back down the hall.

When I am sure Lexi is gone, I jump up and go exploring. Around the corner is a lab. It's enormous, with a beautiful view of the ocean. There are four machines, strange and intimidating. I am glad to be in jeans. In my white sheath I would feel like an ancient relic surrounded by so much science.

One of the machines is an MRI. I've seen one of those before. The others I don't recognize. They look like they would better outfit a spaceship than a room on earth. There is a long table and at the end of it a thick, doughnut-shaped white ring, nearly the size of a small car. There is what looks to be a stainless steel bathing cap, with wires coming out of it, and another cap made of a strange white mesh. In the far corner of the room is some sort of chamber, like the ones that scan the body at airports.

What *is* this place?

What am I doing here?

Maybe I should go. I feel like a foreigner, or an alien, new to this unfamiliar world and unsure how to inhabit it.

Then, out of the corner of my eyes I see the photos. They are side by side on the internal wall of the lab, away from the windows. They seem to hum, to pulse with light, and my feet pull me to them. Each one holds an image of a single person, with a tiny card below that gives their name followed by their age and talent. They aren't normal talents. Not like *gymnast* or *pianist* or even *math whiz*. They are the strange kind that most people think are fake, the kind you might find in a circus or on a show about magic or, well, at a church like the one that grew up around me.

James Halloway. Sixteen. The Weatherman.

Nicole Matthews. Thirteen. Telekinesis.

Chastity Lang. Eighteen. Internal Sonar.

Will I end up on this wall? Is that what Dr. Holbrook hopes? To add me to her collection of freaks?

I am about to turn around and leave this place, grateful José promised to wait outside, when Dr. Holbrook appears in the doorway.

"Marlena! How wonderful to see you." The warmth in her voice is soothing. She is dressed in a loose-fitting button-down shirt and flowing pants that end at her calves.

"Hi, Dr. Holbrook." I tug at the bottom of my tank top, then hook my fingers into the belt loops of my jeans. It's so strange to do these things with my clothing. It's strange not to be dressed like a ghost who might haunt someone's attic.

"Please call me Angie. Let's talk in my office." She beckons me into the big bright space around the corner.

There is a simple white table that must be her desk, with only a laptop and a lamp on it. Facing the glass walls and the ocean are an overstuffed white chair and a fluffy couch to match. They seem out of place among the minimalism and machinery. A thick knotted white-gray rug lies across the floor. Dr. Holbrook, *Angie*, slides open a tall glass door in the wall, and the warm breeze and the sounds of the waves surround us. She gestures for me to sit in the big white chair. I watch as she kicks off her heels and sits on the couch, tucking her legs underneath her like we are friends having a visit. I sink down into the soft cushions, my feet still flat on the floor, hands tight on my knees. My muscles are tense. I am still ready to flee.

"What brought you here today? Why now?" Angie asks, when I don't speak.

I shake my head, side to side. I don't know where to start.

How can I possibly start?

SEVEN

I am eighteen. It is three months ago, in early June, the start of summer. This is the day everything around me comes crashing down. The day I meet Finn.

So many things about my audience are typical that morning. The church is packed to the brim. My mother, ever more the expert pageant director, has everything under control, fitting more and more seekers inside the room. In the corner, petitioners chant and pray on their knees. Their pant legs are grass- and dirt-stained and shredded. There are people from the town. I see Mr. and Mrs. Almeida, who own the bakery. I don't need to see Gertie to know she has a table set up out front, selling her souvenirs.

But one thing is unusual. Mrs. Jacobs is here, arms crossed tight, wearing an unreadable expression. She's never come to an audience, not that I remember. Maybe she decided to see what in the world we do here on Saturdays. Most people in the town have come at least once.

José is helping with crowd control. During the audience, he plays the part of bodyguard, always somewhere nearby, making sure that no one takes a dive at me, some desperate soul who has no idea where else to turn. But now he is making sure I will have space to walk through the aisles. Gently, he clears a path. The room is tender, like a wound. Tourists aside, the people who fill the seats toward the front are the vulnerable, the needy, the sick. I watch the preparations through a hidden window backstage. I am ready for them.

Fatima futzes with my dress as I stand there. The air has grown warmer, the heat capturing the smells of the sea and drawing them inside.

"Marlena," Fatima commands. "Stay still."

I do as I'm told at first, but not for long.

"Stop touching your hair. You're going to make the comb fall out, and the veil is just right!"

I don't have to look at Fatima to see her exasperated expression. I do my best to stop moving as she begins the labored work of figuring out the complicated bustle.

My mother knows exactly where I am, exactly where to look. She catches me watching through the window and smiles. I give her a wave.

The roller coaster of our relationship has flattened itself into a taut sense of peace. I've been painting and creating my visions on a near constant basis. Collages take over the house and I've even tried my hand at sculpture, though only once and probably not again.

The work occupies me, brain and body, heart and soul. It pushes other things out of view. When I give myself over to my work, those strange and uncomfortable questions and thoughts fade so far into the background of my mind they've nearly disappeared. My mother is only too happy to get me whatever materials I need to feed my art. Clay. Metal. Paper. Oils, watercolors, canvas, paper.

It was probably just a phase.

That's what my mother said the other day, in passing, with respect to our recent fights and friction, with respect to the things that were upsetting the balance of our lives. Her words have been ringing through my insides since.

"Turn and look at me," Fatima says.

Fatima stares down her nose at me, since she is taller, appraising my dress, the state of my hair, the artful folds of the veil that trails down my back. She makes a circling gesture with her finger and I do one slow twirl. "Lovely," she says, more to herself than me.

"Really?" I ask.

She looks at me strangely. "You always look lovely at your audiences, Marlena. Don't you feel lovely in your beautiful dress?"

"I don't know," I answer. "How I look is not supposed to matter," I say, parroting my mother's words.

Fatima is on the verge of saying something else when José enters the back room. He nods to tell me that we are about to begin. I resume my place at the window, watching for my mother's cue.

In the third row on the right are five girls dressed the same, with ponytails high on their heads. They are wearing some sort of sports uniform. They must play together on a team. Maybe soccer or lacrosse or field hockey. I decide that it's soccer, and wonder how they found their way to doing something like getting up on a Saturday morning, putting their hair up, and running around outside chasing after a ball and trying to make a goal in a net. How do normal girls decide who and what they'd like to be and do? What would it be like to wear a soccer jersey? To kick the ball as hard as I could, shouting to other girls on my team? To let my limbs go wild instead of keeping everything so still and controlled?

The girls stare at their phones, occasionally sharing whatever is on their little screens, pressing their heads together and laughing. Jealousy scuttles across my insides on its little crab legs.

My mother is on the stage making her opening remarks, talking to people about the history of my healings. "The History of Marlena the Living Saint," it actually says in the program.

One of the soccer girls leans her head on the shoulder of the one next to her.

No one has ever asked me what I want to be or do with my life. The question has never occurred to anyone, I suppose. It's never even occurred to me before now. What would I be if I wasn't a healer? What if I could be anyone I wanted? Maybe I would work as a waitress in a diner, and wear my name on a pin stuck to the pocket of my uniform shirt, or be a teacher of mathematics, or even a competitive swimmer who goes out each morning to practice different strokes, gliding through the ocean. Or maybe I would be a doctor, like Hildegard, but the real kind who wear stethoscopes around their necks and do things like deliver wailing, squirming babies to their exhausted but happy mothers.

The nod finally comes for me to start.

"Thank you, Fatima," I say on my way to the door.

"It's okay if it matters, Marlena," Fatima whispers from behind me, just loud enough that I hear. "It's okay to care whether you are lovely."

For a second I stop, wanting to give her words a chance to physically enter my body and take hold, but my mother is gesturing for me to hurry and now I am on the stage, and Fatima's comments slide off me. My eyes immediately go to the soccer girls, curious if maybe one of them is here for a healing, but they seem bored, three of them staring down at their phones, two with their eyes closed, maybe asleep.

"Marlena!" and "Over here!" begin the usual chorus.

I head toward the special guests my mother has gathered. They seem to mostly be babies held by one of their parents. As I lay my hands on each one, I think about the doctors who delivered them, trying to imagine myself as a kind of doctor. All that is missing is my white coat, a pen in my breast pocket, and the stethoscope. The church is full of that delicious scent of summery ocean, and once again I am that figurehead on a ship, carrying the people across a storm toward calmer seas. My arms are spread wide, angled backward, protective toward this precious cargo I must ferry to safety. Rich shades of wood-smelling brown and fresh clean green wash through me to replace the fiery, rancid pain of suffering and sickness under each of my hands.

You'd think I wouldn't be able to heal on demand, but I can.

As long as the person who needs me is willing and open.

As long as I remain open.

I have tried describing what it's like, but I'm always falling short. Miracles are fleeting, fickle things, and the words we use to try and depict them, or the drawings, the poetry, are just as fickle. For the mystics I'm always reading it's the same. They strain and grasp at the miraculous but it never turns out quite right. Like, in their attempts to tell the world what they know and have seen, to reveal it in all its glory, they've instead offered a puzzle with key pieces missing. A treasure map without the X.

Healing usually starts in my body.

The tingling in a fingertip or the very end of a toe. A static that runs across my left thigh or my right kneecap. Sometimes it's the back of my neck or the base of my spine. Usually the place it begins corresponds to the person in need of healing. If it's a leg that is withered, I will feel something in my own leg. If the problem is in a person's speech, my lips will grow numb. It's the same thing with the eyes or the ears. At the beginning of a healing, I may grow blind or deaf, or the reverse might occur. My senses will be heightened, like I can suddenly hear every single thing in the room, the softest whispers, even the unspoken thoughts in people's heads. Or my sight gets sharper, so sharp I nearly want to close my eyes against seeing so much at once.

Then comes the color, followed by the scenes, usually of the future, of what will be or should be for the person, if the healing involves part of the body, or if the healing involves grief, the possibility of happiness again. I can't decide which is the best part. Sometimes I think it's the colors but sometimes it's the scenes. When I am seeing into the person I am healing, it's like a window into their soul, like I've somehow found the door to the core of who they are, and there I am, Marlena, just a girl wandering around in the deepest parts of their being. The intimacy of it, the access, the burst of hope and wonder, is the most extraordinary thing I've ever felt. It is why the experiences of mystics like Hildegard and Julian are described as ecstatic. It is ecstasy to know a moment of pure unity. To have that with another person for even a single second. I've often wondered if love is something like this.

When this moment of intimacy, of ecstasy, falls away, the person is healed.

The way I've described it makes it sound like a process with steps, *first this, then this, and then this and this.* One, two, three, four, five. In a way it is like this, but also in a way, everything happens at once.

There is one part, though, that usually comes last.

The healing, or whatever you want to call it, eventually spreads into me, to my body, and for a while, I take on whatever it is that left the person I've healed. That's the part that hurts. It's like the post-miracle hangover I get, because God or whatever divine being exists is exacting payment for drawing on his (or her?) power for a few precious moments on earth. I am the conduit drawing down the divine to the people around me, and that conduit eventually sparks and flares and burns out from too much energy flowing through it. It's like God is laughing, or angry, at the audacity of it, great belly laughs, speaking between them and saying things like *You thought I wouldn't notice what you were doing, Marlena? Well, you thought wrong and now you will pay.* The pain in my own body, my own heart, my own mind and soul is the punishment for having the audacity to make miracles happen with my human hands.

Sometimes, in the darkest moments, I wonder if there is a larger punishment out there waiting for me, something far worse and more horrible than these hangovers. One I can't yet conceive of because it is still being cooked up to account for a lifetime of miracles, of hubris, of taking from where I shouldn't. Sometimes I wonder if that punishment is close, but then I wake up to heal another day. And then I am left to wonder, how many more healing days do I have left?

"Faker!"

I open my eyes. It feels like I've woken from a trance. My vision is blurred.

The soccer girls' heads shoot up from their phones.

"Faker! She's a faker!"

The words grow clearer, louder, marching toward me from a distance. I turn toward the voice.

"Marlena the Saint is no saint. She's a liar!"

Murmurs and gasps swirl through the church like pollution in the sea. My vision clears. I see the person who is shouting. Mrs. Jacobs. It's Mrs. Jacobs.

"I've brought proof," she yells.

Nine, no, maybe ten people stand up. I don't recognize any of them, not outright, though a few seem vaguely familiar. I head in their direction, and I see José and Mama doing the same from their corners of the room, but the crowd is thick and they are struggling to move forward. I make sure to get there first.

"Good afternoon, Mrs. Jacobs," I say quietly, looking into her face, trying to read her expression. There is triumph in her eyes.

My greeting seems to unsettle her, and her expression falters, her face growing blank before returning to its fiery red righteousness.

"Marlena," she says, this time without yelling.

"Yes."

"I've brought some people you supposedly cured."

My heart clenches, but I remain steady, the weight of my gown on either side of me like scaffolding. "Supposedly?"

"Yes, supposedly, because you didn't cure them. They suffer just as much as before. And one of them has since died. Your gift is one big lie."

I look into the faces of the people around her, tempted to touch the hands of each one to try and read their souls, their pain, their sicknesses. I search their eyes and the space between them as though the ghost of the person Mrs. Jacobs said has died might be hovering there.

"Is this true?" I ask the group.

The entire church is deadened with silence. No one moves. The people Mrs. Jacobs has brought are stone-faced. A tall man, the only one whose eyes are full of grief, twists his mouth, like the words behind it are distasteful so he refuses to let them out.

"It is true," Mrs. Jacobs snaps.

"I didn't ask you," I snap right back.

One of the women has her head bowed. Now she looks up. "You said my son was cured," she whispers, her voice nearly too hoarse for me to hear.

I reach out. Place the edges of my fingers on her forearm. Peer into her eyes. "And was he?"

There is a gaping pause, and I feel it like the jaws of a shark opening wide around me. "My child died," she says quickly.

My mother is suddenly next to me. "But how long after the Healer cured him? Days, weeks, months? Did he die of something unrelated?"

I grab my mother's arm to make her stop saying such things. "Does it really matter?" I hiss.

She looks my way, peeling back my hand. "Of course it does. It means everything."

My mother beckons for José to hurry. A chasm opens between her and me. In the beat of this silence, chaos erupts in the church, people standing, talking, shouting over each other, debating my existence as though I'm not here. My mother is called away to try and calm people down, a role she is good at. The chaos creates a moment of intimacy between Mrs. Jacobs and me. We are like the eye in the hurricane. Everyone seems to have forgotten us. She reaches out, nearly touching me, but stops just shy of my elbow. Mrs. Jacobs lowers her head toward mine.

"Marlena, it is not you I'm against, it's your mother." Her words are a quickly whispered stream. "Well, I don't believe in your gift, but I do feel sorry that you've been trapped into such a life. It's a shame for such a young girl like you. You need to open your eyes and see what is really happening around you."

"Okay," I find myself saying. "What do you think is happening?"

José has almost reached us.

Mrs. Jacobs leans closer. "Did you know your mother won't let you cure anyone unless they pay ahead of time? Do you even know what she charges?"

"She does not," I say, but my voice is faltering. "People sometimes send money in gratitude following a healing, which is where the money we have comes from."

"That's what she wants you to believe. But it's not the truth. Somewhere deep down you know this. She tells you who to heal before each audience, does she not?"

"Yes, but only because they've come from so far away," I reason, which is of course my mother's reason.

"Stop lying to yourself."

"*Señora*, ma'am, please come with me," José says. He doesn't wait for her to answer, just places two hands on Mrs. Jacobs and begins to steer her away.

Mrs. Jacobs's words crash through me, questions and doubts piling up haphazardly, punching holes through my skin. I am a ship, taking on water through this series of fissures and seams. I can feel myself listing to the side, going down, down, down to the dark ocean floor as my mother finally seems to be gaining control of the room. I almost wish she wouldn't. I want to lie down. Disappear, never to be seen again. I am no longer the brave girl steering the massive ship toward tranquility and peace. The emotions swirling in the room are sharp spikes, piercing my sides, my ribs, my heart. I pitch and keel and falter.

By the time I reach the stage again, I am a shipwreck.

Afterward, my mother is all business.

"You're going to keep your head high, your chin up, and you are going to go out there and do the receiving line just as you do every Saturday. Sarah Jacobs or no, this is what everyone expects from you."

I look up from the floor, where I've collapsed in a heap of tulle and satin. My mother's expression is determined. There is that sharp glint in her eyes, love that will cut and maim. I pull myself to standing, dazed. Fatima and my mother tug and fix the skirt of my dress.

The receiving line at the front of the church turns out to be consoling. Things seem to go back to normal. Maybe my mother was right.

"Don't listen to that woman," a man says to me early on.

I hear some version of this from so many people. Or some version of "You cured me once and it was real." I nod like I agree until I hear this so much my faith comes crawling back from its cold hiding place at the bottom of the sea.

Then I notice a woman a few people back in the line. She is unlike everyone else. Her clothes are different. Jeans with a silky cream blouse, an expensive suit jacket over it, wire-rimmed glasses adorning her pretty, pale face, dressed so unlike the tourists in their shorts and T-shirts. She isn't trying to take my picture or video me so she can post an image of the freak she saw on summer vacation. Tourists aside, the people who fill up the United Holiest Church are true believers, mainly Portuguese and Italians, with their brown and olive skin, Latinos and black people crowded together for worship, for the hope of my divine touch, dressed in their Sunday best even though audiences take place on Saturdays.

It is the woman's turn in line.

The look in her eyes is a mix of skepticism and curiosity. "I'm Dr. Holbrook," she says. Her makeup is perfect, despite the heat.

She doesn't offer her hand, so she must know enough not to try and touch me. "But everyone calls me Angie."

I stare, trying to get a better read on her. "Hello. And what brought you here today?" I ask, as I always do. As I am trained to do.

"I was wondering if you believe in yourself." She says this simply, as though every person asks this. "In your gift."

A wave of dizziness passes over me. That shipwreckedness again. Everyone else has been quick to brush off Mrs. Jacobs's protest, like it meant nothing. "Excuse me? Are you referring to . . . what happened earlier?"

"I don't know what happened earlier," she says. "I arrived late. My grad assistant is still looking for parking." Her stare is unwavering, but also kind. "Now that you are college age, do you ever wonder about your abilities? If they are real?"

My lips part. College? Does she really think this life would allow me to go to college? "Of course not," I try, but once again, I can feel myself breaking apart.

"Hmmm," she replies, studying me with those kind blue eyes. She presses a small rectangular card into my hand. "Call me. I'd like to talk to you. Maybe you have some questions that I can help you answer."

I take it.

In this moment, a boy comes rushing up to her. He is breathless. "I can't find parking, so I'm in the car, idling outside."

He hasn't looked at me and maybe he won't; his words and eyes are all for Dr. Holbrook. *Angie.* His hair is a mess, and a sheen of sweat is covering his skin. I want him to turn my way. I want to know him, to know his name, to know everything about him. I don't know why. But the force of this want is powerful, immediate, and total. It comes on like one of my visions, lifting me up and out of my body and taking me over completely.

Is this love at first sight?

He glances my way for a brief second. No, a half. A quarter.

"I don't want the car to get towed," he says, looking between Angie and me, so I'm not sure to whom, exactly, he is telling this information.

He runs off.

"That's the grad assistant I mentioned. Finn," she says. "I'd better go. I hope you'll call me." She moves to exit the line but I stop her.

I reach out a hand and place it on her arm. A murmur of surprise ripples through the crowd behind her in line, followed by hushed whispers. The Healer doesn't ever touch someone without purpose.

The professor turns back, eyebrows arched over those curious eyes.

I lean in close. "Do *you* believe in my gift?"

She looks at me for a long time. "I don't know. But if you like, we can try and find that out together."

This time, when she walks away, I let her go. I look down at the card.

Dr. Angela Holbrook, Neurobiologist
Director, Center for the Mind & Brain Sciences

There is a series of tall rocks, ledges really, near my house. You can reach them if you walk down a path lined with tall sea grasses and bright-pink beach roses that are pretty but will draw blood with their spiky stems. People are always jumping from those rocks into the churning ocean below. It looks reckless.

I've always wanted to try it. I feel as though I am standing on them now, the flat gray slate hot beneath my bare feet, looking down into the dark sea.

Of course I will go to this doctor, this scientist. How can I not, after today, after Mrs. Jacobs? It was decided the moment I laid eyes on her. Well, and after I laid eyes on him, too. Finn.

PART TWO

Now

EIGHT

The sun shines bright on Angie's face. "Marlena? Why now?" she asks again.

"What do you want from me?" I ask in return.

"I have no agenda, one way or the other, aside from the truth." She stops, then backtracks a bit. "I study the brain, Marlena. The brain is an amazing organ that we know so much—and so little about. I'm interested in understanding the full capacity of the brain, exploring the unusual talents some people are lucky enough to have. And you seem to be one of those lucky people."

I stare at her, trying to take this in, her use of the word *talent* as opposed to *gift* or *power*. "But my 'talent' comes from God." I say these words with confidence, but they suddenly sound crazy. Potentially fake, like Mrs. Jacobs claims.

The same mixture of curiosity and skepticism I saw in Angie's eyes the day she came to my audience appears in them now. She leans forward, her clear lacquered nails gleaming. The warm breeze blows wisps of blond hair around her face. Even her eyebrows are blond. "Is that what you believe, or just what you've been told to believe all of your life?"

I stare at her, unsure how to answer.

I know this must sound weird, but I've never been a person of faith, someone who believes in God and prays to God or gods, if there is more than one. My mother grew up Catholic, but the church that grew up in my honor is not officially Catholic, and technically, it's not even a real church. More of a sideshow with me as the star. But because of it, I've always been around people who believe, whose lives are devoted to prayer, to worshipping within a particular religion. People who have no qualms naming a girl like me a living saint.

Faith is a filmy thing, like a vapor or fog. You can see it, sort of, in the air, wafting around believers, but if you try to grab it your fingers close around nothing.

Healings, though, have substance. You can touch them, feel the newly strong muscles with the pads of your fingers, place your palm against a now-pounding heart, see the smile on someone's face that was once vacant and despairing. Healings have physical markers, physical proof, like a smooth white stone at the beach or mother-of-pearl shimmering in a tide pool. You can reach out and pick them up, admire them.

Healings appear on us.

This, I suppose, is what you could call my faith. Maybe it's why I began drawing my visions. To make them into something real. Something I can see and study and touch.

Lots of religions and cultures have healers. Shamans are healers, and the *sangomas* in South Africa fulfill this role. Catholics will pray to St. Jude or St. Peregrine. But when someone is desperate for help, desperate for hope, it doesn't matter who I am or from what religion and culture I hail, if any. No one cares if I might be a witch, like the women they tortured and drowned and burned in Salem. All that matters is that I work my magic.

Healings, miracles, whatever they are, do not discriminate. Not the way people do and especially not the way religious people sometimes do. All these things we use to divide ourselves up, none of it matters. Healings don't work like that.

They just are.

Angie is watching me, still waiting for me to say something.

"I believe in my gift," I tell her. I decide not to mention Mrs. Jacobs and her claims, which have been floating in and out of my brain like a tide of jellyfish all summer. "But being a healer will never let me be normal. And I'm tired of it."

Angie nods, like she knows exactly what I mean. "You asked me what I want from you. Well, I want to study you. I want to understand your gift better and help you understand it better. I can't promise what we'll find out, but I can promise we'll know more after we study your gift than if we never ask any questions."

I nod. I believe her. I want what she offers. Understanding. Knowledge. I look straight into her curious blue eyes.

"Study me then," I say.

Later, when I am leaving Angie's office, I come around the corner and there he is, sitting in one of the chairs in the waiting room. Finn. He jumps up when he sees me, nearly stumbles, rights himself. Then he leans against the wall and crosses his arms. His lips stretch into a smile.

"Well, if it isn't the fraudulent healer girl."

His voice is playful, but I can detect the mistrust underneath it. It is a rude greeting, but I don't care. I am too taken with him, with that smug look on his face—such a beautiful face—and the gleam in his eyes, intelligent, a little angry maybe, and curious. I recognize that gleam. Angie has it. I like seeing it there.

"I'm Marlena" is all I say to Finn in return.

He tilts his head. My face grows hot as we stand there, watching each other. I am so exposed in my stretchy jeans that show the outline of my knees and thighs, the tank top that forms itself along my body, with the too-large holes for my arms that open to the middle of my ribs, showing off the sides of my bra. I wonder what Finn is thinking. If he is noticing any of these things about me.

Then, out of nowhere, I stick out my hand. I know that's what normal people do, but not me. If I go around touching everybody then the mystery of my healing hands might dissipate, my reputation diminished, according to my mother. My touch must be the rarest of gifts, she always says. I have lived without hugs and affection all my life.

Finn is looking at my hand like it is an alien thing. Maybe he is afraid of it. Maybe he is afraid of finding out I'm not actually a fraud. I wonder if he knows that I never do this, if Angie told him. I wonder if he realizes that this gesture makes him special. Finn uncrosses his arms and extends his hand to me, closes it around mine.

His touch goes straight to my brain and down through my torso into my legs, making them weak and wobbly. His fingers are warm, his palm is warm, and as it presses into me a filmy vision of Finn surrounded by light flashes in my mind, then is gone. The color of it is pale. Washed out. Maybe because I am so nervous.

"Hi, Marlena," Finn says, still hanging on to me. "Nice to meet you. I'm Finn."

I stare at our clasped hands. It is the first time I've ever touched a boy my own age voluntarily, because I want to, and not because I am meant to heal him.

Is this why I feel so many things at once?

My gaze shifts upward to Finn's hazel eyes.

His body is surrounded by light.

I let go of his hand and the light disappears.

We don't say anything else.

I head toward the exit.

Maybe Finn is the angel, not me.

NINE

José peels out of the driveway after dropping me at the house. He doesn't want a run-in with the woman who is standing in the open front door, hands on hips, a scowl on her face. Even the scowl can't ruin my mother's beauty. Her long dark hair that waves just slightly. Her brown eyes and thick lashes, her delicate nose and lips like a bow. All that smooth, olive skin.

"Marlena Oliveira," she barks, the moment I start toward her. She's wearing a white short-sleeved blouse and loose white pants.

My long cotton dress billows around my ankles and wrists. I changed discreetly in the car, jeans and tank top shoved safely at the bottom of my bag. "Yes, Mama?"

"Don't you *yes, Mama* me!"

I study the woman who is my mother, with whom I've grown so far apart this summer, who I now make so angry when before I made her so pleased. People see me in my mother and my mother in me. Some of the T-shirts and trinkets they sell in town show the two of us together. The image is usually of the classic Madonna and child sort, my mother holding me in her arms when I was a baby. Occasionally I see one of those little saint cards with me as a child of nine or ten, my mother sort of floating above me in the background. A divine figure watching over her blessed daughter.

"Where have you been?" she asks.

I breathe in, mustering innocence. "I was at the healing rocks," I lie. The healing rocks are a place I like to go to think and watch the ocean, and where I sometimes prepare for an audience. "I asked José to take me there, Mama. Don't be mad at him. I felt like I needed to recenter myself."

The hard look in her expression softens. "Why didn't you leave a note? Or better yet, why didn't you wait so we could go together?"

I grip the sides of the white cotton dress, my hands sweaty with the humidity. "Next time I will."

She nods, but she is still blocking the doorway. I'm not off the hook yet.

"You forgot that you had a private audience today."

I bite my lip. Realize that my mother is right. I've never done this before. "I'm sorry," I whisper. I might be fighting my mother's rules, but I don't want other people to suffer because of this. "I did forget."

A sheen covers my mother's face. The sun is beating down on her directly but she doesn't narrow her eyes against it. "They've been waiting for you all afternoon."

My legs grow unsteady. "They're still here?"

"Yes, Marlena! Do you think they'd come all this way and then just leave?"

"I don't know, Mama," I say, shoulders starting to hunch. "I'll go up to the receiving room now."

I reach the landing on the front steps, about to pass my mother, when she drops, "I heard about your little escapade in town this morning."

I stop. "Oh?"

"Don't play dumb, Marlena." She turns around. "Fatima!"

A long moment passes before Fatima appears. She's looking at me, apology in her eyes. The dress from my swim, sandy and wrinkled, is in her arms. She holds it out to my mother.

My mother takes it, and sand glitters to the ground. Fatima hurries away. My mother holds the white sheath up to me. "What were you thinking?"

I hang my head.

"What in the world possessed you to go swimming? In front of all those people! In your dress! The tourists have come here to see the healer-saint, not the wild girl-child!"

"I don't have a bathing suit," I respond, which is true. It's something my mother and I have fought over, so not the best answer. Especially since it produces another glare.

"It was hot," I try again, which is also true. The rest of the truth is that I don't really know what possessed me. Something did, something drew me into the water, something mysterious and unnameable. "I just wanted to go for a swim. I'm eighteen. I'm not a child anymore."

I've said the wrong thing again.

"Marlena!" My mother takes a step forward, out of the doorway. The roar of the ocean is loud behind the house. "You must never forget who you are, and lately you can't seem to remember! I don't know what to do with you! I don't know who you are anymore." Her voice trails off, a soft tail of sadness.

"I need a little room to breathe, Mama." My voice grows smaller and smaller.

"Just go," she whispers.

Her quiet is worse than her upset. "Go?"

"Those people are waiting." She finally steps aside to let me pass. As I move by she shrinks away, careful not to touch me.

I wish that instead she would reach out and hug me like other mothers hug their daughters. A storm surge of doubt and uncertainty rises through me. "And what if I can't heal today, Mama? What if my gift doesn't work, like Mrs. Jacobs says? What if I fail? Would you tell me if I did? If you found out from them later?"

"Marlena." My name from her mouth is hard, the pit of an olive.

We are not supposed to speak about that day with Mrs. Jacobs.

My mother closes her eyes. When she opens them they are glassy. "My gifted miracle of a daughter. You still do not know what it is like to love someone with all that you are and then lose them completely. You are lucky to have avoided such an experience, while so many others have had the misfortune of losing everything. Everything and everyone they've ever truly loved." She is thinking of her own parents and my father. When people come asking for a healing audience, I know my mother feels a special connection because of her own losses. For that reason, she also feels a special rage that Mrs. Jacobs did what she did in front of those suffering, grieving people. "Those who come to us, who come to *you*," she goes on, "most of them have lost hope. You are their last hope in this world." My mother tilts her head, and wipes her fingers across the tears that have fallen down her cheeks. "You *will* heal and your gift *will not* fail you. It just can't."

"Yes, Mama," I answer, and head inside.

The receiving room is in a special wing off the side of the house. Long gauzy white curtains billow in the breeze and in the center of it is a long couch, covered in pale-blue linen, where the petitioners sit. They face a single wooden chair, made by my grandfather with careful hands. That is where I am to sit. There is a big white vase on a side table. Fatima fills it with flowers whenever there is an audience. Today it is bursting with pink peonies.

Squeezed into one side of the couch today is a man, not too old, not too young. Maybe forty. He is clutching a woman who must be his mother. Her hair is graying but not totally gray, and she is dressed smartly, in dark-green pants and a cream-colored blouse, her wrists draped with bracelets and her fingers with rings. I see a big diamond on one, with a wedding band pressed tightly against it. She has the look of a woman with style and confidence, who cares for herself and her appearance. Yet to see her face, anyone would immediately know otherwise.

The woman's eyes are vacant. Her mouth is twisted in pain. She is nearly catatonic. When the man hears the soft brush of my slippers on the wood floor he turns. While his mother's face displays a bottomless emptiness, his has the full bloom of desperation and hopelessness, like a black flower that swallows all the light around it. He is quiet and hesitant, uncertainty on his face as he takes me in and I stand there, in front of my grandfather's chair.

"Hello . . ." His mouth is a round O, but nothing else comes out.

"Don't worry," I tell him, because I know just what to do. I have remembered, once again, who I am. I am ready to perform the duties of my gift. In an instant, I am Marlena the Healer. It is like slipping on old, comfortable shoes.

"What is your name?" I ask him.

"Pedro," he says quietly.

"And your mother?"

"Guadalupe."

I nod. I don't bother to sit. There will be no small talk like sometimes with seekers who are nervous, who have questions, who want to have a conversation with the Healer before anything else happens. The son, Pedro, looks at me with fear, afraid to let his mother go, to cede her to me, even though this is what he came here to do.

"Really, don't worry," I tell him again.

"But don't you need to know what—"

"—please," I say, and he presses his lips together into a tight straight line, his arms retracting from his mother. He gets up from the couch and stands aside. She still hasn't looked at me. Not with eyes that can see.

My mother was right.

I have never known grief, or loss, not personally. Not the kind that breaks a heart, never to be the same again, or that immerses someone in a fog for months, even years, the world dimmed and dull and cloaked in perpetual gloom. But I know when I see grief on the face of another person, and it is what I see in Guadalupe, who sits, shoulders slouched, body leaning to one side now that her son is no longer there to support it.

Pedro is pacing in front of the couch, eyes on the floor.

I sit down next to Guadalupe and take her hands into mine. She doesn't acknowledge my presence, doesn't flinch or react. But I think touch must be a basic human instinct. I know just how to smooth my fingers over the lined palms of this sad woman, how to rest my forehead against the thickly veined backs of her brown hands, how to coax the person hidden inside this shell of a body into the world outside again.

I clutch at my chest when I feel the sharp pain of Guadalupe's grief in my heart, and as the colors come. A burned rust sweeps through me first, burned like the dead leaves of fall that turn to dust in your hand. It's followed by the dark red and orange of age, of exhaustion, of a forest after a fire has swept through it. I push past these scenes, the despair that enshrouds Guadalupe in darkness. I see that she has lost a son, her youngest, and her husband, too. My heart cries out at the depth of her pain. Pedro has lost a father and a brother, but people move through grief in different ways, and some, like Guadalupe, enter it as though it is an underworld that traps them in its grip forever.

Visions of tragedy, of untimely good-byes and trauma, wash over me in sepia tones. I draw them into myself, into my own body, taking the burden from Guadalupe into my mind and heart and soul, into the hands that hold tight to hers. I absorb the worst of it, the depths of her affliction. That is my job.

Then, I see a glimmer of yellow. Then another of green and blue. Hues of pink and lilac, accompanied by happy memories, the beautiful and the bright, the ones that lie buried under the cloak of Guadalupe's despair. They are there. The life and future of Guadalupe is buried deep, but waiting. I uncover it for her. I draw it back into view.

And I stay, holding her hands, forehead pressed against her skin, chasing away the thick storm of her affliction until I feel the hope stirring in her again, until I feel the sight returning to her eyes, and until I feel the life in my own body draining away.

❖ ❖ ❖

When I wake I am staring up into the face of Fatima.

I am lying on the couch on my back in the receiving room. Pedro and Guadalupe are gone. I must have passed out.

"Marlena," Fatima says. "Are you okay?"

She holds a glass of water. I struggle to sit up. My head swirls and tips. "I'm fine," I croak.

She nods.

I take the water and gulp it down. Watch as Fatima leaves. Wait for enough strength to stand and to walk. Did I heal Guadalupe's pain? Did I remove enough of the despair from her heart so she can make her way back into the realm of the living?

Will my mother tell me if I did or didn't?

I get up slowly, my legs unsteady. The sun is on its way down along the horizon. I wonder where my mother is, if she showed Guadalupe and Pedro out while I was asleep. I pass by the kitchen on my way to my room. Fatima is there, standing behind the island. Her hands are powdered with flour, palms pressed into a fat ball of dough for the sweet bread she knows is my favorite.

She stops kneading when she sees me. "I didn't show your mother that dress from your swim, Marlena," she says. "I would never. She found it on her own. If I'd found it first, I would have washed it before she could have known."

"Don't worry," I tell her. "It's okay."

Fatima's dark hair is streaked with gray even though she is not yet forty. Like Mama, Fatima came here from São Miguel as a child, with her fisherman father and her seamstress mother. She has four children at home and no husband to help her. Mama pays Fatima well, pays her quadruple what anyone else would because she knows how difficult it is to make a new life in a place where you weren't born, when you are alone and have people who depend on you. It is good to remember that Mama has a lot of kindness in her. Kindness she shows to Fatima.

Fatima is still watching me, hands balling and pushing at that pillowy dough. "Marlena, is there anything you want to talk about?" she asks. There is a beat of silence, broken only by the hollow sound of her palm against the dough, but she seems to want to say something else. "You can talk to me. I'm . . . I'm here for you."

I stare at her, considering this strange new offer, and the deal Fatima and I made earlier today to not tell on each other. But then the handle on the front door turns, my mother about to enter the house from wherever she's been. "See you later," I say and run to the stairs before Fatima can respond and before my mother sees me there.

A big bag of mail, of letters and petitions, has been deposited outside my bedroom door. It rises nearly to the top of my knee, a drawstring pulling it closed at the top. I get one every month. Tonight I walk by without touching it. I've had enough of healing today.

I shut the door of my room carefully, hoping my mother will think I'm asleep and not come up to see me. I wonder if Fatima is telling her she found me passed out on the receiving room couch.

I wonder what my mother will think it means that I did, or if she won't think it means anything at all.

I grab a book and sit in the chair by the open windows, grateful for the evening breeze. My attention floats from the pages to the wall. Across it are my careful drawings, my paintings, my collages of favorite visions. More than one—if you look closely—take the shape of a human heart, hearts I've healed. Colors define them. Hues of purple, green, yellows and reds and oranges. One is dominated by bright, hot pinks. Some of the drawings are a collection of the tiny scenes that sometimes accompany the vision about the life and future of a person I've healed. But mostly they are intricate, detailed bursts of light and color. I have never chosen to paint the dark gray and black storm of despair like I saw today. I've always tried to capture the light that peeks out from those murky depths, the yellow of hope and the aqua blue and pink of joy.

My easel stands nearby, in the far corner of my room, waiting for me to go to it.

Tonight I'm too tired to paint.

I try to focus on the book that sits open in my lap, but my mind keeps drifting. My thoughts shift to Finn. The waves beyond my windows are crashing against the rocks, and I hear his voice intermingled with these sounds, calling me a fraud. Images of him fill my vision, a flush starting to burn across my skin.

Who am I kidding?

Gorgeous, genius Finn surely has a million girlfriends, probably has a girlfriend now. Why would he ever want someone like me? These thoughts send me into bed, pulling the covers up to my chin. I don't care that it's humid, that my body sweats, that I haven't eaten dinner.

A strange thing happens while I sleep.

I have a vision, the kind I get when I'm about to perform a healing. The strange part is that I'm not about to perform a healing and the vision is about Finn. I've only had visions of people I'm meant to heal, and usually that is only while I'm touching them.

In the vision I see Finn, clear as day, as though he is standing in front of me. He's looking at me in a way that no one has ever looked at me. This vision is less about color and more about scenes, scenes of the future, but in this one, I am a part of Finn's future. In Finn's eyes, I see love. Real love. Romantic love. *Finn loves me*, my vision reveals. But then, I watch as Finn turns and walks into a dark tunnel, or maybe it's a dark wood. I try to follow him but I can't. I'm rooted to the spot where I stand. I call out, but he keeps on going, walking until he disappears into the darkness.

It's so vivid, so powerful, so upsetting, that it wakes me.

I sit up in bed, covered in sweat, sheets drenched. My stomach groans with emptiness and my heart is pounding and pounding in my chest. I get up and stand by the open windows and let the breeze cool my hot skin. Try to breathe.

If my vision is right, it means something wonderful and terrible at once.

Finn will fall in love with me.

And then he'll break my heart.

I press my hands against the frame of the window.

Maybe I'm mistaken. Maybe it wasn't a vision at all.

Maybe, maybe, it was only a dream.

TEN

Over the next two weeks, I go to see Angie every afternoon.

I am an addict, José my reluctant dealer.

Finn and I have reached an unspoken agreement to remain at a safe distance. I think he is keeping this distance out of respect. I wish he wouldn't. I wish for less respect.

I learn bits and pieces about him. He's three years older. He's a prodigy. At twenty-one he's already far along in his PhD in neuroscience. He finished his undergrad at nineteen, just one year older than I am now. He is an actual, living, breathing genius. He and Angie are close, almost like a mother and son. I am jealous.

Today when I enter Angie's office she is sitting cross-legged on the floor, piles of paper spread in front of her. Finn is nowhere to be seen. The windows are open even though it is hot. Angie doesn't like the air conditioning. The sounds of the sea help her concentrate, she told me.

Angie pats the spot next to her on the rug.

I sit down and cross my legs like Angie's, sink into the luxurious wool of the rug and wait for her to speak. I can tell she is thinking about something. Her eyes are halfway closed, and she breathes slowly, like she might be meditating. Angie's blond hair is loose and falling around her shoulders, all that thick butter yellow.

Her lids fall open and her eyes are on me. "Tell me something, Marlena. What do you think about our visits so far?"

"I don't know," I answer carefully. "It's weird, to be studied. By someone who doesn't believe in me," I add.

Angie doesn't seem offended by my comment. "You think I don't believe in you?"

"Well, you're a scientist."

Her fingers press deep into the rug. "And you think scientists can't believe in the unseen?"

"I think scientists don't believe in miracles."

"Do you believe in miracles?"

Her question comes so quickly, so easily, it almost seems she hasn't just asked me whether I believe in the very thing that has defined my entire life. "Of course I do," I say.

Angie switches the cross of her legs. "You don't sound certain, though."

She's right. If she'd asked me several months ago, the certainty would have been plain. "There was this woman who came to my audience in June. Actually the same day you showed up." I tell her about Mrs. Jacobs and what Mrs. Jacobs claimed.

"Do you think she might be right?" Angie asks.

"No. I mean, I didn't think so before." I pull my knees into me and wrap my arms around my shins. "But I don't know anymore. So many people come in and out of my life at my audiences, it's not as though I keep track of everyone. Maybe some of my healings work, and some don't. That would make sense, right? For me not to have a perfect track record?"

"It seems reasonable," Angie agrees. "But what do you think might make the difference between a healing that 'worked,' as you said, and one that didn't?"

Her question makes me laugh. "Talking to you is like what I've imagined it would be to talk to a therapist."

Angie waits for me to say more, the good scientist-therapist she always is.

I roll my eyes. "Okay. Your question is good, but I don't know how to answer it. I don't think I've ever articulated out loud that some of my healings might work and some might not, until right now."

She picks up a pen and takes a few quick notes. "Would you feel okay if it turned out that you didn't have a 'perfect track record,' as you put it?"

I shake my head. "No."

"You seem pretty certain of that."

I think of what my mother said the other day, about how I am people's last hope. How my gift isn't allowed to fail. "It wouldn't be fair to those who depend on me."

"You feel responsible for a lot of people."

I rest my chin on my knees. Grip my shins tighter. The understanding on Angie's face, the sympathy, makes me want to hug her. Like I wanted to hug Fatima the other day. Does growing up and turning eighteen make you more affectionate?

"I am responsible," I tell her simply, but there is a force behind those words. A strong gale of something not quite identifiable. "To the townspeople and their shops, to people I haven't even met who need me, or who will. What if I suddenly couldn't help them? What if they died and it was all my fault?"

Angie leans forward, the papers in her lap sliding off. "But . . ."

She does this. Angie inserts a single word, then a pause, because she wants me to finish my thought. I do my best to keep going, to give her a real answer, the gale slicing through me. "Sometimes I don't want to be responsible for anybody. Sometimes I want to go to school like everyone else my age. Sometimes I want to walk down the streets of town and not see a single image of my face on a T-shirt or a key chain or . . . or even a kite. Sometimes I want to know what it's like to not have people whispering about me, or treating me like I'm special, or worse, treating me like I'm some freak." The list pours from me like a poison my body needed to purge. "I've had healing audiences every week since before I can remember. I've been given gifts and treated like I'm a saint and I don't want to sound ungrateful, but . . ."

"But?" Angie presses again.

Anger flashes in a fiery orange ball and I wish I could hurl it at something. "But sometimes I *hate* it, I hate *all* of it." The word *hate* comes out hard and cold and vicious. I dig my fingernails into the woolen knots of the rug. "I don't have any friends. I've never been out, just to have fun. I'm never, ever touched." I push my fingers deeper into the rug, prying the fibers apart. "I've never had a boyfriend. I'm eighteen and I've never kissed anyone and I probably never will." I look up. "All because of my *gift*." My breaths come fast. "Sometimes I don't care if not being a healer means that people will die," I add, these words flying out of me.

Right then, Finn slinks around the corner.

Our eyes meet.

Then mine flee his.

How much did he hear? The last part surely. But the part about never having a boyfriend, never having been kissed or touched? I wait for Finn to tell me I'm a horrible person, who he'd never consider touching if I was the last girl on earth.

All Finn says is "Nice outfit."

Angie gets up, a little awkwardly. Her eyes narrow at him.

But Finn's eyes are on me. I am wearing one of my white dresses today.

"The girl-in-an-asylum look really suits you," he says.

Angie looks like she wants to kill him. "Finn!"

I cover my mouth and start to laugh, and Finn grins.

"Ignore him, Marlena," Angie says.

"No, he's right." I pull myself off the floor. "I've often thought I have that escaped-from-an-asylum thing going on."

Finn's grin settles into a smile and it's hard not to smile back. "What, did your mother drive you here instead of your chauffeur today?" He makes finger quotes around the word *chauffeur*.

"He's not a chauffeur, he's José," I say. "And no, my mother didn't drive me. She'd never let me come here if she knew about it."

"Marlena!" Now Angie turns her exasperation on me. "You have to tell your mother."

I lift my chin. "I'm eighteen. I'm not a minor. I signed those release forms you gave me, so it's none of her business whether I do this."

Finn whistles, then eyes Angie.

Angie shakes her head. "That may be true, but you are not just a study subject. You are a person, a girl, and one who depends on her mother. I do not want to put your well-being at home in jeopardy. I'd be a bad researcher if I did."

"More like *she* depends on *me*," I say under my breath. Then I glance at the clock on the wall of the office. An hour has gone by already. "I should go, actually."

"How do you feel about an MRI before you leave?" Angie searches my face for a reaction.

Angie has asked to scan my brain each time I've come. The

thought of being inside that machine in her lab makes me shudder. I'm not ready for anyone to see inside my head, even though I'm also curious what Angie might find out. "Not today," I say.

"What are you so afraid of, Marlena?" Finn's tone is edged with something.

"Finn!" Angie scolds again. "Stop reminding me how young and difficult you are. If you weren't so smart . . ." She trails off.

"I don't know why I'm resisting it," I answer. "I just know I'm not ready."

Finn's stare cuts through me. "Maybe you're afraid we'll find out you're as normal as everyone else."

"That's enough from you, Finn." Angie's voice is firm, the topic closed. "That's fine, Marlena. If and when you're ready, please let me know."

Finn sighs. I know he's disappointed that Angie let me off the hook so easily. His gaze drifts to a pile of papers on Angie's desk, then it returns to me.

Our eyes catch.

I take a step closer. "What?"

Finn shrugs. "We put out a public call for people you've supposedly healed to contact us for an interview. What it was like. How long it took before they were well again. Before-and-after reports from doctors. That sort of thing." Finn stops there, but there is something else in his expression.

"What are you leaving out?"

Finn places a hand firmly on that stack, fingers wide and pressing down. "These are emails from people who think you're a fake."

Something in my chest tightens. "Really?" Finn nods. Angie's eyes are on me. I guess I should have been prepared for something like this. There must be plenty of Mrs. Jacobses in the world. Maybe it is time I face them. "Um, what if I want to read them sometime?"

Angie's eyebrows arch. "You don't have to—"

"—maybe not," I interrupt. "But at some point, I might want to." My eyes seek the machines in the lab beyond Angie's office door. "Kind of like the MRI, I guess. I'm not quite ready yet, but maybe I will be. Eventually."

"Of course," Angie says quietly.

"I really have to go. It's getting late."

"I'll walk you out," Finn offers.

I keep to the middle of the hallway, wanting to be close to him, but he stays all the way to the other side, his hand dragging against the wall.

"You're a surprise, Marlena," he says.

"Good. You could use a little excitement in your life, Finn."

"I hear you could use a little yourself," he shoots back.

I blush slightly. "Fair enough." Then I announce, "I have an audience this Saturday."

Finn stares straight ahead. "I know."

I glance at him. "Aren't you curious?"

"I'm skeptical," he warns. "And maybe like the MRI, you're not quite ready for me to be there yet."

I slow my pace. "How can you work with Angie on this project and not come to see me?"

He grows quiet. We pass Lexi and get closer to the exit, closer to good-bye with every step. We reach the doors and I think I might leave without Finn saying another word. But just before I go he speaks.

"I *am* curious," he admits.

I stare into the parking lot. José is standing next to the driver's side of the car, arms crossed, looking anxious. Then I look at Finn, who's leaning against the wall inside the vestibule of the entrance, arms crossed too. People are always crossing their arms around me. I think they're afraid if they don't, they'll touch the sacred object that is me by accident. "Why don't you come then? See for yourself what it's like?" My heart pumps hard in my chest as I say this. It almost feels like I am asking Finn out. "You can be my special guest."

Finn laughs. "You have special guests?"

"No." I shake my head. "But I will make you one. I can do whatever I want. It's my audience."

"You sound spoiled," Finn says.

"Probably," I say, and look at him hard. "Or maybe it's just that I am lonely and undersocialized and don't know any better. I'll see you on Saturday, Finn," I add, before I hurry outside into the heat.

ELEVEN

The next morning when I go to the kitchen looking for breakfast, the best kind of surprise awaits me.

"Helen!" I yelp, and she looks up from the coffee she is drinking. Her hair has grown longer since the last time we saw each other. It is thick and lustrous, a cascade of brown butterscotch, and her skin is tan from the sun. From all that tennis she plays, I suppose.

"Hey there!" Helen gets up from the stool where she was sitting at the counter.

"I've never been so glad to see you," I say. Helen is the closest thing I've ever had to a friend. Or maybe more of an older sister.

She eyes me, then she eyes my mother, who has just entered the kitchen. "Oh yeah?"

I nod.

Helen is the first person I remember healing.

❖ ❖ ❖

My memories of that day are potent. I am six, Helen is nine. She is in a wheelchair, a tall thin man behind her, rolling her up the aisle. She wears a short, yellow dress, yellow like the sun in August. Her legs seem spindly, like they can't hold her up. They are bent at sharp angles. Her eyes are sunken into her face. I skip toward her, liking the way my dress swirls around my knees. Does her father think I am mocking his daughter? Does the rest of the audience? By the time I am at her chair I can hear her quick puffs of breath.

"Saint Marlena, please heal me," she begs. Then she lowers her gaze. "I am at your mercy."

I am at your mercy.

I remember these words most of all. At the time I didn't understand them. I had to ask my mother that night about mercy, what it was and why this little girl thought I had it.

I grab onto Helen's armrest and look into her bottomless eyes. She blinks back, scared.

"Don't be afraid," I tell her. "I like your dress."

"I like yours," she whispers.

I get down on my knees. I've nearly forgotten the crowd around us, though now I can remember them, the way they seem to draw close, holding their breath. Helen watches me, big eyes stuck to mine, her father's too. I study her legs, the way the muscle has withered away along the left calf, the way her kneecaps are plainly visible underneath pale, sagging skin. I press my hands flat against her shins.

That's when the vision starts. A bright, pulsing red.

The color spreads like a sunburst, a whirling blur of images, of this little girl, her eyes, her mouth, her limbs. They swirl until they are me and I am them, until they are all that I am and ever will be. Until the girl and I are the same, an instance of perfect wholeness, like merging with the universe and taking another person with you.

As the vision settles, Helen's future flashes before my eyes.

I see her legs. They are fleshy and healthy and shaped the way a young girl's legs should be, the legs of a girl who plays soccer and tennis and goes out for runs. They are strong legs, beautiful legs, legs that any boy would admire, and they are, without a doubt, most definitely hers.

I look up at the girl again. "What's your name?"

"Helen," she says.

I gather her thin legs into my arms, the only hugs I am ever allowed. Rest my cheek against the bones of her shins. I feel the transformation begin, I can nearly see it happening, the shift from these sick and neglected legs to the legs that Helen will have someday soon. "Helen, you will walk. You will see. We will run together." I let go and get up. "Come and see me when you're better," I tell her.

Helen *did* come back; she's come back many times. On each visit she walks straight and tall on her beautiful legs, legs that run and jump and play soccer. Legs that all the boys admire at the college where she's on the tennis team, but legs that all the girls admire, too. It turns out, Helen prefers the girls' admiration to the boys'.

Helen is living proof, I suppose, that my gift is real. Inexplicable maybe, but true.

As Helen and my mother exchange greetings, I notice a big white plastic bag sitting on the counter. I bet that inside is a lemon cake from a bakery where Helen lives. She knows I love them. "You don't have to keep thanking me," I tell Helen every time I see her, telling her to stop bringing gifts, that her friendship is plenty. She brings them anyway.

My mother places a stack of documents in front of her on the kitchen island. "Good morning, Marlena." Her tone is formal. Polite. Helen will always be welcome in our home because of our history, but my mother doesn't like it when I get close to someone else. "Did you sleep well?"

I shake my head. I had another vision of Finn, the same one as before. Another maybe-dream. "It was too hot in my room."

"Why didn't you turn on the air conditioning?" she asks. Her expression darkens. "You're not getting sick, are you?"

"No, Mama," I reply, my tone formal to match hers. "Don't worry, I'll be fine for the audience on Saturday."

She nods. "Good. We have important people coming and you need to be at your best." There is a covered plate next to the sink. My mother points to it. "Fatima made some bollos for you." Her voice is accusing, but the promise of Fatima's Portuguese bollos, little individual round breads shaped like English muffins, overrides this.

"Helen, are you hungry?" I ask, even as I'm uncovering the plate and slicing one in half so I can toast it. Sometimes I'll eat them only with butter, but often I make sandwiches with them.

"I ate on the way here," Helen says.

I peer into the bag Helen brought, and I was right: lemon cake. I suddenly feel loved. "I'm starving," I tell her. "I hope you don't mind."

She takes a small sip of her coffee. "Take your time."

When my two halves of bollo pop up from the toaster I butter them and gobble them down. "You're missing out, Helen. No one makes bollos like Fatima."

She laughs. "Really. I don't want to get in the middle of the romance you're having with those."

"Your loss," I say, shoving the rest in my mouth, a too-big bite, but I don't care. I wait for my mother to say something cutting about my poor manners, about talking with my mouth full, about eating too fast, but she doesn't seem to notice.

I am about to dig into Helen's lemon cake when my mother looks up from the documents she's been studying. "Marlena, I have incredible news. One of the major networks is going to do an eight-part series about you for television! The lawyers sent over the proposal from the network." She turns to Helen to share her joy, but Helen stares into her coffee cup like it might tell her fortune. "The producers of the show want to come here to follow you around for a few weeks, see you at home, film at your audiences. They want to tell the story of your life. You'll be even more famous!"

A television show? Follow me around for weeks? I'd have no privacy. No chance of escaping to see Angie or Finn. I would have to be Marlena the Saint, Marlena the Healer, perfect and demure, performing my role 24/7. I feel Helen's eyes on me. I slide the lemon cake away from me.

"Isn't that wonderful?" my mother presses.

"Yes, Mama," I agree.

No, Mama. It's horrible.

"We will need an even bigger church than we have now after it airs!"

"I'm so excited," I say, though my tone communicates the opposite. I refuse to look my mother in the eye. Instead I look at Helen. "Come on, let's go for a walk." I head out the back door of the house and into the garden, still in my robe and pajamas. I don't care. I want to be in the fresh air. I hear Helen's steps behind me, but I don't slow down. I take the path in our yard that leads to a stairway down to the ocean. I sit on the top step and wait for Helen to join me.

She kicks her shoes off onto the grass and arranges herself at the other end of the wooden slat. "Marlena, what's going on?"

I stare out at the water, at the way the sun shines across the ripples, creating moving slivers of light. I inhale the briny smell. I never tire of it. "I don't know." I turn to look at Helen, envious of the jean shorts that show off her long perfect legs, her clingy cotton

T-shirt. The casual way she wears her clothes. "I don't want to be on a television show. I don't want the church to be any bigger. I don't want any more attention than I already have."

"Marlena . . . you sound so . . . so conflicted," Helen says. "And upset."

I close my eyes, tears welling. They spill down my cheeks and drip from my chin onto my robe. I wipe my hand across my face. "Let's talk about something else. I want to hear about you. Why the visit? Shouldn't you be starting fall classes or something?"

Helen rests her arms across her knees and leans forward. "I start school on Monday. But I'm here because I got a phone call from a Dr. Angela Holbrook, who wants to interview me about you." She takes a deep breath. "Is *she* part of why you're so upset?"

I sniffle. "No. Angie's nice. You'll like her."

"Angie? So you *are* working with her. She told me she had your permission to interview people, but I wondered if it was true. I wanted to talk to you before I went to see her." Helen is still bent forward, close but not close enough to touch. "I wanted to make sure you were okay if I spoke to her. That she wasn't doing some shitty exposé on you, trying to prove you're a fake or something."

I mimic the way Helen sits, resting my arms across my knees. I scoot toward her, relieved when she doesn't shift away. "It's okay to talk to her. Really."

Helen's hair shines against the backdrop of blue sky. "Tell me about Dr. Holbrook then. What's the deal?"

A seagull is pecking at a clamshell at the edge of the surf, trying to pry it open with its beak. "Angie is a neuroscientist and she studies the brain. She's interested in my gift. Where it comes from. What it is. How it works. Whether it's real," I add.

Helen huffs. "You don't need a scientist to tell you about your gift. And you certainly know for a fact that it's real. I'm living proof!" She crosses and uncrosses her long tan legs as if to remind me. She places her hands on her bare, toned thighs.

I rest my chin against my forearms, watching the gull attack its breakfast. "But what if it wasn't? What if everything is falling apart?"

Helen shifts so she can peer into my face. "Marlena, please tell me what's going on. Stop talking in half statements. You can trust me. I'm your friend."

Tears sting the backs of my eyes again. "You really are my friend, aren't you? You're the only one I have." I nudge my foot against a pebble until it falls off the edge of the step, tumbling toward the rocks below. "You're my friend despite the fact that you bring me gifts as payback. Friends don't owe each other like that. Friends are equals."

Helen looks away. "I know you always say that, but it's tradition. An expectation. Not something I can simply decide not to do."

"My mother's tradition. Not mine."

"Okay. I won't do it anymore," Helen says. "I'm sorry. You are my friend. You are." She repeats this, as though she knows how hard it will be to convince me. But then she does the one thing that makes me believe what she says is true. She reaches out a hand and places it on my back. She leaves it there, her palm warm and soothing.

A sob escapes my chest, despite my trying to hold it in.

Helen reaches her arm around me and draws me into a hug. I feel her chin pressing on the top of my head. Soon I am crying hard.

"Oh, Marlena," Helen says after a while, once my sobs turn to hiccups and my breaths grow more even. "It's going to be okay."

"Don't let go of me."

"I won't, I won't," Helen says, rubbing her hand up and down my arm.

Eventually the tears dry and my body grows calm. Helen and I sit there in the quiet of the morning, pressed together, watching the waves as they come into the shore and recede. I hope my mother doesn't see us clutching each other. I try and memorize the feeling of being touched by someone who cares, someone who wants nothing from me other than to help, someone who calls herself my friend and means it. I wonder what life would be like if a comforting touch was a normal occurrence, if it would make me into a different person. Maybe there are other people who would be willing to comfort me, too, and not only because my touch could heal them.

"You are just as much a healer as I am," I tell Helen.

She laughs softly. "I wish that were true. I wish I were gifted like you."

"Sometimes it makes my life hateful."

"But your ability to heal is something incredible. The kind of thing people want to do a television show about."

I pull back. "Maybe they should do a television show about you and your tennis and your romantic girlfriends and your college friends and your nice college life." My voice is fiery.

Helen stares at me, like she is trying to figure out if I'm kidding.

"I'm serious," I tell her.

Helen laughs. "What in the world are you talking about?" Helen shifts and our knees touch. "Now you have to tell me what's going on. No more stalling. I want to know everything."

I stare at the place where our skin touches so casually. Wish that everyone in my life could act this way, grateful Helen mustered the courage. "Everything is changing. I'm changing, but maybe my gift is changing, too."

"What do you mean?"

"It's just, it's always been who I am. I've never known how to be anyone else other than Marlena the Healer, and before, I never wanted to be. It was enough. But lately I've wanted more, different things, the kinds of things other people take for granted, like school and friends and parties on weekends. Which makes me sound shallow, I know—"

"—Marlena—"

"—but then, I also can't stop thinking about whether my gift is real, if it works, or if it only sometimes works." The words are spilling out, and I let them. "And I wonder if that is a new thing, like, if my gift is a kind of reservoir in me, and I've almost used it up. Like maybe sometimes when I reach for it, I only touch dry land, and other times I reach the place within me where it still remains, but soon those places will have dried up too." I tell Helen about Mrs. Jacobs. It feels good to get it out again, like when I discussed it with Angie, this thing my mother has forbidden us to speak about.

Helen's cheeks turn bright red as she listens. "I already hate this Mrs. Jacobs-lady."

I shake my head. "I don't. Maybe I needed her to do what she did. To open my eyes."

"You don't owe her anything."

A tall, spindly blue flower rises through the steps and I catch the petals gently in my hand, admiring them. "You're in good company hating her. My mother wants her banished from the town."

"I bet. Your mother is a formidable woman. She is not to be messed with."

I let go of the flower. "That's the other thing. My mother and I are fighting constantly about the ways I'm changing. I'm just so tired, Helen, of being this person, performing Marlena the Saint all day, every day. The thought of a TV show following me around twenty-four seven. I can't even . . . God, it would be horrible. Sometimes I feel like a machine that people use at will, that the whole town uses to generate itself."

"Oh, Marlena," Helen says carefully. "I don't want you to feel that way."

"My mother wishes I could still be ten years old," I go on, "and tries to dress me like a little girl and says it's to protect my reputation, but I don't care about my reputation anymore. I want to be irreputable. Like not reputable at all. *Disreputable.*"

The serious look on Helen's face evaporates, replaced by laughter. It makes me laugh with her, a laughter that feels good. "Yeah, I'm sure your mother wouldn't like that," she says, rolling her eyes. "No way. No boyfriends—or girlfriends—not for saints." She seems thoughtful. "How about this for a title for their television special: *Marlena Oliveira: The Ruining of a Former Saint.*"

This makes me laugh even more. "Or: *The Miracle Healer of New England: Depurified Before Your Very Own Eyes!*"

"I'd watch either one of those shows," Helen says.

My arm is wrapped around my middle from laughing so hard. "Maybe Angie will prove I'm a fake and then no one will want to do any television shows about me."

Helen's brow furrows. "But why would you want that? Without you, without your miracles, my life wouldn't be my life." She sounds slightly betrayed.

This is the last thing I want. "I'm sorry Helen. I promise that's not what this is about. But sometimes, lately, my gift feels like a curse. I wouldn't want to trade my visions. But I don't want to be a business anymore, to be the center of an entire church." I think of Guadalupe yesterday, and the desperation inside her son's eyes. "I want a normal life. A television show would kill that." I pick up a stone and grip it tightly in the center of my palm. "Sometimes I want to wish away this so-called gift."

"But Marlena, can you even imagine life without your gift? It would be such a drastic change."

"Sometimes I don't care. Sometimes I just want to be free."

Helen sighs. "You may not always feel that way. You may not like the life that comes afterward."

"Yes," I say, sure this is true. "Yes I will."

"So you trust this Dr. Holbrook?" Helen asks after a long silence.

I nod. "I do."

"All right. I'll make an appointment to talk to her."

I suddenly think about Helen meeting Finn. All thoughts of Finn make my heart flutter, and I smile.

"Marlena." Helen draws out my name. "What else aren't you telling me?"

Warmth creeps up my neck. "There might be a boy." I try and keep my eyes on the ocean. "Dr. Holbrook has a grad assistant. I kind of might . . . like him."

Helen drums her thighs. "You have a crush!"

I cover my eyes with my hands. "He's so gorgeous. And tall. And perfect. His name is Finn." I love the way his name sounds when I say it.

"How old is he?"

"Twenty-one."

"An older crush!"

"Yes." I slide my hands down my face and look at her over the tips of my fingers. "He doesn't believe in me. He thinks I'm a fake."

The playfulness in Helen's eyes dims. "That doesn't bother you?"

I shake my head. "If anything, it's a relief."

Helen stands up. "Okay then. Get dressed. We're going out."

I rise to my feet. "Where?"

"To Dr. Holbrook's center so I can make an appointment in person, since I already came all the way out here. I may as well, right?"

"But—"

"Marlena! Because maybe Finn will be there and I want to check him out!"

"Oh!" I put my hand over my mouth.

"And afterward we're going out to eat. I want all the gory details about this crush of yours. Then I can offer my expert advice." Helen's eyelashes flutter. "I am rather an expert in the romance and love department."

"You really want to do all that stuff?"

Helen smiles and stands up from the step. "Of course I do. Friends are there for each other where romance is concerned."

"I wouldn't know." I get up to join her.

Helen is already heading across the lawn toward the house. Her hair swings from side to side as she walks. "Well, now you do," she calls back.

TWELVE

"What, exactly, did you tell my mother so I could spend the afternoon with you?" I ask from the passenger seat of Helen's old, beat-up Volvo.

She shifts into gear when the stoplight turns green. "Just that I wanted to take you to lunch as an offering after the healing walk we'll be going on." The car speeds up. "I told her my legs have been bothering me."

I look at Helen, at her long legs, the way her right foot moves easily between the gas pedal and the brake. "Have they?"

She laughs. "No, absolutely not."

"So you just lied to my mother?"

"Yup," Helen says with a shrug. "People lie to their parents all the time. Today, we're giving you an education in normalcy. First, hugs while you're crying. Next, your friend—because I am your friend—lies to your mother on your behalf, so we can get the hell out of your house for a few hours." Helen reaches behind my seat and pulls a bright-green bag off the floor and plops it into my lap. "Now, you're going to go through my stuff and pick out a real outfit to wear and not this nightgown thing"—Helen pinches the gauzy material at my shoulder—"because this just will not do, and also, one of the most typical things girls do in high school is go out of the house wearing what their mothers approve of, and immediately change clothes into something totally slutty once they're with their friends."

My jaw has fallen open as Helen goes through this list, her eyes still on the road, driving us past the town as naturally as José. "I've done that a couple of times now."

"You've done what?"

"Gone out in an outfit my mother would never approve of, and on the way home changed back into one of my hateful nightgowns so she wouldn't know."

Helen smiles. "You're getting more normal by the minute. And you don't even have to stop being a healer, Marlena. You can be both, see?"

I ignore this comment. Helen means well, but it's hard for anyone to understand what it's like to be me. I think back to my outfit yesterday. "I haven't worn anything slutty, though."

"That part doesn't matter. I was mostly kidding about the slutty part."

"But," I go on, "one time, the jeans were skinny jeans, and you could see my bra through the armholes of the tank top."

"Just the right bit of slutty then." Helen rounds the corner and heads down the road along the sea. "Perfectly normal where someone you have a crush on is concerned."

A question has been brewing in me and I muster the courage to ask it, reminding myself that I can talk to Helen about anything. That she's a friend. She says so herself. "In the vein of helping me be normal," I start, then trail off when I see where we are.

"Tell me."

"But we're almost to Angie's center."

Helen pulls the car over and turns off the ignition. "We have time." She grabs the bag from my lap and starts digging through it. "Besides, you need to change clothes. What if Finn is there when you go to see Dr. Holbrook?" She pulls out a green dress with spaghetti straps and a wide scoop neck. "Put this on and talk."

My eyebrows arch. "Now?"

Helen turns away. "In the effort to not overwhelm you with so much normalcy, I won't watch. Now say what you wanted to say."

I unbutton the sleeves of my white cotton shift, trying as best I can to wiggle out of it in the passenger seat of the car. At least the road is deserted. "My question," I begin, but again can't manage to finish the sentence. I'm not used to having someone I can really talk to, especially about things that are slightly embarrassing.

"Marlena . . ."

I pull the sundress over my head and slide it down my body.

Everything I've been wondering comes pouring out. "What's it like to kiss someone? I mean, how do you even do it? How does it work? Like, is there a magic formula or something?" I wait for Helen's laughter, for her to mock me.

But she doesn't. "Such excellent questions. So you want to kiss Finn."

My cheeks grow hot. I yank the hem of the sundress as far as it will go over my thighs. "He doesn't think of me that way. But I wish I could kiss him. I've thought about it. Or tried to think about it. I don't really have much experience to draw on. Or any," I add, my eyes on my bare, knobby knees.

"If you really like him, and he likes you back, experience won't matter," Helen says. "You'll find your way."

The sound of the waves crashing comes through the windows and fills the silence. "I want him to like me so badly."

Helen sighs. "I want him to like you, too."

I shake my head slightly. "Why would he? I'm such a freak."

"You are not. Don't try and convince yourself of things that aren't true."

Helen sounds so sure of this, and I want to believe her. "The whole town thinks I'm a freak. The other kids my age talk about me like I am one. I hear Fatima and José discussing the gossip about me that goes around town."

"They're just jealous of what you can do," Helen says.

"Right. Everyone must wish to live in total isolation, then draw crowds hoping for photos and begging for help on the weekends. It's such a blast. Way better than going to homecoming and prom."

Helen turns the key in the ignition and the car rumbles back to life. "Marlena, you perform miracles." She glances in the side mirror and pulls onto the road. "You may not believe that people could be jealous. But trust me, to have the ability to change someone's life, as you do over and over, is amazing. Something you can't dismiss without at least a little admiration."

I try and take in what Helen said. "You really believe in me."

"Of course I do," she responds, with the same confidence as earlier. "Don't you?" she asks. It sounds almost like an afterthought, a question she doesn't expect me to answer because the truth, at least to her, is so obvious.

So I let the question hang there, suspended on the sounds of the ocean as it rises and falls around us, beautiful and loud and unpredictable.

We get out of the car. Goose bumps rise along my arms and legs even though it's hot outside. It seems like this heat isn't ever going away. "This dress is so short."

Helen appraises me. "Calm down. That dress is perfect for you."

I try to ignore the strange feeling of air along the skin of my shins, my knees, my thighs. "If you say so."

Helen heads to the door of the center. "Are you coming or what?"

"I'm right behind you."

We head inside, Helen first, all confidence, like she's been here before and knows exactly what she's doing, where to go. She marches right up to Lexi, who I now know is studying neuroscience, like Finn, and who told me once while I was waiting for Angie that Angie has dozens of students competing for the chance to answer phones at the center. Just to be in Angie's vicinity.

Helen explains to Lexi why she's here and I wander down the hall, skin prickling with static, curious if Finn is around somewhere, if he might be sitting on the floor of Angie's office sorting papers, like he often is. I enter the lab with the machines, the blinding sunlight pouring through the windows and giving everything an otherworldly glow. There's something about the MRI machine that both calls and repels me. Today I am drawn to that big white tunnel. It looks like something you would see on a spaceship.

I put my hand out, nearly touching it, but not quite.

I wonder what it would be like to be inside it.

What would it discover about my brain? Anything useful? Would it show that my brain is as normal as the next person's? Maybe I should just let Angie test me and be done with it. Maybe I would learn something important.

I lean closer, pressing my palm against the cold metal. A blinding shock goes through me and I retract my hand. The skin is an angry red, like I've just laid it against a hot iron skillet. I flex my fingers, then rub them, trying to soothe the burning.

Did I touch something I shouldn't have?

Maybe I'm stupid, but I reach out and press my hand against the metal again. I want to know if the burning was real or my imagination playing tricks. At first, there is nothing more than the feeling of cold contact between me and the machine. One minute passes, then two, and the sunlight shifts, just enough so that it beams directly at me through the windows, thick rays of it, hot and blinding. I turn my face toward it and close my eyes, absorbing the warmth on my skin.

Images dance across the back of my eyelids. Glowing shapes, figures and objects surrounded by halos of light. There isn't one color that dominates, but many. Pinks and pale blues and yellows, greens and a deep magenta; some hues are shades of gray and a black that nearly swallows the light and all other color. At first, I can't tell what the figures are. Then, slowly, they become clear.

Minds. Brains.

I'm seeing into the brains of the people who've been inside this machine. The ways that certain pathways pulse with light and others are dark as night, as though they've died. I see growths with sinister tentacles reaching through every part of the mind, and tiny tumors, contained and compact. They flash faster, one after the other, bright and dizzying. I can't pull myself away. It's like the machine is playing a movie it produced only for me.

A loud rushing fills my ears and my entire body starts to tingle.

"Oh no," I hear myself say.

Then everything, the noise, the flashes, goes blank.

❖ ❖ ❖

"Marlena?"

It's Helen's voice, but it sounds far away.

"Are you okay?"

"Marlena." This time, I recognize Angie.

I open my eyes. The two of them are peering down at me, worried looks on their faces. I am lying on the couch in Angie's office, a blanket thrown over my body. Cool air is pouring into the room from the vent, despite Angie's prohibition on air conditioning. My head is pounding. Spots shine across my eyes. "I Ii," I manage, but it comes out hoarse. I try and use my hands to stabilize myself so I can sit up.

"Don't," Angie says. "You should stay lying down."

Helen shoves a bag of pretzels at me. "Eat these."

I shake my head. "I'm fine." I tug the blanket around my legs, though not because I am cold. My legs feel bare in this dress. Angie and Helen are skeptical. "Really," I add. Then I gesture between the two women. "Angie, this is Helen, by the way."

Helen crosses her arms. "This isn't a joke. You passed out. You're not fine."

I look at Angie and try for a laugh. "Wow, I must have really scared you for you to put on the air conditioning." No one else is smiling. I proceed to shed the blanket so I can stand up. I want to reassure everyone. At first I'm unsteady, but then the dizziness subsides. With my bare feet planted on the soft rug, I am feeling stronger. "Really. It's no big deal. That happens sometimes."

"What happens?" Angie asks.

"I faint. You know." But the two of them don't seem to get it. "After I have visions? It started a year or two ago."

"Is this part of what you meant when you said your gift might be changing?" Helen asks.

"Maybe?"

"You've never told me about this before," Angie says. "Not so explicitly. You've talked of getting tired, but not of passing out."

"Because it's not that big a deal?"

"Wait—did you say you had a vision, Marlena?" Helen asks before Angie can say anything else. "What prompted it?"

I pull the blanket from the couch and drape it around my shoulders. Angie touches a panel on the wall and the vents stop working. "It was the MRI machine. I had my hand on it, and, I don't know, I responded almost like it was a person in need of healing, except I started seeing all the people who'd ever been inside it, and what was going on in their brains. It was a lot to take in. So, eventually I passed out, I guess?" Angie is opening each of the windows in her office.

"I really wish you'd let me see inside your brain," she says. "And not just because I'm curious about you. It worries me that you're passing out."

I wave her off. "This is just another day in the life of a healer. I swear." Something occurs to me. "Um, where's Finn? He wasn't around to witness my dramatic collapse?"

Angie looks away suddenly. "No. He had somewhere to be this afternoon."

As much as I want to see Finn, I'm relieved he wasn't here to find me crumpled on the ground, skirt hiked who knows how high, my face slack.

Helen is staying at a safe distance. Like she's afraid to touch me again, like my fainting and talk of visions reminded her of who I am. "You really are okay?"

I nod.

"All right." To Angie she says, "Call me and we'll set up that time to talk. I'm going to take Marlena out for a big meal, since I think she needs one."

"I agree." Angie stares at me hard. "Marlena, promise you'll think about an MRI soon. Not for my sake, for yours. For your health."

"Sure," I say as though I'm really considering it, as though it's no big deal. But as Helen and I are walking toward the exit, a rolling shiver passes over my body. I can't bring myself to look in the direction of that big white tunnel that has the power to reveal all the secrets of the mind.

THIRTEEN

Helen takes a call on her phone after we arrive in town and get out of the car.

"Sorry," she mouths. "I have to take this. Give me ten, fifteen minutes?"

I nod, and wander along the sidewalk of Main Street to kill time. A weird sensation stirs. Not like a vision. More like déjà vu, or when a place you know well suddenly seems unfamiliar, like if you leave your house and come back and someone has rearranged the furniture, but only a little. It takes me a minute to pinpoint what's different. It's seeing Gertie that does it.

She's standing in the doorway of her shop, like always. The kite in the window is gone, replaced by long-sleeved T-shirts emblazoned with an image of me as a baby surrounded by a glowing halo, my tiny fist reaching, one finger outstretched. Next to it is something else I've never seen before. A doll, maybe a foot and a half tall, on a shelf. It's made to look like me in one of the wedding gowns I wore at a healing. I recognize the dress from an audience last year.

It was an unusual audience, because it went on for hours longer than normal and I'd healed forty people instead of my usual six or seven. It caused a sensation, both for the sheer number of people I cured and also because I collapsed at the end of it. It wasn't the first time I ever fainted, but the only time this has happened during an audience. The people present for my marathon healing began to call it the Day of Many Miracles. Word spread and the anniversary is coming up in October. My mother has been preparing for triple the number of people and tourists as usual.

Maybe that's why this doll has appeared, with a perfect miniature replica of that dress. Gertie and the rest of the town plan to make money from the anniversary.

Of course they do.

A burning starts across my skin. Splotches of color dot my vision and all I can see are the rocks that pepper the garden lining the sidewalk. The urge to take one of those rocks into my palm and shatter Gertie's window rises as the burning spreads deeper and hotter. I want to break the doll into a million pieces. I crouch down, push my head between my knees, and try to breathe slowly.

"Honey, are you all right?" Gertie asks.

I let out another long breath before I stand up again. When I turn to Gertie, I realize what is out of place. She doesn't recognize me. She's looking at me like I might be anyone, some tourist girl who wandered off from her parents. "Do you need me to call someone, sweetheart? Your mother?"

The burning I felt before retreats like a cool cloth across my skin. "Sorry. No. I'm fine. Thanks for asking." I stare at her, unable to believe she doesn't know that it's me. A giddiness bubbles into my throat.

It's my outfit.

The blue sundress. The sandals. The thin cardigan sweater I shrugged over my shoulders so I wouldn't feel so bare, and that swallows me in a way Helen swore was both fashionable and practical after my fainting spell. The oversized movie-star sunglasses Helen lent me in the car, so big they practically cover the top half of my face. The fact that my long hair is pulled up into a high knot.

I look like a regular girl. Like I could be anybody.

Like I might be *nobody*. Nobody special.

But Gertie is looking at me strangely now, and I can't decide if it's because I am acting strangely or if I am starting to seem familiar and she's trying to place me.

"I'm fine. Really." I hurry off before it dawns on Gertie she's talking to the real version of that stupid doll in her window.

I continue down Main Street. People pass by like it isn't me they are seeing. Like they can't see me at all. Like I'm not worth noticing.

Is this all it takes to become anonymous? To be free?

A pair of sunglasses? A sundress? A topknot?

I glance behind me. In the distance, Helen is still on the phone, waving her hand in the air, as though the person she's talking to can see her. I veer a little, like I might be drunk. One after the other, the souvenir shops of the town appear and recede. I am tempted to enter, to see what else people are hawking in my name, something I don't usually do. But I don't want to press my luck and risk someone recognizing me, bringing this unexpected reprieve to an end. The ice cream shop appears on my right and I can't resist. I duck inside and the cool air makes me shiver.

I've always wanted to go out for ice cream, to visit this place not as me, but as a person in the mood for a treat. The bell on the door rings as I enter, but Mrs. Lewis, the owner, is engrossed in her magazine. Some of the ice cream flavors are fluorescent in color, others more muted. There are the normal ones, like strawberry and chocolate. But some of the names have a theme.

Miracle Mash and Healing Hazelnut.

Espresso Ecstasy and Raspberry Rapture.

Visionary Vanilla.

Whatever. I don't care. It's not as though I'm surprised the flavors are like everything else in this town. This is my hour off from being Marlena the Healer and I'm going to enjoy it.

Mrs. Lewis must sense a customer, because she looks up. "Would you like to try anything?" She takes a pink spoon from a cup that is full of them, ready for me to direct her to a flavor I want to taste.

"Sure," I say slowly, surveying the possibilities. There are so many and they all look so good. "How about . . . Miracle Mash." I have to cover my mouth to stop from giggling. I have a secret. Anonymity, I decide, is my new best friend.

Mrs. Lewis smiles. "Miracle Mash is one of my favorites." She leans forward to scrape some ice cream out of its tub. "Are you here on vacation with your family?"

"Um. Yes," I say, a little uncertain. I'm not used to lying. Or pretending. At least not with anyone other than my mother.

Mrs. Lewis reaches over the counter to hand me the spoon, now covered in what looks like chocolate ice cream dotted with a million things. Toffee. Chips. Marshmallow. Maybe streaks of peanut butter? I take it from her.

"Will you and your parents be going to the Healer's audience this Saturday?" Mrs. Lewis asks as I lick the spoon clean. "Most people who visit our town attend even if it's not their thing. They go out of curiosity. It's not like you have to believe to go."

The ice cream melts on my tongue and I chew all the delicious things in it, made even more so because Mrs. Lewis doesn't know that it's me. Freedom is tasty. I swallow, and realize that Mrs. Lewis is waiting for me to answer. "Do you believe in the Healer?" I ask, realizing I genuinely want to know what she says.

Mrs. Lewis glances at the candy-coated pink ceiling of her shop. "I do."

My heart speeds up. I drop the used plastic spoon into a container on the counter for them. "You sound so sure. Why? What makes you believe?" Why do I suddenly care so much about the opinions of the nice lady who owns the ice cream shop?

"It's difficult to describe, but . . . I suppose there's a couple of reasons," she starts. "I think miracles are possible and they happen all the time." My eyebrows arch and she laughs. "Not necessarily big miracles like walking on water, but little, everyday ones. Someone smiles at you for seemingly no reason, out of the blue, when you are having the worst moment of your life, and somehow that smile gives you the strength to get through the afternoon. You know?"

No one ever talks to me like this. "I think so."

"But I also think bigger miracles are possible. That they're rare, but they exist, and sometimes lucky people who walk among us are their source. I believe something sacred resides in them, that they have the power to connect us, to remind us that life is a beautiful mystery. They can transform us into something better. Something whole."

My eyes are getting watery. I blink. "Do you think that . . . the Healer can do those things?"

Mrs. Lewis's eyes are glistening a little, too. "Yes."

My heart is galloping, stars are exploding and blurring my vision. "Is there anything you've ever wished for Marlena to heal?"

Mrs. Lewis grows quiet. She takes a long, labored breath before speaking again. "It wouldn't work for me."

"Why not?" For the first time in as long as I can remember, the desire to heal someone, to do it of my own free will and because I want to help, not because my mother is making me, rises up as powerful as any vision I've ever had. "You live right here. Maybe you should take your own advice and go to one of the Healer's audiences. Just to see."

Mrs. Lewis goes completely still. The statue of a late middle aged lady, humble and sad. "It costs money," she informs me. "To get a healing. Like everything else in this life. If you can't pay, the Healer won't attend you at an audience."

I shake my head back and forth. "That's not right. It's just not."

"I agree," Mrs. Lewis says, misunderstanding my meaning.

"No, that's *literally* not right. I mean, I read up on the Healer and how the audiences work before my family came here." My cheeks flush a little with the lie. "And that's not how it works. You have to ask to get on the list for an audience. But you don't have to pay to be on the list! And afterward, people send their gratitude in donations and offerings, which is why the Healer's family lives so well."

Mrs. Lewis is studying me. I bet she's wondering why a tourist would know so much. "I don't want to upset your idealism, sweetheart, but I promise you, the money gets paid up front. No money, no healings. And they are expensive. *That* is why the Healer and her family live so well. I tried myself once, and the mother turned me away because I didn't have the funds."

My lips part.

Could she be right?

It would make so much sense. How we could afford all that we have. That the money is so consistent. Shame pours through me that my mother would turn away this nice lady, that she is charging for healings up front, like they are a mattress or a new car, making me into the car salesman. This shame covers every inch of skin. I can smell it, taste it, hear it. "If this Marlena girl is worth anything at all, she'll heal you for free."

Mrs. Lewis smiles weakly. She thinks I'm being idealistic again. She sniffles and a tear rolls down her cheek.

"Go to the audience," I say. "Really."

"Maybe I will." She wipes a hand across her face and starts to laugh. Shakes her head. "Look at me, getting all emotional with a customer who just came in to get some ice cream! You poor thing!" She sniffles again and this makes her laugh more. "Did you like Miracle Mash or do you want to try another flavor? I want people to be sure when they choose their ice cream. I like them to enjoy it."

I laugh a little, too, the sound of it releasing us from some of the intensity of our conversation. Mrs. Lewis seems serious about the business of picking flavors. Like choosing the right ice cream is as important as anything else. As important, even, as a miracle.

It occurs to me I don't have any money. I never do.

"Um, I, um, my parents have all my money. I'm so sorry." The last word comes out a squeak.

"No worries, honey. Really." Mrs. Lewis plucks a baby-sized cup from a teetering stack and reaches into the tub of Miracle Mash. She comes up with a scoop that she plops into the cup. She plants another pink spoon into the ice cream and hands it over the counter. "This one is on me."

I stare at it.

"Take it," she says. "Really. It was nice talking to you, sweetheart. I'm glad you stopped in. You made a slow day more interesting. Besides, it's nice to see a girl your age with an interest in big things like faith and miracles and doing the right thing."

I reach out and she hands me the cup. As she does, I make it a point to touch her hand, to press my fingers against her own, hoping that some relief for Mrs. Lewis, even a little bit, might be transferred to her in this brief instant. "Thank you so much," I tell her, holding on a beat longer, as long as I can. "This is so nice of you."

"Sweetheart, it's nothing. You have a good rest of your day."

I nod, my throat tight. "You should go to one of those audiences. If anyone deserves to be healed, it's you," I say, then head out the door. It chimes with my exit.

I make my way back toward Helen, taking one bite after the other, wondering if ice cream always tastes this good or if the way I received it, like a gift, a tiny, miraculous offering given freely and joyfully and without the need for anything in return, makes all the difference.

"Are you ready to eat?" Helen asks when I reach her.

I nod. "I'm starving." The word *starving* comes out with emphasis on *star*. I adjust the sunglasses higher on the bridge of my nose.

Sunglasses are my new favorite thing. But not only because they give me precious anonymity. I guess because that anonymity turned out to mean more than freedom from recognition. It gave me that conversation with Mrs. Lewis, allowed me to realize that I could find it inside myself to want to be Marlena the Healer. Not out of obligation. Just because. That it is more important than ever that I stop allowing my mother to control my gift and all that comes with it. To put a price on it.

Helen searches my face. "What happened between now and twenty minutes ago? I was worried about you. You looked so out of it and now you look so much better."

I shrug.

"I thought you'd be disappointed about missing your chance to see Finn," she says.

"I guess I just needed to take a walk."

"Marlena?" Helen's voice is singsong. She draws out each syllable of my name playfully. "Did you see Finn or something?"

"No. But I did eat some delicious ice cream."

Helen flips her sunglasses up onto her head. "Well, that's it, then. I bet your body needed the sugar." She pushes her hair behind her ears. "Now let's eat something healthy so you don't faint on me again."

"Let's," I agree, and slip the sweater from my shoulders, hanging it over my arm as we walk. We pass groups of tourists window-shopping on Main Street. Not one of them turns in my direction. Maybe it's because Helen and I are unremarkable in the way we're chatting, two girls who want nothing more than to tell each other their secrets on a beautiful day by the sea.

FOURTEEN

"I don't want this lipstick." I pluck the tube from my mother's hand and pick up a different one from the box of makeup. I am staring into the long mirror hanging in my mother's bedroom, the two of us engaging in the weekly ritual of dressing me for my audience. "I'll wear this one."

My mother is looking at me like she doesn't know who I am. "You never care which lipstick you wear. You never care which dress either. You let me do everything."

Earlier, I rejected one gown after the other until I found the one I liked best. "Well, today, I'm not letting you."

"That dark shade will be lovely with your coloring," my mother says. She doesn't seem to notice I'm being cold. Or she's choosing not to. Ever since that talk with Mrs. Lewis, I can't look at her without getting angry. "A bit of smoky shadow would be lovely, too. It will help make your features stand out against those bright stage lights." Our eyes meet in the mirror. "It's good to see you taking your audiences seriously again. Whatever has gotten into you, I hope it keeps up."

Finn. The hope of seeing Finn at my audience has gotten into me.

All I respond is "Yes, Mama."

My mother turns to the tiny buttons of the sleeves on my dress.

The gown I chose is simpler than the typical princess dress that bells at the waist that my mother always picks. She thinks they make me look regal. This one drops straight to the floor. The lace makes it beautiful. Hand sewn and so intricate it's difficult to believe someone was born with the talent for such masterful work. My hands might be able to heal, but there is plenty of other amazing artistry that human hands can produce.

My mother takes out a small brush and begins painting my lips. I try to imagine the moment when Finn sees me. I wonder if he will think I am beautiful, if he doesn't mind when a girl wears makeup, if he might like the cascade of my long dark hair against so much lace.

I smile at myself in the mirror and imagine that I am smiling at him.

"It's good to see you happy, Marlena." My mother starts to hum a song she used to sing when I was small.

I wish I could enjoy it. But it's difficult not to snap at her.

"Mama, do you charge money for my healings? Up front?" I ask. My mother is still humming, like she hasn't heard my question. "I thought people made offerings after healings. You've always told me they were donations. Not payments. That you couldn't put a price on a healing."

She sings to herself, softly, in Portuguese.

Cheia de penas, cheia de penas me deito.

It's "Lágrima," one of the beautiful, sad ballads from the fado tradition, sung by a single voice, often with only a guitar or even without any accompaniment.

"Mama," I press through the lyrics of her singing. "Answer me."

"Yes," she says simply. She doesn't raise her head. Returns to her song.

My heart beats hard against the pristine lace of my gown. "Mama, are you serious? Is there a specified fee? Do you turn people away who can't pay? Do you tell them I won't heal them?"

Desespero, Tenho por meu desespero . . .

"Yes," she drops, nearly imperceptibly, between lyrics.

"Mama!" She is down by my feet, fixing the hem of my gown. "I can't believe you've been lying to me all this time! If my 'gift' is really that, a gift, then shouldn't it be given freely? If there's money involved, shouldn't it be offered afterward? In gratitude but not in payment? Mama, you turn people away!"

She doesn't speak now, or sing. The room goes quiet, as she works on the bustle of the dress.

"If the healing doesn't work, do you give the money back?" I whisper.

My mother rises up from behind me in the mirror. "Sometimes it surprises me, how naïve you are, Marlena."

Everything in me hardens against her. "But isn't that how you like me, Mama? A child, naïve and stupid and sweet?"

Bright hot lights flood the stage.

One of the staff at the United Holiest Church has thrown the light switch, signaling that another audience is about to begin. Other staff scurry around, sweeping, moving pots of plants from here to there, placing great cascading flower arrangements at the entrance of the church and at the end of each aisle. Two women heave a small tree toward the stage. I am ashamed to admit that I don't know their names. Shouldn't I?

"Marlena?"

José is at my elbow, beckoning me into the back room.

"Marlena?" José prompts.

"Sorry. I was just thinking."

He chuckles. "Don't do too much of that, *cariño*. Too much thinking is never good for anyone."

I follow him, nodding at Fatima, who is waiting for me. "Hello, Marlena," she says. "You look especially pretty today."

I want to reach out to her, but I settle for words. "Thank you, Fatima."

She picks up the veil that is draped across the chair.

"I'm not wearing that today," I tell her.

"But your mother—"

"—my mother has no say in the matter."

Fatima's mouth closes.

I turn around, look out across the stage through the open door. This place was once just a garage, with folding chairs that my mother, Fatima, and José would set up, forming rows theater style. There was no stage, no other staff, no floodlights. If there were flowers, they were daisies or black-eyed Susans, handpicked from a nearby field. Occasionally there was a cactus, because they're easy to maintain. A rickety table served as an altar. There was no platform. Audiences were simple affairs.

I wonder if my mother was demanding money back then, too. Or if it was something that started gradually. Every now and then we've gotten an enormous donation from a wealthy benefactor. That's how we built this church, in fact, and how my mother bought our beautiful house. Maybe those experiences gave my mother a taste of something she decided she wanted all the time.

"Marlena?" José asks from behind me.

I don't answer. My eyes seek out my mother. She is in the middle aisle talking to one of the staff, gesturing at the seats she wants reserved for the people on her list. I wonder how much they paid her, how much she demanded, how much she promised. I wonder how many people she turned away who didn't have the money, people like Mrs. Lewis. My mother looks every bit the queen, beautiful and thin and tall, confident and self-assured as she talks to the man who is roping off those seats. A plan forms in my head.

"Marlena." José is sounding desperate, like he gets when I have conned him yet again into taking me to Angie's center. "People will start arriving and you cannot be seen here when they do."

"Sorry." I turn around. "I was just thinking about the audience and how I want it to go."

José shakes his head. "I told you, *cariño*, too much thinking will get you in trouble. It's not worth it, whatever is going through your head. Your mother will not like it."

I go to him now, shutting the door behind me. "You're right. But maybe that's the point."

Later, when I walk out, the crowd is hushed but murmuring.

I take one step, then another, left, right, until I can grip the edge of the altar. Beautiful, flowered branches sit in a tall cylindrical vase. Cherry blossoms, which cost a fortune because they aren't in season. My eyes adjust to the bright lights. Mama is standing at the podium, talking. I've come out before I'm supposed to. She hasn't noticed me yet. She's still reading a history of my healings, a litany of proof that my miracles are real, to convince people that I am truly a saint. She's always loved this part, the proving, the convincing.

Am I the only one who can see the snakes curling through her hands?

Or am I the snake she's handling?

I reach the end of the stage.

My mother turns, sees me, stops speaking. The eyes of the crowd have forgotten she is there. They are only for me.

I look around.

Finn. I wonder where he is. If he's coming.

There is the usual crush of tourists, craning their necks to catch a better glimpse, some of the children giggling, hands over their mouths. Some of the adults, too. The rest are seated, or half seated, since plenty rise from their chairs, or sit on the edges. I see Gertie way in back, table set with souvenirs to sell when seekers are at their most vulnerable, their most likely to hand over cash for a memory. I wonder if Gertie gives Mama a cut. In the last row I see Mrs. Jacobs, arms crossed, defiant, her entire posture seeming to say, *I dare you, Marlena. I dare you to convince me.* I stare at her until she is squirming in her seat. It's the first time I've seen her at an audience since June.

I am not worried. Something is happening in me, to me.

I'm done with obedience.

I put a hand over my eyes to shield them from the glare.

Soon I am in the aisle.

The front row of seekers has gotten to their knees, heads bowed. They look to be of the same family. They have shiny black hair and their round, brown faces match. A little girl glances up at me, afraid.

I don't want her to be afraid.

I go to her, rest my palm on her head, feel the soft silky base of her ponytail, remembering the child on the beach who asked if I was an angel. Her mother and father gasp that I have chosen to grace their little one. As I let my hand fall from the girl, the rest of her family draws around her, touching her on her arms and back, like I anointed her the saint and they can touch me through touching their child.

To my right, my mother is gesturing at the seats occupied by the people I am supposed to heal. The ones my mother promised miracles in exchange for cash. They sit there, backs straight, eyes on me, two women, one man, an older man with a girl, who might be my age. They don't shout. They are quiet.

Confident.

But others jockey for my attention, shouting my name, some of them begging in the aisles until José forces them back.

"Marlena! Please!"

"Please, miss!"

"Over here!" A woman in the middle of the fourth row to my left is waving a photo of a man in a military uniform. "I need your help!" She is wailing.

There are people in wheelchairs, people on crutches, people with dark glasses over their eyes to cover their blindness. The tourists, the unbelievers, glance around; some of them are laughing, some of them have hands on the pockets where their phones are kept, like they're reaching for a gun, fingers twitching. Mama doesn't allow videos or photos during healings, only before an audience and afterward if you wait in line. Everyone always wants proof, wants a souvenir, a piece of me they can show to others.

"Marlena!"

"Marlena!"

"Marlena!"

The room is a cacophony of need, of desperation, of hope and hopelessness. The paying guests watch me, wait for me quietly, secure that their money has guaranteed my attention.

I turn away from them, and two things happen.

My eyes meet Finn's. At the end of the center aisle.

He stares intently. Like he can't tear his eyes from me.

A flood of emotion flows underneath my feet and lifts me up until I am floating. I am carried away even though I haven't moved an inch.

"Marlena," my mother hisses, from the side of the room. "What are you doing?"

And then, sitting in the very last row, I see Mrs. Lewis.

Her eyes are deadened, so unlike the woman I spoke to in the ice cream shop, who sent me away with a treat, kind and sweet and earnest, a woman full of love, ready to give it away. Her face is tilted down into her lap, like she wants to disappear, or is ashamed to have come. I stare until finally, her hands balled into fists, she looks up.

I move in her direction.

FIFTEEN

"Why me?" Mrs. Lewis and I are standing in the aisle, face-to-face. She is shaking. Her deep-brown skin is covered in goose bumps.

I don't want to frighten her away, but I don't answer her question. I don't mention the ice cream she gave me, our conversation about faith and miracles. Our conversation about me. I want the chance to walk the town again anonymous and free. I want this so much I let sweet Mrs. Lewis hover in doubt and confusion. The saint is selfish.

Mrs. Lewis's eyeglasses hang on a metal chain along her front. She's wearing pale green like she is dressed for Easter, the straight skirt reaching down to wrinkled knees. Her shoes are the same green, with heels maybe two inches high. Her hair is set, like she took the time to put in rollers last night, to sleep in them, and carefully take them out before making her way to this church.

"Shhhhhhhh," I tell her. I hold out my hands, palms up.

So many people grab at me once it is allowed, once they are sure they are not violating Mama's laws about touching the Healer. But Mrs. Lewis is reluctant. She twists the gold ring she wears, round and round.

"I'm not going to hurt you."

"But . . . but I don't . . . I don't have . . ." The metal chain she wears shifts and shudders with uncertain, worried breaths.

Money.

Mama turned her away once, because she couldn't pay.

Before she can stutter more words of hesitation, I stop the wringing of her hands with my own. The second I do, the vision starts.

Black is the color that dominates, black and gray, charcoal gray and light gray. I hear the rough, hoarse breaths from her lungs, sense the shaking in those wrinkled knees. The world spins, I am barely able to see. Someone, some merciful person—José I think—brings Mrs. Lewis a chair and she sits. I kneel down before her, never letting go of her hands. The blacks and grays grow shiny, bright and glaring like a newly washed car in the sun. They take the shape of a human heart.

Mrs. Lewis's pain is physical, not emotional. She is dying, or will die soon. I hold the vision of her heart steady, and see the way the left side is collapsing, caving in on itself, the blood in her veins unable to reach it with the force her heart needs. As we sit there, me on the floor, Mrs. Lewis in the chair, scenes begin, first from the past, of doctors and hospitals, the helpless faces of her husband and her grown son, her grandchildren still small, the swell of responsibility to care for them in this graying, kind lady.

But then, nearly eclipsed by this expanding bubble of misery, something else stirs, powerful and certain and full of light. The blacks and dark grays gradually turn green and blue, as bright and strong as new blades of grass and as light and delicate as a robin's egg. I can see her, literally see her. She watches her grandchildren graduate high school and college, she has dinner with her son, whose own hair is now gray with age. Little by little, her breathing eases.

I get up, knees shaky. In the far back of the room I see Mrs. Jacobs start to stand, shaking her head. I am not afraid. I lean in toward Mrs. Lewis so I can whisper, "You're going to be okay." I kiss her cheek.

When I pull back, something else starts to happen inside me.

The tingling, the colors, the scenes from Mrs. Lewis's future are pulsing through me and won't stop, even though I've let her go. Everything in me shifts, expands to include other people, the other seekers who are here. I can see all their need at once, their wounds, their pain, the same as when I touched the MRI in Angie's lab.

I am once again that figurehead on the ship. I carry them on my back.

I hold my arms wide and begin to speak. I can't not speak. Names fall from my mouth. "Joseph. Benicia. Amanda. Christiano.

Malcolm. Pilar. Jeremy. Concetta." The names come from every-where and nowhere.

Soon I am surrounded by a crowd, someone in a wheelchair, others limping, one man with a woman sagging in his arms. Someone grasps my left hand and another my right. There are hands along my forearms and hanging on my elbows and shoulders. Across my back. People are everywhere, reaching for me.

I welcome it. I welcome them, all of them. I have never been less afraid and I have never been more myself. The world is full of color and music and beauty and I am at the center of it all.

Somewhere in the room, sounding far, far away, I hear Mama's voice calling out. "Marlena, Marlena, Marlena! What are you doing?"

"Dennis. Sarah. Claudio," I say.

The crowd around me grows and grows. They murmur, they pray, and I am taken up into their prayers and whispers. Taken over by them.

"That is all for today," my mother is saying into the microphone on the stage. No, she is shouting. "That is all. José? Help me here!" My mother cries for people to pull back. Eventually they obey, falling away, letting go of my hands and my arms, until once again, I am alone in the aisle. All that beauty and life, gone.

I begin to weep. I am empty. Hollow without it. Without them.

Everything grows silent.

I place a hand to my temple. It feels like my head has split apart, straight in half, like a dropped bowl that hits the floor just right. I am depleted.

But I am real.

And now I am weeping for joy. I have never been more certain that I am real, that my gift is real. This is my job, my purpose, my reason for being. Nothing else matters. I don't need Angie to study me, to prove whether my gift is real or a fraud. I am a healer and I always will be. It is what I am made for.

How could I ever have doubted this? Doubted myself?

"Back away. This audience is over," my mother is saying, her voice booming through the church. José is next to me, gingerly taking my arm even though he's not supposed to touch me, lifting me off the ground and carrying me away.

Time goes by as I gather my strength backstage, enough to walk. Thirty minutes. An hour. My mother has yet to appear and I don't know why she hasn't come to speak to me, to scold me. Despite José's protests, I make my way out into the church for the receiving line. I emerge into the sea of seekers and tourists who have waited for photos. People erupt into chatter and shouts.

"Marlena!"

"Marlena, I need you!"

"Marlena, over here!"

"Amazing," shouts a woman.

"I didn't believe, but now . . ."

I stand on the stage and look out over everyone. Then, in the very back, I see Finn, his face, the tilt of his head, the intensity of his eyes. I take in the fact that he just witnessed what happened. Witnessed me.

What did he think?

I descend the stairs and move through the crowd. "I'm sorry, excuse me," I tell the people swirling around me. "I'm tired," I tell them, in apology. It's not a lie.

I plow through everyone, and they scurry to move from my path. I am making a scene and I don't even care if my mother witnesses it. I see Finn, hold him there with my eyes. I know he's not going anywhere, that he's waiting for me, but I feel as though he might slip away before I can get to him, that I will be unable to reach him before he does. He is beyond me somehow, beyond me already, or at some future date.

What, what, *what* is this feeling? Where is it coming from?

It's like a half vision, an unformed premonition.

When I reach him I head straight through the exit and signal for him to follow. I wait under one of the gnarled old trees whose branches are a canopy from the September sun. Me, in my wedding dress, breaths short and bursting, hem dragging through the dirt. Finn comes through the door and looks around.

"Over here," I call out.

He heads toward me. "Well, that was dramatic."

"I guess it was," I agree. Was he referring to my audience, the swell of people around me, or the way the crowd parted as I moved through it? Or maybe the fact that I look like some runaway bride, and Finn the boy come to rescue me. "I don't have much time. My mother . . . she's angry about what happened in there." The feeling that Finn might disappear is ever more potent now. It makes me want to place my hands on his shoulders and hold him there.

A leaf flutters to the ground between us. "How could she be angry after *that?*" he asks. "Whether it was real or not, you have this way with people. You help them. You have something they *need.*"

A pain spreads through my body. "Whether it was real or not?"

Finn takes a step closer. The sunlight shines through the spaces between branches, the dappled light giving him an otherworldly look. "After what I saw today," he says, with a mixture of fear and reverence and maybe a little bit of awe, "it's difficult even for me not to believe."

SIXTEEN

It is Monday, and I wake to noise throughout the house. Not the kind from Fatima cleaning, dragging the vacuum over the plank floors that double as sand catchers in the summer, or the use of a blender in the kitchen. I hear scraping and banging, like builders are getting ready for a renovation.

There is a knock on my door. It opens a crack. "Marlena?" It's Fatima. "Your mother wants you downstairs."

My mother and I aren't speaking. Not since Saturday. In the tension and silence, I've been painting nonstop.

"You're supposed to shower and get dressed." She shuts the door again.

Uh-oh.

Fatima didn't even wait for me to reply.

Intentionally slowly, I get ready. I step across the art supplies on the floor, careful not to kick anything over. I spend a nice long time under the hot water in the bathroom, then dry my hair until there isn't a bit of moisture. I pull one of the white sheaths over my head and a long pale sweater over it. The weather has changed, the temperature finally dropping. Something in me has changed, too. I search inside my soul for what it is until I find it.

Faith. A kind of faith.

I am awash in it, in the tender, bright green of its newness. But it's not a faith in God. A faith in myself is unfurling. My doubts have browned and turned to dust, replaced by the sense that using my gift can be a choice of my own making.

A shrill, high-pitched burring noise pierces my ears.

Is that a drill?

I shove my feet into my white ballet slippers, hurry out of my room and down the long hallway, past the rustic walls painted white. Now there is a banging sound, like a hammer. Did I miss the memo about a renovation? But why would I be needed downstairs for that? I stand at the top of the stairs, listening.

Fatima emerges from the gift room, duster in hand. She won't look at me.

"Fatima," I say. "Please tell me what's happening."

She scurries away. Before she heads into one of the guest rooms on this floor—not that we ever have guests—she calls back, "Just go see your mother. You know how she doesn't like to be kept waiting."

"All right," I tell her, not wanting Fatima to get in trouble. I descend the staircase, step by step. *Thump. Thump.* Dread is a mist wafting up from the first floor. I walk straight into it.

"Marlena!" my mother is shouting. "Get down here!"

When I head into the living room there are workers everywhere. Some with tool belts, building some sort of freestanding wall in the corner. Two others are dressed professionally, women in sophisticated skirts and heels. There's even a man in a suit, like the kind someone would wear on Wall Street. They barely notice me.

"We need that to be just a little bit taller," says a woman in cobalt blue to a man who is working on the wall.

People navigate around me like I'm a column or a piece of furniture. Someone is fitting a long, thick roll of paper, or maybe canvas, in two hooks on either side of the wall.

Then I notice the cameras.

Tiny video cameras have been attached to the ceiling in every corner of the room.

"Yes, exactly," the woman in blue says to the man who's straightening the backdrop.

"Marlena!" my mother yells.

Since Saturday I've enjoyed the fresh taste of independence, bright on my tongue. But this—this is my mother's effort to regain control. To press me under her thumb.

"Marlena!"

I take a deep breath, and walk into the kitchen. The man in the business suit is standing next to my mother, joined by one of the women. In front of them the kitchen island is covered by stacks of paper, grouped in neat piles.

"Good morning, Mama," I say.

She looks over. "Finally, you're here. I've been calling for you for an hour. *Você está sendo mal educado*," she adds in Portuguese.

I ignore her comment about my being rude. "What's going on? Why are all of these people here?"

My mother sighs. "I tried to tell you last week but you didn't want to hear it." She takes a big gulp of her coffee. She always drinks it lukewarm because it's nearly three-quarters milk. She's wearing her favorite white suit. Mama has lots of white suits. I am the miracle healer in white, and she is the mother of the miracle healer, also in white. "You were too caught up with Helen to care what I had to say."

The woman and man are staring at me.

Finally, the woman smiles tightly and moves in my direction. "Hello. I'm Dana Reisner." She obviously thinks I should know who she is, or at least recognize her name, but I don't. She's reaching out her hand to shake mine when my mother barks.

"No! Remember what I told you about my daughter!"

The woman, Dana, yanks her arm away.

I glare at my mother. "It's not like I have leprosy."

My mother turns to the woman and speaks quietly. "My daughter doesn't like to be touched unless she's performing a healing."

"Of course. I'm so sorry," Dana says to my mother, not to me, and the tight smile reappears. Everything about this Dana seems fitted so as to be exact, her suit along the shape of her body, the way her hair is coiffed into a kind of helmet, not a strand loose. Even the expression on her face seems to take up as little space as possible. "Marlena, it is very nice to finally meet you," she tries again. "I've been hearing about you and researching you for a long time."

I take a step closer, and she takes a step back, like I really do have some terrible communicable disease. "Well, that's interesting. I don't know anything about you."

My mother sets her coffee onto the counter and it makes a loud *thunk*. "Marlena, remember what I said about your attitude."

"And you are?" I ask the man, ignoring her.

His arms are crossed. They don't even twitch as he introduces himself. "I'm Joseph Hurwitz. I'm the producer for the television series you and your mother have agreed to do with us. Dana is our lead host." His voice is upbeat, like he expects me to be thrilled.

"You mean my mother agreed to do with you." I start to laugh. Their faces grow confused. Maybe I should do something to scare them, cackle, or start chewing on my hair, or run and scream through the house. Maybe if they think I'm insane they'll be less interested in doing a serious show about the crazy girl-healer.

"Marlena." My mother's tone is ever more frustrated. "I told you about this! We need you to sign these documents before any of the filming can begin." She places a hand on top of one of the stacks of paper.

"Don't I need to read them first?"

"I've already read them for you." She looks at the television people with apology. To me, she says, "All you need is to add your signature."

Lead Host Dana holds a shiny silver pen out to me.

I let her hand hang there until she realizes I'm not taking the pen and retracts it. "I'm eighteen. I don't have to do anything I don't want to do. I'm not signing my privacy away because you ask me to."

"This is one of the most respected producers in the country, Marlena. And Dana is one of the most important journalists on television. You will be famous, after this airs." My mother says this like it is the most wonderful news.

"I'm already famous," I snap.

My mother shakes her head, communicating to the television people once again that I'm obviously the insolent child who doesn't know anything. The bratty, temper-tantrum-throwing, difficult miracle healer. "But you're not a household name yet." She swipes her hand into the air, like she's brushing something worthless away. Dana and Joseph follow this back-and-forth like my mother and I are a riveting show in our own right. Perhaps they are salivating about the juicy conflict between mother and daughter they will get to explore on camera. "I know you feel powerful after that . . . stunt of yours on Saturday. But with this deal, we're talking about turning you into a celebrity. You'll be famous beyond your wildest dreams."

My fists clench. "You mean famous beyond *your* wildest dreams, Mama. This is about *you*, not me."

My mother's face is the picture of calm, and she manages a smile. But her eyes are arctic. "Can I have a moment alone with my daughter?" My mother asks this politely, sweetly.

Joseph nods. "Of course," he says, though Dana seems crestfallen to be barred from the rest of this mother-daughter performance.

Before they can leave the room I go on. "And what will my celebrity fame bring us this time, Mama? A vacation home in Turks and Caicos? A castle in France? Diamonds and emeralds to wear around your wrist and your neck? Will this special come with a national merchandising deal, too? Will I be gracing the breakfast tables of people across the nation? Will I be healing on demand soon, by television and online? Is that the master plan for 'us'?"

My mother's eyes narrow to match my own. "Stop being so selfish—"

"—selfish?"

"—you've been given a miraculous gift from God. Don't you think you owe the world access to it? Do you really want to keep it to yourself, make this all about you and not the needs of others and the grace that God has given you?"

I lean over the counter toward my mother, who's standing on the other side. I stretch my long arms across the marble, the neat stacks of paper shifting as I move, wrinkling as I press into them. "So, Mama, you'd rather I heal until I drop dead? Is my death included in this deal I'll be signing?"

My mother's face drains of color. "Marlena," she hisses. "This is not the time."

"Well, I disagree. I disagree with everything. With all of it. With all of *you*." With every bit of force in me I swipe my arms across the counter, sending those reams of paper sailing into the air and cascading to the ground. Then I grab the coffee mug near my mother's hand, still half full, and hurl it across the kitchen. It shatters against the wall, leaving behind a tiny dent in the plaster, the shape of a small scallop shell. Coffee splatters everywhere. The mug lies in jagged pieces on the floor.

The sounds in the living room come to a stop.

Without another word or glance at anyone, I walk to the front door of the house, open it, and head into the heat, slamming it shut so hard behind me, the entire frame around it shudders.

SEVENTEEN

I walk and walk and walk. I don't even know where I'm going. The ocean appears ahead, the seawall alongside it, and I force my breaths to mimic the slow swells of the water, calm even though the day is gray. No one is at the beach on this cloudy school day, and everything is quiet. I start up the sidewalk that leads into town and the short strip that counts as Main Street. My mind is racing. It won't stop turning over the events of this morning, the workers, the television people. The look on my mother's face when I threw her mug, when it smashed against the wall with that great ugly crash.

I reach the store that sells beachy souvenirs at the beginning of Main Street, one of the few places that doesn't trade off my image. Gertie's shop is open but she's not in the doorway, maybe because the tourists are sleeping late, or because the clouds are keeping them away. I pass Maxwell's Card Shop, Almeida's Bakery, followed by Marinelli's Religious Icon & Candle Store, which is full of pendants and mass cards with the Catholic saints, but which specializes in ones with my photo on them. My destination is next, on the right.

Mrs. Lewis is sitting on the stool by the register, same as the other day, a newspaper in her lap. The bell on the top of the door dings and she looks up. Her face, her eyes, are rested. Calm and relaxed.

Is she healed?

"Marlena?" She sounds surprised. A little wary.

The Healer has never entered her shop as far as she knows. She doesn't realize we had a conversation last week, that she gave me an ice cream out of kindness. She probably thinks our only encounter was at my audience. She glances at her purse.

She thinks I'm here to collect.

"I don't want any money," I blurt. It pains me to have stressed her, especially after what I know about her heart. "I'm sorry. I . . . I'm just so sorry to worry you." I look around. My head pulses with something. I don't know what. I wish I had a disguise. I should've run to my room to get one before storming off. "I can't really go anywhere, can I? Not as me. Not without causing problems."

Mrs. Lewis comes around the counter. "Are you okay, sweetheart?" She plucks a napkin from a dispenser and dabs at my cheeks. "You've been crying."

"Oh," I say. "Yes." I stare up at her. Mrs. Lewis stops wiping my cheeks, then folds the napkin neatly into a small triangle and places it on the counter.

Ugly, arrogant thoughts whisper through my mind.

Will she save it? The napkin that dried the tears of the Healer? Will she sell it?

I reach out to the counter to grab it, crush it in my fist. Mrs. Lewis startles at this.

"Can I use your phone?" I ask her.

Without a word, she hands her cell to me and I make the call I've thought about since stepping over the shards of china on the kitchen floor, intentionally muddying my soft white ballet slippers in spilt coffee, hoping my mother winced as she witnessed me doing it. After I hang up and hand the phone back to Mrs. Lewis, I tell her thank you and head toward the exit. I shove the napkin, still in a tight ball, into the trash can. I actually stick my arm down into it, pushing the remnants of my tears deep into the garbage.

"Sweetheart." The unwavering kindness in Mrs. Lewis's voice kills me. "If you're in trouble, or if you ever need anything, you can come to me." I hear rustling behind me. A little square of paper appears, gripped by wrinkled, spotted fingers. Hands I held on Saturday. "That's my cell number and my home number and the number to this shop. My email is there, too. I mean what I say."

I don't look at her. But I manage to speak. "I know you do." I take the paper. Slip it into the pocket of my sweater.

Then I walk out and wait.

The happy jingle of the bell on the door rings in my ears long after I'm gone.

❖ ❖ ❖

I've never seen his car before. It's an old blue truck, beat up and scratched, with a dent over one of the back wheels.

Finn leans over from the driver's side and pushes the passenger door open. He's wearing jeans and an old gray T-shirt. A tattoo of a human heart is visible on his arm. I've never seen him in short sleeves. "Get in," he says.

I climb into the seat and slam the door. The space between us is small. Intimate. I am shaking. I can't stop staring at Finn's tattoo. It's not something I'd expect him to have.

His eyes are curious as always. I love how his curiosity never leaves him.

I am curious too. I reach out and lift the edge of Finn's sleeve to better view the tattoo.

My hands are not my own today.

I lean closer, careful not to touch his skin, studying the beautiful red color of the heart, the skill of the artist, the detail. It is at once real and otherworldly. The kind of thing I might see in a vision and do my best to capture on canvas.

Finn's chest is still.

I force myself to let go of his shirt, to sit back and stare out of the windshield, focusing on the great maple tree growing up in the sidewalk garden next to the car, its roots raising the bricks around it into a jagged hill.

"Where do you want to go?" Finn asks.

"I don't care. Just drive."

He maneuvers to the end of Main Street and out onto the road beyond it. Finn reaches into the narrow back seat of the truck and comes up with a long, gray scarf. He hands it to me. "Wrap this around you. You're shivering."

I take it and wind it around my neck and shoulders. It's soft, maybe cashmere, and smells of trees and wood, mixed with something sweet. I imagine myself wearing it to school, if I was a girl who went to school, proudly displaying it to my friends, the treasure of having the scarf of the boy I like.

"The other day, did you mean what you said?" I ask him.

Finn turns right, heading toward the ocean. "What did I say?"

"After my audience. About maybe believing in me."

"Yes."

My heart lifts.

"At the time," he adds.

It crashes. "But not anymore?"

"I don't know. Maybe. Maybe not. I'm not the type to believe in miracles. But I also can't get the spectacle of it out of my head."

I don't speak. I can't move. I don't want to be a spectacle to Finn.

His breaths are clipped. "Do you want me to? Believe in you?"

"I don't know. Sometimes. Yes, I think."

"Are you going to tell me what's going on? What prompted this urgent outing?"

"Later," I say. Then, "Can we just be quiet for a while?"

"Okay," he says.

We fall silent. Listen to the rumble of the engine. The town recedes in the side mirror and eventually disappears. I slip out of my coffee-spattered shoes and pull my knees to my chest, wrap the hem of my white dress under my bare feet. Turn my head toward Finn and watch as he drives. There is stubble on his cheek, unlike when I see him at Angie's center. His hair is a bit messy, like he's been running his fingers through it. His eyelashes are long, his lips a pale red. Something unidentifiable swells quickly and instantly and I am dizzy with it. I want to touch Finn. I want to possess him. I want to—

"—pull over," I say.

"Marlena, what? Are you okay—"

"—please?"

He shifts the truck into the breakdown lane along the seawall, where people in the town like to park and drink coffee or eat lunch while they look out at the ocean. We come to a stop in a deserted stretch of it. Seagulls circle over a spot in the water where there must be lots of fish. I uncurl my legs. Look at Finn. Stare at him. Grip the ends of his scarf like my life depends on it. My hands can't be trusted. He turns to me.

"Kiss me," I say.

His eyes widen. "What?"

I lean closer. "Kiss me."

Finn blinks.

"I want you to kiss me," I say a third time, like he didn't understand the first or the second, like this one might magically get through to him. I edge closer, nearly climbing over the gear shift, desperate with wanting, wanting him to be mine, wanting to know what it's like to love and be loved. The want is a wave and it's lifting me up, threatening to tumble me straight into the rocky shore. "Finn . . . just . . . just *do it*. I've never . . . just . . . please . . ."

"Marlena." My name is a statement, soft and gentle.

It's also a *no*.

I pull back, ashamed. My cheeks burn. Tears sting my eyes. What is happening to me? What is wrong with me? "I'm sorry. That was so stupid." My voice is a tiny round pebble. "I'm so stupid and I've ruined everything." I shift my body toward the window, pressing my forehead against the glass. My breaths create a fog across it, a pale round disk of crystals. I fumble for the latch on the door. Before I can open it, I feel a hand on my arm.

"Don't go," Finn says.

I stop.

He doesn't move his hand. Instead, he presses it more firmly against me. His touch sends stars streaming before my eyes, bright and bursting. I can't tell the difference between desire, longing, and visions when I'm with Finn. Maybe they're one and the same with him.

"Please stay."

"I'm such an idiot," I whisper.

"You're not."

"Stop being so nice to me. I *know*. I know the deal. You'll never want me now." The glass has gone warm against my forehead. I slump back against the passenger seat. "And why would you? I try to pretend like I might be normal, like I could be, but I'm not and never will be. I was crazy to think someone like me might have a chance with someone like you." My eyes are on my lap. "I'm so mortified," I whisper.

"Marlena," Finn says. "You're not crazy. Don't be embarrassed. Please." His fingers slide along my arm until they reach my hand. He takes it into his and holds it. "I've thought about kissing you," he says.

Red, pink, and orange flashes before me. I don't know what's real and what's not. I turn to Finn, see him through the sunrise in my eyes. "You have?"

He stares out the front of the truck, but doesn't let go of my hand. "Since the first moment I saw you."

"Really?"

"Yes. You think you feel crazy, but I'm the one who's felt crazy. I . . . I shouldn't be thinking of you this way."

"Why? Because of Angie's study?"

He returns my hand to my lap and places his on the gear shift. The colors in my vision fade. He shakes his head. "Mostly it's because of me. And because of who you are. Because I don't know what to make of you."

His words are vague, but I know where he's going. "Because you don't believe in me."

Finn sighs. "That's pretty much the first thing I said to you."

"I don't care."

"Shouldn't you?"

"What I care about is that you see me as Marlena. Not Marlena the Healer or Marlena the Saint, but just as *me*."

"But you're not . . ."

"I'm not normal?" I finish. I wait for Finn to confirm this, that no, I could never be normal to him, that he could never see me as just Marlena. Or to convince me that he *could* see me this way. That one day he will. Instead of responding to my question, Finn changes the subject. "Are you going to tell me what happened to make you call me?"

The air deflates from my lungs. Answers enter my mind and leave the other side.

It wasn't because I wanted to try and kiss you.

It wasn't to confess my feelings for you.

"I don't know. I don't want to talk about it."

"Are you sure?"

"Yes."

"Okay."

Finn rolls down his window. I roll down mine. We sit there, watching gulls circle and dive, circle and dive. The sound of the waves slapping the rocks helps to lessen the tension. I hope the fire in my cheeks is fading.

Eventually Finn speaks. "Let's go get something to eat. You

won't tell me what happened, but I'm assuming you're not ready to go home yet. Right?"

"Yes. Right. I don't want to go home."

Finn shifts into gear and backs up the truck a little. "Okay, then."

We pull out into the street.

"Where are we going?"

He shrugs. "You'll see."

I stare at my gauzy white sheath, the long pale sweater over it. The ends of Finn's soft gray scarf. I wish I could go home and change my clothes. This is definitely not how I thought this day would turn out. The truck rumbles over a pothole and the two of us bounce. The bottom of his heart tattoo is visible, then hidden, visible, then hidden under his sleeve as Finn shifts and turns the wheel. It has the effect of seeming to beat.

"Marlena . . ."

I bite my lip. The heart on his skin flashes bright as the red sun of morning. Or maybe my eyes are playing tricks. "What?"

"I do see you as Marlena. But you are still Marlena the Healer. This . . . this magical creature who I watched walk among the sick on Saturday, like some sort of apostle. I can't exactly forget that part."

"Can you try?" I ask.

I expect him to say yes, but he doesn't.

He presses his lips tight and concentrates on the road.

EIGHTEEN

"I've always wanted to do simple things," I tell Finn.

He looks up, mouth full of lemon merengue. He swallows. "What do you mean?"

We are sitting at a picnic table by the ocean. Long flat rocks jut out toward the sea. The sky is still gray. This setting, the peace and beauty of it, clashes with the angry chaos of my morning. My heart keeps speeding up, skipping, then abruptly slowing down, a child playing tag. But I like the world at this odd, heady angle.

Finn brought us to a ramshackle cottage on the side of the road, painted a pale blue. On the shingled wall next to the windows is a homemade sign that says "THE PIE SHOP" in block letters. Each one is a bit imperfect, slanting to the left or right, wider in some places and narrower in others. Inside the shelves are packed floor to ceiling with chocolate bars from all over the world, the kind that are hard to find. The rest is a kitchen where three people are hard at work cutting and chopping and baking. A long display case brims with all kinds of pies. Savory, sweet. Some vegan, some vegetarian, and plenty for carnivores.

I've lived here my entire life, but I didn't know this place existed. Shows how much I get out.

I look down at the oblong pie I've been devouring, half of it gone, the crust crumbling where I've attacked it with my fork. Steak and cheddar. I don't know why I picked it, but it's delicious. "Simple things like, I don't know, this, for example," I tell Finn. "Eating with a friend."

"So we're friends?" Finn asks.

Something flutters in me. Do I want to confirm that we're friends, when what I really want is for us to be more? Finn answers before I can respond.

"Wow, I see how it is, Marlena," he says, but he is laughing. "Don't let me pressure you or anything. We don't have to be friends."

I hesitate, sensing this moment is important. An image flashes. Is it a vision or a simple thought? It's of me, reaching out, taking a step. Finn is waiting for me, a few feet away. The picture fades. "It's just that, well, um." How can I explain? "It's difficult for me to know what a friend is. I'm only recently learning what it means to have one. I've been sheltered from other people. Everyone but my mother. She keeps me, our life, very private. But lately I don't want to live like this anymore, and the more I want to be free, the more my mother wants to imprison me." I stab at the pie to give myself something to concentrate on other than Finn. "Hence, I do things like demand a kiss from a boy I hardly know at the absolute wrong moment because I have no idea what I'm doing. Or what other people do in such situations."

Finn lays his fork on the table. "I wasn't making fun of you. Or, if it seemed that way, I didn't mean it to."

I resist the urge to dig into my plate again to distract myself from the nervous feeling in my chest. "I know. It's okay."

Finn's hand is flat across the weather-worn boards, not far from my own. "I'm glad you called me," he says quietly. "You should consider me a friend."

"Are you sure that's what you want?" At first I don't realize the different ways this question might be interpreted, but I don't take it back. The breeze floats around us. As I wait for Finn to answer, I want to inch my fingers toward his hand. A car drives by on the road beside us. It sounds loud, like someone turned up the volume on the world. Finn's eyes drop to the table, and he pushes the conversation in a different direction.

"Tell me about the simple things you've wanted to try. I want a list."

I grab my fork, stabbing the pie, trying not to be disappointed. "I don't want to bore you. Or make you think I'm even more of a freak than you already do."

Finn raises one eyebrow, something I've read about in books but never seen anyone do. "I don't think you're a freak, but obviously you think you are. And I'll remind you that technically, I'm kind of freakish, given my age and that I'm already getting my PhD. So let's just say I want to know some of the things on your list so maybe I can assist in the effort to defreak you. Or maybe we can normalize each other, since it hasn't occurred to you that I also might need help in that department."

I swallow the bite I've just taken, then laugh. "I'll tell you some of the things on my list, but only in the effort to help you out."

"Of course. I really appreciate that."

Things pop into my mind. I try to pick through them. There are so many and they appear at random. "Going for a swim on the beach."

"You've never been swimming?"

"Not like a normal person. Not in a *bathing suit*."

"Normal for you is skinny-dipping?" Finn asks, laughing again.

"That's not what I meant." I shake my head, cracking up. "Okay, moving on. Going to a party. You know, with people my age." I keep going. "School. I've never been to school or class or had a locker. I've only read about those things in books." Finn is staring like he wants to speak, but has decided to be patient so I can get through my list. "I've never been to a movie. I've never gone on a road trip. I've never had a sleepover. I've never been allowed to dress like a normal person, at least not openly." My heart rushes forward, beating at the insides of my rib cage. "Even though I'm eighteen, I've never driven a car, never even sat behind the wheel of one. And I've never been . . .

out on a date." My eyes dart toward the spray of ocean rising up from the rocks. "There's plenty more but I'll stop there."

Finn says nothing.

"What? Now you realize what you've gotten yourself into, offering to help me out with this list?" My question sounds cheerful, but underneath it is insecurity.

"No. It just makes me sad that being a healer has kept you from . . . from *living*."

"I'm living." I swallow. "Right now."

The silence that follows is frustrating. I can tell Finn is holding back again. He's like a soda can that started gushing after being shaken but then somehow stopped. I want to shake him up again, like I did when I told him I wanted to kiss him in his truck.

"You've never been out on a date?" Finn asks finally.

And here we are. Where I want to be. But will the outcome be bad or good?

I bite my lip. Then shrug. "Maybe not."

"Ever?"

What is the right answer here?

"Maybe never?"

"Okay," Finn says.

"Does that freak you out?"

There's a beat before he answers. "Stop saying that word. And no."

"Does it surprise you?"

"No," he answers, this time too quickly.

"Is this a date?" I ask, just as quickly.

There is a long pause.

"Maybe?" Now it's Finn's turn to be uncertain. "Do you want it to be?"

I nod, but don't speak. Words might shatter the moment.

"I want it to be, too," he says quietly.

I smile, but only a little so as not to wear my joy too boldly. I look down at my thin cotton sheath and pull at the ends of Finn's scarf. "This isn't how I imagined I'd be dressed for my first date. Like an escaped mental patient."

Finn laughs, loud this time. "You do *not* look like an escaped mental patient."

"You said it yourself once, when I was visiting Angie's office!"

"I was kidding!" He holds out his arms and appraises his T-shirt. The heart tattoo is in full view.

"You literally wear a heart on your sleeve," I observe.

"Oh." He drops his arms and it disappears under his shirt. "Yeah."

"What's the tattoo about?"

He looks at the sea. A little slice of sun has peeked out from the clouds and soft yellow rays slant over the water. "I'll tell you another time."

"Look who's being mysterious."

He shakes his head. I guess he's not giving out this information today.

The breeze has picked up. The afternoon is waning. "My mother is going to kill me when I go home."

Finn's eyes narrow.

"What?" I ask him.

"Your mother . . ."

"My mother . . . ?"

"You can't let her rule you."

I press my fingertip into one of the crumbs on my plate. "Easier said than done."

"You have more power than you realize."

"Right."

"Of course you do. I was at your audience. You have all the power, not your mother. I saw what you did."

My eyes flicker up. Seek Finn across the table. "And what did you see?"

"I saw . . ."

What?

"What?"

"I saw a girl performing . . . miracles." This last word is a disbelieving whisper.

"Did you?"

His eyebrows arch. "Did I?"

I remember the rush of faith I felt this morning. "Yes," I tell him, and in this moment, it is the truth. I believe in myself. I was there, after all, on Saturday. I am Marlena, the Healer, the Saint.

It isn't a fairy tale. *I am not a fairy tale.*

"What does it feel like?" Finn asks.

I push my plate to the side and lean my elbows onto the table. "Honestly, it feels amazing. Like the most intimate moment you've ever had with another person, like your soul and theirs are connected. An instance of perfect unity."

"Wow."

"And it's not just emotional. I see so much. There are colors, and I can hear everything. Like the essence of a person is composed of music."

"Marlena," Finn breathes.

I can tell he is rapt. "Yes?"

"But?"

He knows. He knows there is more. And there is. The anger, the uncertainty bubbles up, as I think of how to go on. "But there is a dark side to my healings. It's exhausting, and it gets more so as I get older." I think of the people Mrs. Jacobs brought to my audience a few months back. "Sometime I wonder if my gift is waning, or growing more unpredictable, if sometimes it works and sometimes it doesn't. And sometimes I've wondered if my gift is not from God like my mother says, but from the devil, like I might be dipping into a spring in hell and pulling up water from its fires for people to drink." I shiver. "Wow, *that* is something I've never said out loud." I pause, and Finn leans forward. "Sometimes, I wonder if the cost of healing someone is my own well-being. Like, I'm draining my health and passing it on to them. Like, maybe one day, I'll end up depleted and sick and incurable. That death will be my punishment for keeping people alive."

"That's horrible."

"But even worse," I go on, because I can't seem to stop, "I'm just . . . alone. We don't even have other family. I have my mother and . . . no one. Nothing. Healing and some books about women who lived hundreds of years ago. It's been nice to have Angie. And you. It's the first time I've disobeyed the rules of this life so that I can do something I want. Something my mother didn't approve."

Finn is thoughtful. Calm. Some of that calm reaches across the table and flows into me, like a balm. "Why don't you take a break?"

"What do you mean?"

"You know, take some time off from healing?"

I shake my head. The idea seems ridiculous. Impossible. "I can't do that."

"Why not?"

"Because being a healer doesn't work that way. Because my mother would never allow it," I add, realizing this is true.

"You said she would never allow you to meet with Angie, but you're doing it. You're eighteen. You can make your own decisions."

A giant wave slaps into the rocks, followed by a loud splash. The force of it matches the feelings surging in me. "But I've never known anything different."

"And you never will, unless you allow yourself to."

Could I really do what Finn is suggesting?

"But my mother . . ."

"Can't force you to do anything you're unwilling to do."

"It's complicated," I say.

He takes a deep breath. "Life is complicated. That's never going to change. It's not a reason to avoid doing something you want to do. And need to." The look in Finn's eyes is sincere and beautiful and open. No one has ever looked at me like this, not even at my healings. I don't think I knew until now how much I've yearned for someone to see me this way. I don't know what to say. I almost want to run away.

"Finn."

He waits for me to go on.

"I should go," I whisper.

"Oh." He sounds disappointed. "I'll take you home."

He starts to get up and so do I, but my dress gets caught on the bench and I go tumbling to the ground.

"Are you all right?"

I try to laugh off my spill. "I'm fine." There are grass stains on the white sheath to add to the coffee-stained slippers. What a mess. I hope that Finn will hold out his hand to help me get up, but he doesn't.

"You've given me a lot to think about." I look at him from my crouch on the ground. "But there's one thing I don't have to think about."

"What's that?"

"I want to see you again. I mean, not just at Angie's center."

"Okay," he says.

"All right."

"All right."

Finn reaches toward me.

When I take his hand, as he pulls me up, I see suns and stars, streaks of color. I see a swirl of red at Finn's center, vibrant and beautiful. But there is something else. Sorrow. A sorrow I can't quite explain or express, a pool of it collecting behind the red.

Once I am standing, Finn lets go. The joyful colors, the suns and stars, the watery sorrow fade. I wait and breathe, breathe and wait, until eventually they disappear. The only thing that remains is the knowledge, the certainty, that my life, my real life, is finally about to begin. That, in fact, it already has.

NINETEEN

When I get home, my mother is sitting on the couch in front of the windows, still in her white suit and heels. The ocean is a stormy dark blue behind her. The workers and television people are gone. The shattered mug and coffee in the kitchen have been cleaned up, the papers piled onto the counter.

"Did you have a nice day, Marlena?" Her gaze goes to the grass stains on my dress, then up to the gray scarf around my neck. Finn's scarf. I'm still wearing it. "Where did you get that?"

"It doesn't matter," I say.

"It does to me. Whose is it?"

I shake my head.

Anger flickers across my mother's face. "Tell me that some boy didn't give it to you. You know that boys are off-limits. We both agreed."

"Yes, back when I was twelve." Finn's words from earlier about my having power pulse through me. "It's none of your business where I got the scarf. So stop asking."

"Marlena!"

I unwind it from my neck and fold it. "Yes, Mama?"

She rises from the couch. Her suit is wrinkled. "You do not talk to me like that!"

I hold the scarf to my middle. It warms the place where it presses against me. I glance around the room at the remnants of today's failed television shoot, at the cameras mounted to the corners of the ceiling, darkened and off. "Well, *you* don't get to use *me* anymore. I'm not some doll, Mama! Some toy you offer people to play with in exchange for fame and money."

My mother inhales sharply. "That's not how this is."

I take a step toward her. "Maybe it wasn't before, when I was younger, but that's exactly how it is now. I know what you tell people, Mama. Stop denying it."

My mother raises her hand. For a second, I think she might be about to hit me, but then something comes over her and her expression shifts. "Such gifts," she whispers. "Such gifts and they are wasted on you."

"Maybe," I say. "But maybe it's time I get to decide how and when to use them, instead of being used by them." *And by you*, I think.

She crosses her arms, like she doesn't trust them. "What are you saying?"

I inhale, readying to tell her what I've been thinking about on the way home in Finn's truck. "I want things to change."

The muscles in my mother's body tense. "Change how?"

"My gift, the healing, it's a part of me, a big part."

"Yes? And?"

"But I want to do things other girls my age do, Mama. I want to have friends. I want to go out for ice cream like a normal person." I tug at my sheath. "I want to wear normal clothes. I want access to some of my money, so I have the freedom to make my own decisions, to buy something I might need or, God, just something I want to eat if I'm hungry." There is still one thing I haven't yet said. "I'm . . . I'm stopping. I'm quitting healing. For now. Saturday was my last audience for a while." This proclamation rings through the room.

My mother shakes her head, back and forth. "Marlena, you can't."

"I can and I am. You can't force me to do anything I don't want." I cross my arms now. "Not anymore."

"Gifts don't work that way. God gave you this gift to use. You have no idea what will happen if you stop."

"You mean God gave me this gift without my asking, so you can use me to make money. And the rest of the town can, too. Let's be honest."

My mother throws up her hands. "Forget about the money for a minute! Gifts like yours aren't to be played with. You can't just turn them on and off."

"Well, I am."

Her head is still shaking. "It's not right." She takes a step back and drops heavily onto the couch. "Marlena, I'm . . . I'm afraid."

"Afraid of what? That you can't live off your daughter anymore? That you can't ask seekers and the suffering to pay up or I won't heal them?"

Her hands grip her knees. She suddenly looks so young. "I'm afraid you will come to regret this."

I close my eyes a moment. I hear honesty in her words. Honesty and worry. Real motherly concern. "If I do, Mama, it can't be worse than the regret of missing out on a normal childhood, a normal life. I regret that most of all. More than anything else that could possibly happen from this decision."

My mother's gaze drops to her lap. "You say that now."

"It's the truth." I watch her there, so still, like she's not breathing. "I don't want television specials, Mama. I don't want to be famous. I don't want to be needed by everyone. I just want to be like everyone else."

"You've never been like everyone else and you shouldn't want to be. I saw you on Saturday, Marlena. I saw what you did. We all saw. You should be . . ."

"Grateful?" I supply with a long sigh.

My mother's eyes flicker up at me. "Proud. I was going to say proud." Then, "Being a healer is who you are."

My throat grows tight. "But it's not all that I am, Mama."

There is a long pause, the two of us staring at each other, roles reversed, my mother slumped on the couch, rumpled and defeated, me standing before her, confident and unyielding. "You're not a little girl anymore," she says. There is sadness in her tone. Real sadness, and longing.

The air around us is fragile. I'm afraid to move through it.

Carefully, I step out of my stained white slippers. "No, I'm not," I say. Silently, I turn away.

"Marlena," my mother calls after me as I climb the stairs. "I do love you, you know. Never forget that. I always have."

In my room, I take down the evidence of my visions, the things I've painted and made and drawn. I carry them to the gift room, setting them on a shelf and stacking them in the corner. I take my collection of books about healers and mystics, the writings of Julian of Norwich, Teresa of Ávila, Margery Kempe, even Hildegard, and bring them to the gift room, too. Next come the white sheaths. I ball them into a big heap on the floor by the paintings and the books. I don't care if they get ruined. I go back and forth, back and forth, replacing the stuff of my life as a healer with the stuff of normalcy. Jeans. T-shirts. Platform sandals and baggy sweaters and flip-flops and short skirts. I pick through the offerings for anything I like. Stacks of novels that people thought I might like to read, probably because other girls my age do like to read them. Soon, aside from the clothes and the books, my room is nearly bare of everything that ever marked my life as a healer.

My mother is right. I know nothing else aside from healing. But so much blank space is more exciting than daunting. The change makes me feel different.

Lighter.

Freer.

More hopeful.

But it's also strange.

I'm strange. Like I'm not quite here. Like I'm floating in some in-between space, wedged between reality and the unseen. Teresa of Ávila wrote of this place she called the interior castle, which she had to move through, fight through, to get to God. Maybe I've entered something of a castle myself, but an exterior one. I must pass through it to finally enter the outside world. I wonder how hard I'll have to fight, or if I'll have to fight at all. Maybe it will be easy.

As the day wears into night, I feel a shift, my entire being changing. All the cells in my body are remaking themselves to reflect the girl I am going to be from this day forward. The girl who is not a healer. The girl who is not too sacred to touch. The girl who is not responsible for the livelihood of an entire town, for the future of so many seekers. The figurehead, removed from her ship.

It's like the cells in my body know what is happening.

Does God know?

Will God throw a tantrum, taking my gift away and more

besides? Sometimes I think, if there is a God, he is a salesman on the side of the road, a con artist hawking shiny baubles, acting as though you already promised to purchase them, as though you begged for them when you never did. Yet somehow he still tricks you into thinking it was your idea to hang them around your neck in the first place.

A shiver runs through me.

I sit in my chair by the window, curl my feel underneath me, and look out onto the water and the darkening sky.

The human body, our muscles, our hands, have their own memories. Healing is like that, a muscle I've been flexing my entire life. I don't even have to think about it. Calling on my gift has always been as simple as rustling around in a pocket for a charm I know is always there. But it's also strange to have a gift whose source remains a mystery. A charm I've come to depend on, but one I've never fully understood.

Is it possible that just as I can call on my gift at will, I can as easily will it away? That in removing the stuff of my life as a healer, I can remove the gift from my body? Or is it more like the charm getting lost, fallen through a hole in my pocket? And if so, where will it go? Will it be resting between the floorboards, waiting for me to find it again?

TWENTY

When I wake up on the first morning of my new life as Marlena *Not the Healer*, I do a number of things.

I pick and choose from the clothing now hanging in my closet. There is a glittery tank top I might never wear but decided I wanted anyway. There are jeans and jeans and more jeans. Skinny. Ripped at the knees. Cut off at the bottom. Jeans with studs. Jeans with embroidered flowers. T-shirts are piled on my shelves and cute, colorful dresses hang in a row, a bright tempting rainbow of choices. I decide on one of the T-shirts. Pale violet, with a V-neck. A pair of jeans with studs in the shape of tiny stars. Bright-green flip-flops. I've always wanted to wear flip-flops. I've seen girls wearing them at the beach, in town, on the boardwalk by the wharf, on the way to some takeout restaurant, thwacking along as they chat with their friends or hold hands with their boyfriends.

Boyfriends.

Am I going to have a boyfriend?

T-shirts, jeans, flip-flops, and a boyfriend, too?

There is a rush in my ears, a dizzying lightness in my head to accompany it.

I grab a deep-fuchsia sweater in case I get cold. I love the bright color.

So much color!

The sun shines through my bedroom window. I turn my face to it, my whole body, a flower discovering warmth and light.

My stomach grumbles low and loud.

I thwack my way down the hall and the steps and into the kitchen, smiling.

What do healers on vacation eat?

Candy bars? Ice cream? Cheeseburgers and fries?

"Marlena, you look nice." Fatima looks up from the counter where she is chopping vegetables. Carrots. Celery. Onion. Kale. Kale, of course. She is making one of those Portuguese stews that take forever to cook, that she makes sometimes when my mother is feeling homesick for her own mother's cooking, though she never admits this out loud.

Is Mama feeling homesick today?

"You really think so?" I ask Fatima. She smiles an uncertain smile, like she's not quite sure what the rules are at the moment. I wonder what she overheard yesterday. If she overheard everything. What my mother told her, if anything.

"Yes. But Marlena?" Fatima comes around the counter to where I'm standing. "May I? Fix something?"

"Sure," I say. But she hesitates. "Fatima, please don't be afraid. I'm not a sacred object." Fatima blinks. She looks around the kitchen like she's expecting my mother to jump out of the fridge and scold her for being too close. "Besides, I need your advice on my outfit. Too much color?"

She shakes her head. "No. I think the color is nice. Different, but a good different." She tugs a little at my T-shirt, where I've tucked it in. Once it's completely untucked, she fixes it so it hangs to the edge of my hips. "That's all. But it's better."

"Thank you." I shrug on the bright sweater and hold out my arms, wait for Fatima's verdict.

"I like the pink," she says, then places a hand over her mouth.

We both start to laugh. I don't know why.

Fatima returns to the other side of the counter. I think our conversation is over, but then she says something else. "Your mama told me this morning that things would be different, but she didn't tell me how. Do you want to talk about it? I . . . I won't tell her."

My good feeling falters. "Where is she?"

"I don't know. She left early. She didn't say where she was going." Fatima has gone back to chopping carrots, but she keeps looking up.

"I decided I'm not going to be a healer anymore, Fatima."

A startled sound escapes her and the knife clatters to the counter. "Marlena? Really? But that is a *big* change."

"I just . . . I needed a break. It's just for a while."

She takes a dish towel and wipes her hands. *"Tudo bem, tudo bem,"* Fatima says while nodding. "I suppose it makes sense, *querida.* I can imagine you might want a break. It's a lonely life you've had." Fatima draws in a deep breath. "Marlena, I . . ."

I climb onto one of the stools in front of the kitchen island and wait for her to continue.

". . . I've always thought that things could be different for you."

I lean my elbows on the counter. "What do you mean?"

"That being a healer, being who you are, doesn't require that you live how you do. That you could be a normal girl, but one who is *also* a healer. That you could be both things." She's not looking me in the eye. "It's your mama who's made it seem like it's one or the other. Your mama and maybe those books you're always reading by those ancient women. Like it's all or nothing."

What Fatima has said is so simple it should be obvious, but it's never been obvious to me. "I don't know. It's hard for me to think of things any other way. So, for now, I think it just has to be all or nothing. And I want it to be nothing."

Fatima sighs, picking up her knife again. "That makes me sorry, Marlena. And sad. I hope you can find your way to a place where you can be both."

I tug at the bright-pink ends of my sweater sleeves. "Do you think it's real, Fatima? My gift? Ever since Mrs. Jacobs . . . I've wondered about it."

Fatima's eyes shift upward, toward heaven, then flicker back to me. "Yes, Marlena. I do."

I go out the back of the house.

José is on his way to pick me up. I want to tell Angie about my decision. I feel like she should know that I'm quitting healing for a while. But I'm also going because Finn told me not so casually he'd be there today, and that maybe—if I stopped by to see Angie—he and I could hang out afterward. Do one of the things on my list of normal.

The ocean shines with sunlight, the waves lapping at the shore.

The air smells warm.

Inviting.

What's that saying again?

The world is my oyster.

I take a step forward, and another, walk through the world, let myself be absorbed into it, embraced and beckoned and called. I wonder if today I am its pearl.

The moment I get in the car, José reaches his arm back and hands me an envelope. His eyebrows arch, his round face searches mine.

On it is my mother's handwriting. "Marlena."

I open it. Inside is a pile of cash. No note. Just money.

"*Rosado, cariño,*" José says. "I like you in pink. I think it's your color."

"I didn't know I had a color."

"I didn't know either. But maybe you do now. Maybe you have more than one."

"Maybe."

José is still watching me. "*¿A dónde vamos?*"

"Where do you think?"

"Your friend Angie's center?"

"Yes. Please," I add.

I count the money. Then I count it again. Twenties, tens, fives. There is six hundred dollars. I've never held so much money in my hands. Huh. I told my mother I wanted money, and here it is, like magic.

Apparently I do have power.

I count the money again. I can't help it.

With money, a girl can do things. Go places. Buy stuff.

Maybe I'll go shopping. Maybe I'll go to a store and try on outfits like other people do when they're looking for what to wear. Maybe I'll find something I like that isn't the choice of someone I've healed. Something that isn't a thank-you, an offering, for services rendered, miracles completed. Maybe I'll buy it just because I like it.

"José?"

"*Sí*, Marlenita?"

"Will you pull over at that gas station?"

"*Por supuesto.*"

He stops and I hop out. Before I go inside, I gesture for him to roll down the window. "Do you want anything?"

José seems surprised. He's not used to me asking such things. I'm not used to being able to offer. "*Limonada,*" he says. "*Con gas.* You know which ones I mean?"

I nod. I do know. I've seen Fatima drinking them in the kitchen.

Suddenly, an image of Fatima and José hanging out after work, drinking fizzy lemonades by the seawall, pops into my head. I wonder if they spend time together when they are off the clock.

"*Gracias.*"

"Sure thing, José," I say, and go into the little store.

First, I head to the fridges and find the familiar soda can I always see in Fatima's hand on her break. The cool air rushes out when I open the door. I don't take anything for myself. I'm not here for a drink.

I want magazines. Fashion magazines.

I've never looked at one.

I've never been allowed. It's just not what healers do, I guess.

There is a shelf at the front of the store full of them and I go to it now, cold soda sweating in my hand. I pick up *Vogue.* I know it's famous and I've actually heard of it, so I figure it's a good place to start. I tuck it under my arm and keep looking. *Glamour. Elle. Harper's Bazaar. Marie Claire.* There are so many and they are so shiny and beautiful. I skip over the wedding ones, feeling allergic to anything white and sparkly and weddingy. When I go to the register I have a pile of seven magazines to go with José's fizzy lemonade. They are heavy and the stack makes a loud thud when it hits the counter. Before the man rings up the total, I add two chocolate bars. One for me, one for José. Twixes. I've seen José eating them. The man keeps totaling and then asks for way more money than I expect. I guess magazines are expensive. I fish two twenties from the envelope. He hands me back a five, two ones, and change, which I put away while he's placing everything into a plastic bag. I grab the lemonade before he can put that away, too, say thank you, and head outside.

José's window is still open.

"Your drink, *señor*," I say, handing the can through the window.

He chuckles and takes it.

"Marlenita," he laughs, shaking his head.

"What?"

"Nothing, *cariño*." He eyes the bag, which is sagging with the weight of the magazines. "What else did you buy?"

"Girly things," I say, and shrug.

I'm about to get into the back seat when I stop and bend forward again, looking through the passenger-side window. "Can I sit up front? Or is that weird?"

José's eyebrows arch again. "Of course you can. It's not weird."

I open the door and settle in. I've never sat up front. I guess because Mama always set the precedent of sitting in the back. This seems silly now that I think of it.

José puts the car in gear and pulls onto the road. I glance over at him, but his eyes are facing forward. I reach into the bag and pull out *Vogue*, with its glossy cover and a woman in a frilly, strapless black gown with her head thrown back laughing. She's frolicking among some trees, their leaves golden and red and a fiery orange of fall.

If I put on a dress like this, would it make me that happy, too?

I flip through it, mesmerized by so many beautiful things.

"You looking for style advice, eh?" José asks as I'm reaching into the bag to pull out another glossy tome.

I nod, a little embarrassed by how many magazines I bought. It makes me look either desperate or like I have no impulse control. Maybe both. But maybe it doesn't matter? It feels like I've been let out of jail. Maybe, on my first day of freedom, I'm allowed to go a little crazy. Maybe on my second day, too.

The pictures on the pages are so exquisite. The women, the clothes. They are elegant and funky and sexy and so many other things I'm not used to. The wedding gowns for my audiences are lovely, sure, but they make me into the portrait of innocence, the virginal bride. Of course, I am a virgin, but still. These clothes make me wonder whether, if I put them on, I'd become a different person, like putting on a new skin.

I page through the magazines like a hungry monster. I gobble them up.

I want everything at once. Clothes, friends, boyfriends, road trips, shopping trips, parties, lazy days at the beach, cookouts, school, homework, epic makeout sessions, and movie nights. It's like I've been starving for years, but just realized I'm ravenous. The world has always been there, but it feels like I am only now seeing it. My heart pounds.

I need to calm down.

"Oh!" I dig around at the bottom of the bag until my hands close around the candy bars. I nearly forgot I bought them. "Here." I drop one of the Twixes into the cup holder. "That's for you."

"My favorite!"

"I know."

José's palm rests on top of the wheel as he steers us alongside the ocean. He's quiet for a bit and doesn't reach for the chocolate, but then I hear him take a breath. "Did something happen between you and your mama? Well, I know *something* happened, but are you okay, *mi niñita?* This seems like a lot of sudden change."

I look down at the pile of magazines in my lap, slipping and sliding around with the movement of the car. "I'm okay," I tell him. "Maybe for the first time in a while."

"That's good to hear," he says, but I can sense hesitation. "Your mama," he starts, but then stops.

I almost don't want him to continue.

Is it weird that I don't wonder where my mother is? Or when I'll see her again? Or what will happen when I do? Like, what in the world will we talk about or say to each other if it's not about the audience coming up this coming Saturday or, I don't know, a television special about me? Will we suddenly talk about boys and clothes and get manicures and hang out in the lawn chairs in the back of the house and sun ourselves? Will she ever forgive me for stopping being her perfect child-daughter-healer?

Instead of asking José what he was going to say about my mother, I change the subject to something that has just occurred to me in my newly freed state. I watch as José turns the wheel, just slightly, but enough to round the bend in the road. "José, would you teach me how to drive one of these days?"

José belly laughs so hard it's nearly a minute before he answers, and so long that Angie's boxy glass center has come into view. "I'd love to, *cariño*. I thought you'd never ask."

TWENTY-ONE

I thwack my way through the front door. I decide I love flip-flops, the way they are seemingly so low-key and unassuming, flat and rubbery and made so you can get them caked with sand and wash them off later with a garden hose if you want, but at the same time just a little bit obnoxious because of the constant, rhythmic noise they make as you step. *Thwack, thwack, thwack.* Rhythmic like the ocean waves, yet plastic and man-made and entirely unnatural. Profane.

People can hear me coming, I think.

Unlike before, when I wore my silent, white ballet flats.

I am no longer a ghost.

As usual, Lexi is buried in a thick book on her desk. She glances up. "Hi, Marlena. Look at you!"

"Colorful?" I say, getting used to everyone's surprise. "Um, too colorful?"

She smiles. "No. Cheerful. Different. I like it."

Lexi might be lying, but I don't care. "Thank you."

"Angie's on a call. She should be off in a few minutes. You can wait wherever you like. You know your way around." She drops her eyes back to her reading.

I resist inquiring whether Finn is with Angie in the office and instead head into the wide open lab. The MRI machine glows bright as always in the stark sunlight streaming through the glass. Before I can decide otherwise, I kick off my flip-flops and climb onto the hard table and lie down. Then I inch myself along the platform until I'm inside the dome. The machine is off, so the effect is unremarkable. It's just dark and quiet and still.

I place my hands on the inside of the dome and wait, bracing myself.

I wait and wait.

Nothing.

Just silence. Lifelessness. No visions. No sensing other people who've been inside this machine, no wounds either physical or emotional. The visions were here just the other day. So where did they go?

I swallow.

There is tension in my muscles, my shoulders especially. I let my hands fall away from the hard, cold metal. They come to rest on my chest.

"Marlena?" Angie's voice is muffled by the machine. "What are you doing?"

I inch my way out, using my bare feet to pull myself and sit up.

Angie is standing by the wall of the lab, seemingly frozen. I suppose it's not something that happens every day, a girl randomly climbing inside her MRI.

"Hi." The bright-green flip-flops are still on the floor, waiting for me. I hop down from the table, acting like me being inside an eerie MRI without it being turned on is the most ordinary thing in the world. I slip my feet into the shoes and *thwack* over to her. I will never tire of that sound.

"I'm glad you're here," she says, slowly coming back to life. I wonder if she notices how today I'm sporting an outfit other than my typical dressed-for-bed attire. I try to look around inconspicuously for Finn to see if he's hiding in some corner of the lab, but I don't see him anywhere.

Maybe he's not coming? Maybe he changed his mind about hanging out with me?

Angie searches my face like she's trying to see inside my mind. Her eyes shift to the machine and she nods her chin at it. "Thinking about getting an MRI?"

"Maybe?" I say.

Angie's hair is long and loose today, and it brushes her shoulders. She's wearing a blue button-down blouse that matches her eyes. Casual but somehow dressed up. Like she could go to the fanciest restaurant around and fit right in. "Did it feel scary, to be inside of it?" she asks me. "Or not as bad as you thought?"

"Not as bad as I thought, I guess?"

"At least this time, you didn't faint when you touched it."

I nod. I didn't. How can a person feel this different overnight? Be this different? Maybe it's all in my imagination. My attention drifts to the photos on the wall behind Angie. James Halloway. Nicole Matthews. Chastity Lang. All teenagers with gifts like mine, or something like it. "What are you really looking for when you talk to us?"

Angie's brow furrows. "Who do you mean by 'us'?"

"You know. All the weirdos you study." I point to their photos. "Sonar girl and telekinesis boy. The weatherman. And me," I add.

"You're not a weirdo," Angie says. "None of you are."

"Did you put them in these crazy machines?"

Angie clasps her hands. "Eventually. Yes."

I think about how an MRI is designed to allow someone to see through you, to literally see through your skin and muscles and bone. Designed to expose all of your secrets, to photograph them in black and white. What would an MRI reveal about me? What's inside me that you can't see just by looking? "What do you think you might find in my brain?"

Angie cocks her head. "I don't know," she says, but I don't think that's the whole story. She has a theory. She's not telling me what it is. "That's why I want to do an MRI."

"Do you have any scans I can look at?" I ask, realizing I'm curious what they look like. "You know, so I can see what I'd be getting into?"

Her expression brightens. "Sure. Of course I do." She beckons me to follow. We pass her office and keep on going, into a different part of the center. She leads me into another lab of sorts, but this one is small. Three of its walls are covered with giant screens. Angie picks up a tablet from the table in the middle of the room. The lights go dim and the screens grow bright. My eyes take a second to adjust.

"Oh wow!" I reach out instinctively, toward the glow suddenly emanating from the wall. "That's . . . . those . . . they're beautiful!" All across the screens are images of human brains. Well, images in the shape of a human brain. The colors are startling. I didn't know they would be so colorful! Lines and splotches and lakes of red, blue, green, yellow, purple saturate the scans like maps, like winding bodies of water, like . . . "Angie, I . . . I . . . they . . ."

"What?"

Longing, as powerful as a wave crashing into shore, permeates my every cell. I swallow, I breathe, I try to start over. "This probably won't make any sense, but I recognize these."

Angie is close in the dark. She's watching me, not the screens. "I don't understand, Marlena. Say more."

"I recognize them from my visions. My visions look like this. Not *exactly*. But very similar. Like, incredibly, incredibly similar."

"*Really.*" Angie's voice drops an intensely interested octave.

"Yes." I walk up to the screen to my right, until this one image is only inches from my nose. It almost looks like a sea anemone.

There is a stem—the brain stem, I assume—that mushrooms up into a million tiny waving threads, which are dominated by blues and bright purples. I want to touch it, like I might touch a person during a healing. It's like I am looking at something that came from inside me, that is somehow mine, yet there it is on the wall, as though I painted it and hung it there. "Why does the brain do that? Light up aqua here, and lilac there?"

"It has to do with a person's activities at the time of the scan, and what emotions they are feeling, their thoughts. Different emotions will light up different parts of the brain." She points to the purple sections. "These colors can indicate sadness, depression. The blue is associated with anger." She points to another scan on the wall full of pinks and reds. "Those colors indicate happiness, excitement, engagement with the world."

I stand on my toes to look at another scan, this one a wild swirl of rainbows. "It really is like one of my visions. And the colors from my visions tell me something, too, about the person I'm healing. What they're feeling or going through. Though shades of gray and black are what indicate pain and grief in my, um, scan of a person." I turn to Angie. For once, she's staring at me like she doesn't know how to respond. "I'll show you them sometime," I offer, wishing she'd stop looking at me that way. "My art, I mean. If you ever come to my house—not that my mother would be happy about that."

"Maybe you can take photos and send them to me."

"Maybe," I say. "Maybe I'm like a living, breathing MRI

machine?" I try to laugh. *Maybe all this time I've been painting scans of people's brain activity? Or maybe I've been painting images of my own brain, how it lights up during a healing?* "That sounds crazy."

Just then, Finn walks in. "Um, sorry to interrupt. I didn't know anyone was in here."

My entire body swoops like I'm flying. I wonder how this would show up on one of these brain scans. A bright saturated red? A pink as intense as the color of my sweater? The same hue as my cheeks now that Finn is here? "Hi, um, hi," I say, eloquently.

Angie skips right over greetings and goes straight to the point. "Marlena was just telling me that her visions look like brain scans," she tells Finn. Then to me, she says, "Finn has a photographic memory. I've never seen anyone who can grasp the map of someone's brain like he does. I'm sure he'd love to take a look at your brain scan just as much as I would."

In this moment, I remember Angie is a scientist, like a *really* serious scientist, and I wish she hadn't just revealed this thing about me to Finn, the boy I'm obsessing over, like it isn't a big deal. Though I do like that she just revealed this other, fascinating detail about Finn to me.

"Angie, come *on!*" Finn rolls his eyes.

I guess he must be feeling the same way I do. "You have a photographic memory?"

He nods.

"Wow," I say.

He shrugs.

Then, maybe because I'm so nervous about everything, I drop, "So I've decided to take a break from healing." After which I wonder if this lands like a bomb or just more of a somewhat-interesting revelation that fizzes and sputters.

Angie was about to say something else and instead she closes her mouth.

"Well, that's quite the news," Finn says, finding his voice.

I avoid looking directly at him and instead search Angie's face, trying to guess what she is thinking. I don't want to disappoint her. I worry that I am.

"Why don't we go to my office and talk about this?" she suggests. "We'll leave Finn to his scans."

On my way out of the lab, Finn speaks softly to me. "See you later. Right?"

"Yes," I say, just as softly.

When Angie and I get to her office she sits cross-legged on the floor, and I take a spot on the couch. I almost wish she would sit next to me like a mother might. "Does that mess up . . . this?" By this, I mean the project of Angie studying me.

"Well, that depends." She says this calmly, like what I've just informed her of is no big deal. "Just because you've stopped healing doesn't mean that my research and our conversations have to end. As long as you're okay with it, we can continue as before."

My breath quickens. I'm afraid to tell her the truth. "I don't know. I think I want a break. Not from *you*. But even from thinking about healing. At least for now."

Angie inhales deeply. "Marlena?"

"Yes?"

"What prompted this decision?"

Everyone keeps asking this.

"And just a moment ago," she goes on, "you seemed so excited to talk about your visions and how you saw them in those scans."

"I know." I straighten my jeaned legs, study my toes against the green of my shoes, the windows and the sea beyond them outlining everything. My flip-flops are a glaring hue against the monochrome white of everything in Angie's office. I used to match the decor, blend right into it, and now I'm an interruption. "Yesterday I got into a fight with my mother," I start. "She has, or maybe *had*, plans for a television special about me. Film crews following me for weeks. She didn't consult me, she just planned it. I got angry at her, like I've never gotten angry in my life. I threw a mug. It broke and it was a mess."

Angie nods as she listens, always pulling stories through quiet and the need people have to fill the gaps in conversation.

"Sometimes I think my mother depends on me more than I depend on her. She just wants me to keep going, healing, so our life never has to change. It doesn't even matter to her if my gift is real or not."

"Do you want your mother to believe in you?" Angie asks.

I let my legs relax again. Slump into the cushions of the comfy couch. "I don't know. Her belief in me has come at such a cost. Like, she doesn't really see me as her daughter. I'm a healer first. A healer *only*."

"Is this why you decided to take a break?"

I force myself to be the silent one now, afraid of what I might say. *Yes, and also because I want to go out on dates with your research assistant.*

"Is there anything else?" Angie presses.

"Probably." I only allow myself the one word.

"Are you sure about your decision?"

"Yes," I say, even though inside of me is a jumble of uncertainties. Do I really want a life without my visions, visions that look strangely similar to those beautiful scans? "You know a lot about the brain, right?" I find myself asking.

"I hope so, Marlena, since I've devoted my life to studying it." Angie says. "Why?"

"Do you think the brain can . . . change?"

"Well." The breeze from the open windows floats between us. "It depends on how you mean. The brain is always changing, remaking itself, depending on how we use it. Kind of like the colors that light up differently in the scans, depending on what a person is feeling." She pulls her phone from her pocket. "For example, these things are changing our brains in ways we're only now starting to comprehend. We have a long way to go in understanding this, and no idea what the long-term consequences will be. How they might literally remake our brains." She sets the phone on the ground next to her. "But that's not what you were asking me, is it?"

"I'm not sure. I guess I wonder if we can *will* our brains to change."

"Say more," Angie says.

I search for the right words. "Like, let's say there's a part of your brain you're drawing on all the time? And suddenly you stop drawing on it? Will it forget how to be used in that way?" A thought occurs to me. One I don't like. "Will it go dark of all its color?"

"You're thinking about how your break might affect the way your brain works."

I nod.

"The brain doesn't change overnight, Marlena. Not like you're suggesting."

Angie sounds so sure, like even the possibility it might is just magical thinking. But then, Angie is a scientist, even though she's also a scientist who dabbles with the mysterious and the unbelievable. "Okay," I say, somewhat relieved, but not entirely convinced. I am somehow lighter today than I was yesterday. It's as though the anchor of my gift has been pulled up from the ocean floor, allowing me to float out to sea.

"What would really help to answer your question is if you allowed me to do an MRI," Angie suggests, yet again.

Before I can answer, the door opens and Finn pops his head inside Angie's office. "Can I come in?"

"Of course," Angie says.

Finn's eyes dart to me. "Are you ready, Marlena? Or should I come back later?"

"Finn is giving me a ride home," I explain to Angie, and as a way of giving Finn an answer that *yes*, I'm ready. I watch for Angie's reaction. I don't want Angie to think that Finn and me leaving together is a big deal, even though it's the hugest deal. The biggest deal in my entire, sheltered life.

"Okay," Angie says, the wheels of her mind clearly turning. I wish I knew what it was telling her. She stands up and so I do. "When will I see you next, Marlena?"

I bite my lip. "I don't know."

Angie looks at me hard. "Don't forget, I'm here if there's anything you need. If you have questions. You don't even have to call."

I nod. We hold each other's stare a moment longer.

Then Angie goes to her desk, picks up a book, and flips through it, looking for something, as though Finn and I are already gone. But as he and I exit the center and cross the parking lot toward his truck, I wonder if she has made the connection, the one that has to do with my break from healings and Finn and me spending time together. This thought prompts me to glance back. When I do, I see Angie standing by the windows of her office, watching us. I can't make out her face. The shine on the glass obscures her expression.

TWENTY-TWO

The envelope of money cracks and crinkles in my pocket as I hop into the passenger seat of Finn's truck, like it keeps wanting to remind me that it's there. The driver's side door slams shut and Finn looks at me. He's in jeans again, and a black T-shirt, sleeves long enough that no ink from his tattoo peeks out from under them. "So, Marlena, I had some thoughts about our outing today."

The sound of his voice is like an on button, erasing everything else in my mind. I'm with Finn. He said *outing*, but we both know what this really is. We're going on a sort of date. "I'm up for anything."

"I thought we'd start simple, from your list."

"Oh?"

We are both acting casual. I don't know about Finn, but I don't feel casual right now. I feel like there's a million things I want to ask him. That I want to know.

Finn puts the truck into gear and soon we are on our way out of the parking lot and driving down the road by the sea. "An afternoon movie, and then maybe something to eat?"

"A movie in a movie theater?"

Finn laughs. "Yes, since you said you've never been to one."

"I haven't. We don't even have television in my house. Or a computer. Well, my mother has a tablet, but I'm not allowed to use it." *But my life is changing. Maybe soon I'll have this, too, and more. Oh yeah, and Finn, you have a photographic memory, huh?*

He shifts gears and the truck goes a little faster. I roll down my window. The breeze is cool and soft.

"So you decided to take a break from healing," he says.

I watch him as he drives, so relaxed at the wheel, and wonder if I'll ever drive like this one day, if it will feel second nature. "I told my mother that I'm on vacation. And, surprisingly, you were right. I told her I wanted a break and now I'm on one. It's weird, how it was so easy." The movie theater comes into view ahead. It's a huge gray cube of cement designed to keep out the light. The very opposite of Angie's glass-windowed center. The sign next to it boasts sixteen options for what we might see.

Finn turns into the parking lot. "I'm hurt you're surprised I was right. You do know I'm pretty much a genius." He smirks a little. "Seeing that I've got a photographic memory and all."

"Yeah, I did hear that." I try not to smile. "But we'll have to see. I have a lot of questions and I'm just not sure if I believe in your genius or not. Yet."

He laughs as he drives down an aisle looking for a spot, then pulls into one not far from the entrance. "Touché, Marlena."

By the time the theater goes dark, I am holding a bucket of buttery popcorn, my second candy bar of the day, and a large sugary soda. So much to take in, to eat, and so very gluttonous of me. As Finn and I sit down in the middle of one of the rows, what I really want is to hold his hand. We decided to see some romantic comedy that I've never heard of, because it's not like I'm up on the latest movies. I pop the crunchy, squeaky puffs of popcorn into my mouth to give my fingers something to do, in between sips of Coke, eyes on the screen, not really seeing anything. My brain can only process Finn, Finn, Finn, the nearness of his shoulder, his skin, his palm on the armrest, so close. I want to touch him, turn my head and stare.

At one point I actually think, *My mother was right about boys.* Having an interest in a boy, desiring his attention, just wanting one can apparently become so all-consuming that I can think of nothing else. I don't know if it's just because Finn's my first crush or if it's specific to him, but I do know that I am consumed by Finn in a way I've never been consumed by anyone in my life. I mean, who could perform miracles in such a state?

My insides are fluttery and woozy and drunk. Teresa of Ávila believed she had to shut out the world so she could wind her way to the center of her soul where she believed God awaited her, while all sorts of creatures and obstacles battled her progress. In Teresa's visions, she fought her soul demons with sword in hand. But I feel like I've been residing at the center of my soul for years, and my task is to fight my way out, push past Teresa on my way.

The darkness of the theater makes everything surreal and magical, makes me bolder, like how my anger yesterday made me throw mugs and call Finn and get in his truck. I set the bucket of popcorn on the floor and shift just a little in his direction, tiny increments, closing some of the distance between us. I lean on the armrest.

What will happen if I touch him, this time? What will I see? Something? Anything? Nothing at all?

His cheek is so close. If I turn my head my lips will brush his skin.

The movie plays in the background. I hear it like music in a restaurant, distant and faint. "Is this really happening?" I ask Finn, and I don't mean the movie.

He turns. The two of us stare at each other in the shadows. "This is really happening," he says.

"Can we go?" I ask.

"But the movie," he starts, yet he's already up out of his seat.

I'm up in a flash, too, following him out of the theater, my heart tripling the speed of my steps, my breath doubling it, the air and my mind fizzy and sparkling. The light of the theater lobby is blinding, my surroundings a blur as we push our way through the doors into the afternoon, returning to Finn's truck. He drives out of the parking lot without speaking. It isn't until we are on the road by the sea that he asks, "Where to, Marlena?"

"I know a place," I say. And I do. I want to share something of me with Finn. No, I want to share everything. "Just a little farther down the street, there's a place to pull over." Finn lets me guide him where to go. He parks in a narrow lot along the low-lying park by the ocean. "This way," I tell him after we've gotten out of the truck.

We slip off our shoes and pick our way across the grassy bank and over the rocks, some of them round and difficult to cross, all of them ringed by seashells underneath, some broken, some whole, and small white pebbles, smooth from the ocean. The rocks are dry, the tide low, everything dusty with sand and salt. We keep going, me leading, until we reach three great boulders that rise up to form a wall of sorts, a tiny cove of granite and slate. Beyond it is a wide gray ledge. This is where we stop.

"What is this place?" Finn asks.

"I've always called it the healing rocks," I tell him. "I've been coming since I was small. I love it here."

Finn nods, taking in the view of the ocean, wild with white-caps, but far enough away to keep us safe from the crashing waves. Seagulls glide overhead, the air is brisk and tangy, the sun bright and high. The sky is blue, streaked with white cotton clouds. "It's beautiful," he says.

I look at Finn's hand, tempted to take it, but I keep my arms pinned to my sides.

How do people do this? Is it always this fraught? This confusing?

"Over here," I tell him, tiptoeing across the wide, rough stone until I reach the edge of it and sit down. I've always loved how the tall boulders that shelter this place are close enough that I can lean back against them, like sitting in a comfy chair. A sofa made from the life of the shore.

"You didn't like the movie?" Finn asks after he's settled next to me.

"I don't remember much of it, so I don't know. Maybe I would in another circumstance?" I glance at Finn. "If I was there with someone else?"

Finn's eyes shift from me to the sea. "I don't remember any of it, either," he says. Then, "Can I ask you something?"

"That depends."

"On what?"

I pick up one of the smooth stones sitting on the ledge and begin to press it into the center of my palm. "Is it a Finn-and-Angie-research question, or just a Finn-who-is-curious-about-Marlena question?"

Finn sighs. "Maybe a bit of both. I want to understand you better. If it's something you don't want to answer, then just tell me."

"Okay. But you can ask me something, if I can ask you something afterward. I have questions, too, Finn."

He smiles. "All right. It's a deal. But me first." Finn leans over and picks through the pile of shells and pebbles next to the rocks, and comes up with one that is small and flat. Perfect for skipping. "So, how did you end up this way? I mean, as a healer?" He laughs. "Let me be more specific. Did you sign up somewhere at church? Did you go to healer school?"

I give a laugh, too, but it's more of a nervous one. "No, it doesn't work that way. Performing miracles is not a profession a person chooses. It chooses you, and you submit to it. You know the story of Mary, right? And the angel Gabriel? You can be a scientist and still know that story, right?"

"Yes, I've heard it once or twice," Finn says. "An angel showed up and told Mary she was going to have the son of God, like it or not, and she would end up an unwed mother. Not a very nice situation. God's kind of an asshole like that, I think."

"Maybe." The white stone in my palm is warm against my skin. "But, at least in theory, Gabriel gave Mary a choice, and she accepted it as a gift. That's one of the reasons why people venerate her." I pass the stone from one hand to the other as I continue to talk. "Being a healer, or a visionary, can work like that. There are famous visionaries who resisted their visions, or who thought they were sicknesses, but later came to accept and understand them as gifts. For me, it was a little different. I was just a baby when my gift revealed itself, or so I've been told, so there was no choice. I was too little to make choices. My mother made them for me. And then, the community around you sort of ratifies your gift, as they did with me."

Finn's legs are longer than mine and they scrape the rocks below. "What do you mean, they ratify it?"

While we talk I set my stone down and search for a perfect clamshell the size of a coin, pearly on the inside. Then I search for something else I like. It's easier to do this than to look at Finn while I answer. "They confirm that it's real, that your touch is miraculous, that you are capable of healings, and they tell others about your gift. Spread the word. I guess you could say they anoint you as holy, or sacred." I select another treasure, this one a pale-pink rock. "Also, faith healers are a big business. Child healers can make money for their families, for the churches affiliated with them. It's the same with me. It wasn't long after I started healing before I became a business for Mama, for this entire community. People will pay a lot of money for hope. Even a little bit of it."

The waves roll into shore, rising and disappearing, mimicking the feeling of this day, my newfound freedom raising me up with possibility, then spilling me to shore and rocking me with confusion, complication, uncertainty.

I look up from my growing pile of rocks and shells. Finn is watching me with a look I've seen before. Yesterday, when we were talking about my visions at the picnic table, he wore the same expression. "And you've become an image of hope, which is why you're on T-shirts and candles and things around here."

"Even kites," I say with a shrug. "Please tell me you don't own any of them."

"Not yet." Finn chuckles. "I have another question."

"Not fair, you've asked a lot! One more and that's it. Then it's my turn."

"Fine," he agrees, a bit reluctantly. A tiny green crab scuttles across the corner of the ledge where we sit. "You called these the healing rocks. Do you, I guess, no, is it *easier* for you to heal here? Does it put you in the mood to heal? Do you want to heal right now?" His questions spill out in a jumble. There is something there, underneath his words. Something other than sheer curiosity.

I shake my head, my eyes never leaving him. The smell of sea permeates the air and I wonder if the skin on Finn's neck will taste of salt and sun. "No. It was just something I told my mother so she would let me come here. Healing doesn't work like that. It's just something I have inside me, like a treasure in a box I have hidden, but only I know where to find it. It's hard to explain." I change position, crossing my legs. "Now, you get to tell me about you."

Finn slumps further against the rock supporting his back, head tilted toward the sky. "My life is boring. I'm just a graduate student."

"It's not boring," I protest. "Not to me."

"What do you want to know, Marlena?"

"Well, for one, what's it like to have a photographic memory? Is that part of why you're so . . . geniusy?"

He reaches up and grips the back of his neck.

Stalling.

"I answered your questions, Finn!"

"I know." He sighs. "Fine. It has certainly helped me get where I am in my studies. And, I mean, it's pretty much like it sounds. I remember everything I see, like a photograph. You know, snapshots. Images of what's on the pages of books I've read."

"Everything?"

"*Everything.*" He says this ominously, like it's not always a good thing.

"It sounds a little bit like having visions."

This makes Finn smile. "See, Marlena, I told you we were more similar than different."

I shift position so that I am facing Finn rather than the ocean. "Give me an example of how it works."

He's thoughtful for a moment. "Have you ever heard of synesthesia?"

"No. Is that, like, a disease?"

Finn shakes his head, laughing. "It's more like a condition, but a cool one. Sometimes I've wondered if you have some version of it, if that might explain your visions, and I'm wondering it now, especially since Angie said your visions look kind of like the brain scans you saw today."

Of course I want to hear his theory, but I'm torn. "Um, Finn, I hate to tell you this, but you just turned things back to me, which again isn't fair, and you still haven't answered my question!"

He bites his lip. "Hmmm. You noticed that?"

"Yes."

"You just need a little more patience, because I was about to return to me when you interrupted." Now Finn is grinning.

I try hard not to return the grin. "It's also true that I'm intrigued about what you said. So? I'm waiting."

"All right. Photographic memory, how does it work?" He takes a deep breath, then starts to talk like he's reciting something to a teacher who is quizzing him. "Synesthesia is a condition that affects the senses, where the stimulation of one of the senses has a corresponding effect on a different one. For example, a synesthete might say that they can 'taste' the round shape of an orange, or 'hear' the color of the sky. The way a synesthete's senses blend together is usually consistent. The person will always 'hear' the blue hue of the sky, or will always 'taste' the round shape on an orange. If the person is a lexical synesthete, then each different word they hear or see will have its own particular color."

I wait to make sure that he's done. Then I say, "You sound like a dictionary."

Finn shrugs. "A photographic memory can work like that. I've read about synesthesia before, and I can recall exactly what I read as though I'm reading it now." Before I can respond, he goes on. "Doesn't synesthesia sound a little like what you experience with your visions?"

A big wave crashes loud against the rocks, spray darting high in the air. "Maybe? There's certainly a lot of color, and there's often sound, and my senses are definitely all involved and seem connected to the colors. But even though that's an interesting theory, you said that synesthetes experience color and the senses the same, always. And my visions aren't predictable like that."

Finn is nodding. But he looks a bit disappointed.

I raise my eyebrows. "Sad you couldn't scientifically diagnose my situation?"

"Maybe a little? I liked my theory."

I laugh. "So what does your mother think of your, um, *abilities?* And the rest of your family, for that matter, since you haven't told me anything about them."

His expression darkens. "Things with my family are complicated. They don't exactly appreciate my 'abilities,' as you put it, or my path to becoming a neuroscientist."

"What? That's crazy! How could they not! What you do is—"

"—Marlena," Finn interrupts.

I stop speaking.

He closes his eyes. "Let's talk about something else. I'll tell you about my family some other day."

I study Finn's profile, lit by the sun. "Okay," I say quietly. "But there is something else I'm really curious about."

Finn's eyes flicker open and he turns back to me. "And what is that?"

I point to his sleeve. "I want to know about the heart you have under there."

"My tattoo?"

"Yes. You wouldn't tell me about it yesterday, but today you have to."

"It's just a heart."

I know when someone is not telling the truth, and Finn is not telling me the truth right now. Like my healings, there is something intimate about inking an image onto one's skin. Something permanent and alive with meaning. "Is it about another girl?" I ask, then wish the gulls overhead had chosen this moment to cry out, drowning my words.

A smile dusts Finn's lips. "No, nothing like that. It's just a reminder, I guess. Not to be all up in my head."

I pull my knees tight to my chest. "What do you mean?"

He shrugs. "I'm already a doctoral student, and I graduated college when I was nineteen. The intellectual side of me has always been what dominates. I got the tattoo so that I'd have a visual reminder of this other part of me and of life, a reminder that there's more to me than just my brain. Every time I look at my arm or see myself in the mirror, I also remember that it's okay to feel." Finn runs a hand through his hair. "I told you yesterday, I'm also a bit of a freak. People have treated me differently all my life. They have 'great hopes for me'"—he flicks two fingers around this phrase—"so the heart tattoo is there also to remind other people that I'm more than my brain. Even Angie."

Finn's words fade. "I've never needed that reminder," I tell him. "From the moment I first saw you, all I could sense was the heart in you." I exchange this confession in turn for his. The way the sun shines on Finn's face makes me wonder if he is human or something else, an ethereal creature that doesn't belong to this earth, that might disappear into the fabric of this universe at any minute.

"Really, Marlena?"

"Yes," I say.

His hand reaches for mine. "What else did you see, visionary girl?"

The tips of his fingers find the center of my palm. I watch as they slide across my skin. I wait for those half visions I always have with Finn to appear, the sense of *something* with Finn. But this time is different. A feeling in my belly awakens, an unfamiliar warmth, and I find myself leaning into him, reaching my hand to his shoulder, then his neck, snaking my arm around him and pulling him close until our faces are inches apart, his half-lidded eyes watching mine.

"I don't know what I'm doing, Finn," I tell him.

I say this, but then, I also absolutely do know, in the same way I've always known how to heal. Wanting another person is like a tiny stirring of the soul, a spark that spins outward until it is lighting up your insides with fireworks. They spill through the thin layer of skin that contains the body and outward, straight into the body of another. Just like a healing, but also not.

"I think you do, Marlena," he breathes.

When our lips touch, I discover a new way to encounter the soul of another person, to walk within its gorgeous depths, to play hide-and-seek with the most secret parts of who they are. If there were colors, they'd be bright reds and pinks and they would light up my brain like a sunset. Maybe they are doing just that, right now.

TWENTY-THREE

When I walk into the house later on, I stop, as usual, to listen.

There isn't a sound.

But as I head to the stairs, still light-headed from saying good-bye to Finn, I see her. My mother is outside in the backyard, sitting on one of the lawn chairs she never uses, staring at the ocean. Her knees are pulled to her chest, arms wrapped around her shins. Her dark hair is long and loose and some of it falls down her back, some of it over her shoulders. Once again I am struck by how young she seems, vulnerable almost. This and that her clothing is different. She's wearing jeans and a big billowy black top.

She never wears black. It's the color of mourning, she always says. It reminds her of those terrible days after I was born.

Is my mother in mourning?

I open the screen door and step outside.

She turns her head. "Marlenita."

My mother hasn't called me that in ages. I walk over to her chair, the grass a luscious sea underneath my feet in the fading light. "Hi."

"How was your day?" Her voice is soft, her words are soft, but her eyes are difficult to read.

I think about my answer, worrying that her simple question is also a trap. I decide to tell her the truth. "It was good. Really good. The best day I've had in a long, long time."

My mother's face goes blank. Like someone attached a line to her and drained away all signs of life. "José told me you got the money I left."

"I did. Thank you."

"It's yours, Marlena. Just like you said yesterday." She rests a cheek on her knees as she talks. "Today I set up a bank account for you. The paperwork is on the counter. There's an ATM card with the code written next to it. There's more money in it than you could ever need."

"Okay—"

"—also," my mother interrupts, voice monotone, "I alerted the necessary parties that your audiences are canceled until further notice. And Fatima moved all those things you piled into the gift room up to the attic."

I inhale to protest, to inform her that some of those things, like the books, my paintings, I didn't want to be inaccessible, but my mother is still not done.

She lifts her head and stares at me. "You wanted freedom,

querida—well, now you have it."

My insides go to war, debating what my mother is really up to with such lavish offerings, offerings that were just yesterday totally and utterly forbidden. One side of me thinks she has a larger plan, and that just when I think everything is all right she will swoop in and take everything back. The other side of me doesn't know what to think, but I long to believe she is doing these things only because I asked for them, because she thinks that after all this time I deserve a little reward for how patient and obedient I've been during the entirety of my childhood.

"Are we going to talk at all?" I ask her now.

"About what?"

"About this." I gesture between the two of us, and in doing so I guess I'm also pointing at our clothing, which has changed drastically between yesterday and today.

"I thought we said all that needed saying last night."

"Oh. You do? Okay."

I stare at my mother, study her, and finally see what I've been missing since I stepped out the screen door. It's defeat. My mother is defeated. There are dark circles underneath her eyes, purple and bruised. The way she sits may make her look younger, more vulnerable, but the woman I see up close seems like she's aged. It nearly makes me want to go to her, to give her a hug.

I don't.

Maybe I could after she's proven I can trust her. If I can have faith that somewhere inside her, Saint Teresa is waging a battle to release the mother that she is, the mother she used to be. Maybe Saint Teresa is fighting right now, this minute, to release her from the hidden place where she's dwelled for so long. I hope Teresa is prepared, sword in hand, with a spare tucked away.

That night after I get into bed, I can't sleep. I poke around in my body, my heart, my mind, for that familiar feeling of my gift. Sensing it there, waiting for me when I need it, has always been a strange kind of comfort. I do my best not to panic when I can't find it anywhere. Not even a little trace or tug.

TWENTY-FOUR

If I've been an angel before, I am no longer. Every day I am shedding feathers, until my shoulders are so light I can finally stand up straight and tall. With each one gone I become more visible, more human, a thing of flesh and bone.

I smile at myself in the mirror. I like being a real, human girl.

Fatima takes me shopping for a bathing suit. She wears a simple white top and matching slim skirt that reaches her knees. Her black hair is pulled into a bun, frizzled wisps escaping around her face. She looks like the typical Portuguese lady, with her long face and smooth, dark features. Everything is on sale because it's the end of the season, and she has me try on what seems like the entire store. She knows how big a deal it is for me to pick something out that will be all my own. That I've dreamed of wearing a bikini like other girls on the beach. In the dressing room I struggle with the ties and the hooks around my neck and back, but I refuse the help she offers.

"It's okay, Marlena," she says through the door. "I'm a lady, too."

I know this, but I can't let her help. I've been shamed about my body for too many years. After I try on the first bathing suit, I'm almost too embarrassed to look at myself in the mirror.

"Marlena, you're going to wear this in public, but you're afraid to show me now?" Fatima calls from the chair she's been sitting in while she waits. "If I still had a body like yours I'd be prancing all over this store and around town in only a two-piece!"

"Fatima, you're not helping," I call back, but I'm laughing. Then, "Fine," I say and slink outside.

She puts her hands to her cheeks. "¡Ai, querida! Look at you! You're so skinny! I wish I had a behind like that."

My cheeks burn. "Fatima!"

She stands up and starts barking orders. "Stop slouching and stand up straight. Now walk a few steps. Stop hunching over, Marlena! Now swivel your hips a bit."

"I didn't know there'd be catwalk lessons today," I tell her.

Fatima waves her hands as she speaks. "You should be proud of what you look like. You have nothing to hide! Not anymore," she adds, but under her breath. "Go change into the other ones. I want to see all of them."

"Yes, ma'am."

When I come out wearing a bathing suit with tiny flowers that ties around my neck, back, and hips, Fatima's face lights up.

"That's the one!" She smiles. "It has the same green as those flip-flops you're always stomping around in. And it's perfect with your coloring."

"I love my flip-flops!"

She chuckles. "I know you do." She plops back into her chair. "Go change into your clothes. We have a winner."

I do as I'm told. With the chosen bikini in hand, Fatima makes me pick out a big fluffy beach towel, also green, and sunglasses. I decide on a pair with giant lenses, just like the ones that Helen let me borrow.

"Here comes the movie star," Fatima says as she surveys my choice.

"Here comes the nobody," I counter, remembering the bliss of anonymity.

We go up to the register with my purchases.

"You should call that nice girl, Helen, who loves you so much," Fatima says while we wait in line. "You need some friends your age to spend time with and take you places. Not old fogies like José and me. You need to get out more."

I nod. "I know I do."

She eyes the colorful bathing suit in our basket. "Wait till that boy of yours sees you in that little thing."

How could she know about Finn? He's never been near the house. "What boy?"

"Oh, Marlena. I've been working for your mama for nearly a decade. I see you and I see your mother every day. I know things.

More than you realize. And I don't need to see the boy to know that he's there."

"But—"

"*Querida.*" She turns my chin with her hand so I am looking at her, touching me so easily. "Just like there is nothing wrong with that beautiful body of yours, there is also nothing wrong with you having a boyfriend. I know your mother taught you that you can't like a boy because of your gift. But the only thing that is going to ruin your life is you never living it."

I stare up into Fatima's dark eyes, take in the gray streaks in her hair that reach toward her knot. I don't know what to say in response to this simple offer of love. My answer is as wordless as I feel, but I hope it says to Fatima exactly what I want it to. I wrap my arms around her soft middle right there in the line at the store.

"*Ai, querida,*" she whispers, burying a kiss into the top of my head.

"Next!" the lady at the register barks, and it's our turn to pay.

"Turn a little—no, that way—to the right." Helen stands behind me, twisting a lock of my hair and pinning it against my head. She's already done my makeup. It's Friday and we are at her house and she's been working on "my look," as she put it, for twenty minutes. We are going to a party, another thing on my list.

Helen lives only an hour's drive from my town, not far by most standards, but it may as well be an entire continent away. It's the first time I've been this far from home without my mother or José as a chaperone. Helen picked me up and brought me here, to her house. It's small—a bedroom, living room with a kitchen attached, a porch out front—but it seems perfect. It is Helen's and only Helen's. She rents it for college, and it's a five-minute walk from the beach where the party is.

"Now a little to the left," she says.

I've been doing Helen's bidding as I watch my transformation in the bathroom mirror, in between glancing down at my new phone, trying to figure out how to send a text. I took it from the gift room before I left. Helen helped me to set it up. I bring it close to my face. Then I tap the screen. "Oh! I did it!"

"Marlena, stop moving. You did what?"

I am concentrating too hard on tapping the screen in the right place for each letter to answer her at first. Then I finish what I want to say and hit Send. "I figured out how to send a text!"

Helen laughs right as her phone dings. She picks it up from the counter and reads it and laughs harder. "Marlena, I'm right here. You don't need to text me."

My text said: **Hi, Helen, it's me, Marlena! I'm so excited we're going to a party!** "I know, but I wanted to test it out."

"You also don't need to spell everything out exactly," she advises. "Or use punctuation."

"Yes, I do. How else is the person I'm texting supposed to understand me?"

Helen shakes her head and goes back to fixing my hair. My eyes return to the screen, tapping slowly. This time a text to Finn, which appears inside a little yellow bubble.

My first text to Finn!

Hi Finn. This is Marlena. I got a phone today.

I hit Send and stare at the screen like it's a magical object, waiting for it to do tricks.

"Turn a little again," Helen directs.

I obey, never taking my eyes from the phone.

Then, suddenly, a waving smiley face, a tiny image of a truck, followed by a picture of a phone with an exclamation point appears, but nothing else. The name next to the blue quotation bubble tells me it's Finn. My first text *from* Finn! "What does this mean?" I hold the screen so Helen can look at it.

"That Finn is happy to hear from you, that he's excited you got a phone, and that he's driving, which is probably why it doesn't say anything else."

"Oh. Okay. I'm glad you understand it. Thanks for the translation." I type out a really long message this time. It takes me forever.

I've seen so many people staring down at these things and I always think they're going to bump into a pole or a tree but now I know why! I CAN'T BELIEVE I CAN JUST WRITE YOU THINGS! Also, please don't get in an accident!

This time Finn's answer is nearly immediate.

LOL.

I tap my response. I am so slow. **Finn, what does LOL mean?**

Finn: LOL, LOL!!!! Laugh out loud, Marlena. That's what it means.

Me: Stop laughing at me! I'm new at this! Where are you? Will you be at the party, when you said?

Finn: Yes. (Still LOL.) But only if we stop texting so I can get back on the road. I pulled over to answer you.

Me: OH! Good idea. Sorry. That's all from me.

I look up from the screen. I feel breathless. "I can totally see how these are addicting."

Helen plucks the phone from my hand and sets it on the counter next to hers. "You are not allowed to become one of those people who never look up from their phones, Marlena." She slides another pin into my hair. "There." She grabs her beer bottle for another sip. She gestures at the mirror. "What do you think?"

I stare at the girl I see. My hair is up but it's also falling around my face. Wine-colored lipstick stains my mouth and my eyes are dark and smoky. "I look older."

Helen studies her work. "I'd say you look your age. And hot." She laughs and takes another sip. "Perfect for a party."

I roll my eyes. "I have never looked hot in my life."

She plucks at the strap of the black top she gave me to wear. She paired it with jeans and black heels. I can barely walk in them. "Well, congratulations. You do now." Helen gets a knowing look on her face. "Finn is going to faint."

"I don't want him to *faint*," I say, but I'm smiling.

"Not literally." She's laughing. "But you do want to make his heart pound."

"Maybe. Will *Sonia* be there tonight?" I ask, dragging out the name of the girl Helen likes. "Are you going to make *her* heart pound?"

Helen sweeps a hand across her body. "Damn, I hope so! I mean, look at this! What girl wouldn't want this?"

I laugh. "I wish I had your confidence." I reach for Helen's beer bottle and wait to see if she swats my hand away. When she doesn't, I take a sip. It makes me wince. It's only my second sip of beer in the entirety of my life and this one seems even more disgusting than the first.

"Good thing you can't really get that down," Helen says. "I don't want you drunk and puking at your first party." She makes a warning face. "You need to be careful, my darling. You have zero tolerance and the alcohol will go straight to your head, and fast."

"Yes, mother."

"Seriously. You are not getting sick on my watch. Parties are supposed to be fun, not vomit-inducing. There's a difference, and it all depends on this"—she grabs the bottle and holds it up as evidence—"and how much or how little of it you drink. Besides, you can't get sick, because I need to hit on Sonia tonight!"

I stand up and nearly topple over on these heels. "I know, I know." I slide the phone into the pocket of my jeans and follow

Helen out of the bathroom, through the front door, and onto the porch, almost falling again. "You really think I can handle these on the beach?"

She glances over her shoulder. "We'll be on the deck in the back. And until then"—Helen stops and slips her own heels off her feet—"we can go barefoot. And if you want to walk the beach, then voila!" She dangles the straps from a single finger.

I slip mine from my feet too, grateful to be rid of them, imitating the way Helen holds hers. The two of us set off across the grass. Everything about today, this evening, the promise of a party, thrums through me. The sun has just set, and the sky is the bright aqua blue of early evening, the stars like crystals across the expanse of night ahead. As we walk from yard to yard, the soft scuffing sounds of our steps break the quiet. I reach out and grab Helen's hand.

She turns to me, hair curling over her shoulders. "What, Marlena?"

I weave my fingers through hers, searching inside myself, searching for the healing touch that has always been as familiar as the lines on my palm, even the shape of my own face. I find something else instead. "I've seen inside your soul," I tell Helen. "I think I even saw this moment between us, all those years ago when you first came to me in that chair."

As if to prove the strength of her perfect legs, Helen steps gingerly across a series of low, flat boulders that line a neighbor's garden, agile as a gymnast. "What was it like?" She guides me left, her hand still holding mine. "My soul, I mean."

"It was painted with hope and happiness," I say. "With openness. Love."

"I think you're biased," Helen says. Then she asks, "Are all souls like that?"

I shake my head. A cottage appears far down the street, lit up, dozens of cars parked outside and clotting the road. "Some souls are full of despair and darkness. Hopelessness. Sometimes they are gray with it, deadened by whatever troubles or sickens them. But all souls are beautiful, regardless. I feel guiltier now that I'm older, that I've reached into so many, and without anyone's permission."

"But you did have permission. All those people wanted something from you."

The noise from the party grows louder as we get closer. "I guess. But I'm not sure people realize that by asking me to heal them, they're opening the doors of their soul to me. Sometimes it feels like stealing, like I'm some thief who is rummaging around in their most hidden parts, prying into a place where no one else should be allowed."

Helen stops at the edge of the yard. Music and laughter pour through the open windows. Two people, a guy and a girl, get out of a car and head up the walkway and into the front door of the cottage. "It's okay, Marlena. It's okay with *me*, if that's what you really want to know. I've always felt"—she pauses a moment, blinking—"lucky to have this lasting connection with you, after everything I went through when I was little." The shoes sway from her fingers. "I know you've lived a lonely life, but mine was lonely, too. It would have been lonely always, I think, if it weren't for you." Helen's eyes shine in the light of the moon. "I know you don't like thinking of yourself as a saint, but sometimes I've wondered how you are walking this earth as though you're a normal girl."

I shake my head, hard. "Don't do that to me, Helen. It's my mother's dream that I act like an angel. The cost of being a healer is this"—I gesture between us—"friendship. Going to parties. Going anywhere at all. And I want to be free."

"I want those things for you, too, Marlena, you know that," Helen says.

I hear her hesitation. "But?"

"But what if someone is sick? What if I came to you now, in that chair? Would you turn me away?"

This question chills me. I stand there, bare feet planted in the lush, dewy grass, the cool air of evening brushing my skin, trying to figure out what to say. It is one thing to turn my back on people I've never met, but it is something else to think of doing that to Helen, a person I love, someone whose soul still twirls inside me like a child. "It's a good thing I don't have to answer that question. Not with what I know of you now, and who you are to me." *But what if it happened? What if I did have to face that situation?* These questions whisper through me. "I hope I never have to worry about it."

"I hope so, too," Helen says. Then she forces the clouds from her gaze and eyes my feet. "Shoes, Marlena," she commands.

I obey, grateful for the end of this inquiry. Helen slips hers on expertly, and strides up to the front door of the cottage. I totter behind her, letting the thrill of the party flow through my limbs and push all worries aside.

TWENTY-FIVE

When Finn walks onto the deck, I wave at him, trying to catch his attention.

It's a relief to see someone I know amid Helen's college-partying friends. She is dancing in the living room, beer in hand, jumping up and down, hair flying around her face. Sonia is there with her, dancing just as hard. I've been watching them through the window. Helen keeps coming to check on me, but I keep sending her back to her dancing and Sonia. They both look so happy.

I'm learning a lot tonight, like why people are always taking out their phones when they're alone. I'd take out mine, but the only people I know to text are here, or before, they were driving. It's not that people haven't talked to me, or that Helen hasn't introduced me around. But it's strange to try to make small talk with someone I've just met when we have nothing obvious in common, and when the person doesn't need something from me, like healing. I can change my clothes and read fashion magazines and buy bikinis and hold a beer and even sip it in public, but that doesn't stop me from being the Marlena I've always been, which is a Marlena who has no idea, really, how to be at a party.

It's like I am *at* the party, but not *of* the party. Just like I've always been *in* the world, not *of* it. I don't like how difficult it is to shake my healer life, my healer outsiderness. I am ever the anchorite, heavy curving iron wrapped around my ankle and dragging me down to the bottom of the sea.

Finn finally sees me waving and smiles.

"Hi," he says when he reaches the edge of the deck. He eyes the beer in my hand and holds up his own. "I didn't know you drank beer."

I laugh. "I don't. Not really. This one is mainly for show."

"I think that's probably a good thing. You don't want to drink too much."

"Spoken like Helen," I say.

"Sounds like Helen knows what she's talking about."

"Helen told me a party stops being a party when you start puking your guts out."

"Wise woman," Finn says.

I want to fling myself on Finn, throw my arms around him. What is my problem? How does this work, this liking-a-boy thing? I have no idea how to behave or control myself when with one. I lean forward on the railing, because I don't trust my limbs, and look onto the beach. Finn does the same. The moonlight shines off the ocean. We glance at each other briefly. I want to touch his cheek. His neck.

I hold up my beer instead. "Cheers?" I say, then add, "I've always wanted to make a toast."

"Then you shall." Finn tips the neck of his beer bottle until it makes a glassy *thunk* against mine. He grins. "I thoroughly enjoyed getting your messages tonight."

"Well, yours were confusing."

Finn laughs. "You'll get the hang of it. Besides"—he pulls his phone out of his pocket to show me, then puts it back—"these things are overrated."

I study him. "I guess, now that I think of it, I never really see you on yours."

"I try my best to pay attention to the people I'm with. I try not to look at it too much, in general."

"But what if I text you later? Will you look at my message?"

He leans a little closer to me. "If I know it's from you, then definitely."

My heart does a little spin at this, at his nearness and his words.

"If it isn't the famous Finn," Helen calls out from behind us. She is making her way through the crowd on the deck. I'm grateful for the interruption, because without it I may soon act on my inappropriate impulses. Helen is barefoot again. She doesn't hold out her hand to Finn and instead reaches around him for a hug. How does she do that so easily?

"I feel like I already know you," she says to him.

"Nice to meet you, Helen."

We form a circle. Me and two of the people I care about most in the world. A tiny party of three.

Helen looks Finn up and down. "So you're the genius."

Finn nudges me. "Aw, Marlena? Really?"

I like the casual way he touches me and I want to nudge him back. But what if I fell on top of him in the process? "Why are you embarrassed about being smart?"

"Yeah," Helen says, laughing. She gestures behind her at the rest of the party. "There aren't too many other geniuses here. I think it's good to have at least one present. You know, just in case things get out of hand." Helen grabs my beer and holds the bottle up to the light coming from the house. "Wow, it's practically still full." She puts an arm around my shoulder. "Good job. I told this one no puking."

All of this casual touching is bolstering my spirit. And making me wonder how I ever lived without it.

Finn chuckles. "Yes, Marlena reiterated this excellent advice."

Helen lets go of my shoulder and turns to me. "You guys should walk to the old bridge. They took down most of it when they built the new one, but they left a bit for the fishermen." Helen points into the darkness toward a rectangle of lights over the water. "It's just over there." Finn turns to look and Helen leans into me to whisper, "He's supercute. You should take advantage and go be alone with him!" Then she takes a step back, addressing us both again. "Okay, lovebirds," she sings. "I'm back to my dancing and my Sonia!"

"Enjoy. We'll be around," Finn says.

"It's okay if you're not," Helen tells him. "Marlena has keys to my place and no curfew. But be good to her or I'll sic Mama Oliveira on you," she adds with a twirl and begins weaving her way across the deck, beer held high over her head.

"Helen!" I shout after her, but she's already heading into the house. I turn to Finn. "I can't be held responsible for anything that comes out of her mouth."

But Finn is laughing. "I think I like Helen. I think we should take her advice and check out the bridge." The deck is more and more crowded, the biggest group of people circling a keg. "Unless you want to stay?"

I shake my head. "I think I've had enough of my first party." I sigh. "I can't manage to sit through a movie and now I'm ready to leave a party after an hour."

Finn grins. "I think you'd just rather be alone with me."

I bite my lip to hide my smile. "Whatever you say, genius." I gesture toward the stairs on the deck that lead to the beach. "After you."

Finn and I push through the crowd. Before my feet hit the sand, I take off my shoes and dangle them from my finger like Helen showed me. As Finn and I walk, he slips his hand into my free one. A rush flows over my skin all the way up the back of my neck. Each time we touch, something happens to me. I feel happiness, I feel hope, I feel possessive. Like I want Finn to myself and for nobody else. As we step across the cool sand, I'm proud of myself for not tackling him.

How do people know what to do? Why aren't there boyfriend instructions?

Is Finn even my boyfriend?

He squeezes my hand. "What are you thinking? You look lost in thought."

"Nothing," I say. "Nothing I'll tell you."

"In that case, I'll have to convince you otherwise."

We reach the old bridge and sit down on a bench at the very end of it, one that looks onto the blackness of the ocean. Out here, it's silent aside from the soft sound of waves lapping against the pilings beneath us, and the occasional splash of a fish. "Thank you for coming to rescue me from my first party."

"I didn't know you needed rescuing," Finn says.

His profile is lit by the moon. I wish I had the guts to inch closer. "You've saved me more than once. The first time was after I fought with my mother and you came to pick me up in your truck."

Finn shifts, and his thigh presses lightly against mine. I make sure not to move. "Well, I'm happy to 'save' you or 'rescue' you whenever you want," he says. "It's about time someone else does the saving in your life."

I close my eyes to let Finn's words sink in. Without having to ask, without even really knowing, Finn just gave me a gift I've been yearning for as long as I've been old enough to wish for it.

He reaches out and tilts my chin upward with his finger. "What just happened, Marlena? Where did you go?"

"I'm still here," I tell him, opening my eyes. There is longing in his, and I wonder if he can see the longing in mine. People have always looked at me with longing, but the kind I see in Finn is different. It makes me feel real.

The stars are bright in this dark place over the ocean. There's no nearby city to block them out. The night glimmers.

I place a hand over my own heart, feeling it pound. "What's happening, Finn?"

Finn turns to face me. He leans closer. "What do you mean?"

The air is velvety as it moves between us. "I almost can't catch my breath. It's like I've gone running."

A smile drifts across Finn's lips. "I think it means you want to kiss me."

I laugh softly. "I've been wondering how people manage to make second kisses happen after first ones."

"Oh, Marlena, you really are funny," he says.

"Is your heart pounding, too?" I decide not to resist my urges any longer and reach out, placing my hand against Finn's shirt, right where I know his heart resides behind the cage of his ribs. He closes his eyes. I press my palm into his chest until I feel it beating.

Finn lets out a *whoosh* of breath and moves my hand away. He shifts farther from me on the bench.

"Did I do something wrong?"

"No," he says, but too quickly.

I study him in the darkness. What is he holding back? "Okay," I say. Finn will share when he's ready. I can wait. I need to. It's what normal people do.

There is relief on his face when I don't press him. Then his eyebrows arch and he inches my way again, until his face is all I see. "You were talking about kissing me?"

I lean toward him. "You were talking about kissing me back?"

Our lips are close. I can feel the warmth of his breath. Finn's hands find the small of my back and he draws me to him. His lips brush mine, barely, before they press a little harder. His hands find their way into my hair and my hands find their way inside his shirt, across his smooth, warm skin. We stay there, gripping each other, holding each other close, until everything becomes urgent, our breathing, our mouths, our tongues. This is unlike our first kiss at the healing rocks, which was slow and sweet and short. But also like it, too, because somehow I know exactly how to kiss Finn, even though the way we are kissing is completely new. I let my body think for me, speak for me, with words I didn't know I had.

The instinct to heal, the one that flips on in me so my body can take over and reach out to the body of another, is similar to the one that switches on in me now. I didn't know the body could feel hunger like this, for a kiss, for someone's presence, to see their face. I am greedy for Finn as I look at him between our equally greedy kisses. It's all I know and all I can think. I feel like I can see inside Finn's soul, inside his heart, but not in the way I'm used to. It burns red like the setting sun and is as beautiful and powerful as the ocean. I let it warm me. I let myself bask in it. I find myself wanting to paint it.

When the two of us pull apart, I start to laugh.

"What?"

"Wow," I say.

"I know." Finn's hands are still wrapped around me. "Lately, I forget that you're a famous healer. I told you I didn't think I could, but it turns out I can."

"Lately, I forget I was, too," I say, trying not to linger too long on the fact that, without even intending to, I phrased my life as a healer in the past tense.

Maybe my mother was right: it is all or nothing. Either a life as a healer or a life as a normal girl. How could I be satisfied with being a healer after this? I need more, I am more, want more, maybe even if it destroys the person I was. I will only be satisfied with Finn.

This truth blooms like the most beautiful vision I've ever had.

But I don't tell Finn this. I'll tell him soon. We have plenty of time for the secrets hidden inside us to emerge when they are ready, one by one, like bright-red cherries picked from a summer tree.

TWENTY-SIX

My new life as a normal person isn't all candy and fashion magazines and parties. All Finn and freedom. A big bag of mail has been sitting outside my door for days. At first I ignored it. But it grows bigger and fuller every time I see it. The bigger it gets, the greater the wave of guilt that consumes me, like an ocean swell that could topple a massive fishing boat. It is a constant reminder that a healer might decide to take a break, but the pains and sicknesses of others never subside.

One morning I can't resist any longer. I drag the bag inside my room. Then I sit down in my chair by the windows and open it, pulling up the letters and cards one by one.

Dear Marlena, you are my last hope in this world. . . .

Dear Marlena, without you, I may not see the end of this year. . . .

Dear Marlena, I've lost the will to go on, please help me. . . .

Most of the letters are pleading, but some are angry and full of accusations.

You should be ashamed of yourself! God has chosen you and yet you turn away from HIM!

God will surely punish you for having spit in His face!

There's no such thing as a healer! And now you've proven this!

I hope YOU find out what it's like to face down death and have no other choice but to go forward into it! You or SOMEONE YOU LOVE!

This last one I read over and over. It's from a man my mother had promised a private audience, who was later told not to come.

Will there be a punishment for my freedom? Revenge on the part of God?

I've always wondered if I'd be punished *for* healing. For using my gift, and acting the part of God when I'm only a girl. Maybe there's punishment in this life no matter which path I take. Maybe loss and sorrow and grief are simply a part of what it means to live as humans on this earth, and it is our duty to accept this. We can try to outsmart such things, yet they will eventually catch up, no matter what we do. Even if we are living girl-saints.

Then a letter from a girl named Alma goes straight to my heart in a way that none of the others have. *Dear Marlena*, it begins, like the others do. This is where the similarities end.

> *My name is Alma. My mother has spoken of your miracles since I was little. Sometimes I've thought you must be a witch like in stories. I've always wanted to see if you can really do the things my mother says. I have muscular dystrophy. I don't know if you know what that is, but I'm in a wheelchair. My mother keeps telling me you are going to heal me soon, because the doctors say I don't have long to live. Most people like me don't live past eighteen.*
>
> *The other day my mother heard that you've stopped healing. She doesn't know why. "What God gives us, He sometimes takes away," she said. She cried a lot. My mother really believed you'd save me in a way that none of the doctors can.*
>
> *I'm writing because I wanted to tell you that I think it's okay. With so many people needing you, it must be difficult. And I'm not sure if it's right to wish for miracles, or to want to be different than I am. I might not be like other kids my age, but I'm living the life that I have and this is enough, even if other people don't think it should be. The life I have is beautiful in its own way. People who aren't like me will never understand, I guess.*
>
> *I wish you the best. Maybe we'll meet, if you ever start healing again.*

Even if you don't, maybe we'll meet anyway. I don't need anything from you. But I would love to see you, so I know you are real and not just a character from one of the novels I'm always reading.

Sincerely, Alma

I set her letter in my lap and stare out the window.

Alma's words remind me of a girl who came to one of my audiences. Though it's truer to say she was dragged by her parents. Her name was Heather, she was fourteen at the time, and she was deaf. When I touched her that day I was—I don't know how to describe it—repelled? I could tell right away she didn't want to be there. That she didn't think of being deaf as a disability, as something that needed curing. I could feel the rage inside her that her mother wished her different. I dropped her hands and stepped away. The mother looked at me with dismay, but the daughter had this expression of tremendous relief.

"I thought you were a healer," the mother said to me. "I was promised you could help!"

I shook my head. "Your daughter isn't sick."

The mother turned and stomped away.

But the daughter lingered. I was younger than she was and she was at least six inches taller. She leaned toward me and pointed to her lips. I watched them intently.

"Thank you," she mouthed slowly, "for not doing to me whatever it is you do to others."

Is healing something I *do* to others? This made healings sound like something I might *afflict* on someone. A disease or virus in its own right. Something that I do *to* people, sometimes against their will.

I pick up Alma's letter again. Like with the angry words from the man who wants me punished, I read hers over and over, until my eyes blur. Then I pick up a pen and a piece of paper. Shouldn't I say something to her? Shouldn't I write back? But then I put the pen and paper away. If I answer Alma, shouldn't I answer all the others? Why should one child matter more than everyone else?

The thought that I could find a way to be both healer and girl pushes its way to the surface of my mind. That there might be another version of being a healer I've yet to discover. But then it sinks to the bottom again when the echo of my mother's favorite refrain rings even louder. *You are a saint and a healer, Marlena. Or you are no one at all.*

Ever since the announcement about my break from healing, I've avoided going to Main Street. But like with the bag of mail, today I can't seem to resist. Soon I find myself walking up the hill toward the shops. I look through the windows of Almeida's Bakery. There is barely a loaf of bread in the glass case. The streets are empty of tourists. It's like the town has gone dormant before a storm. As I walk down Main Street, I almost expect to see a single dark rain cloud following me, since I am the beneficiary of dirty looks from more than one of the shopkeepers.

Gertie is the first one to accost me. Of course, Gertie.

Her voice calls out from the doorway. "You couldn't have waited for winter?"

I stop midstride, the clacking of my platform shoes stopping with me. I consider ignoring her, but then I take the bait. "What do you mean?"

Gertie steps onto the sidewalk, her loose gray dress rustling. "This so-called vacation. You couldn't wait until January? Until after the Day of Many Miracles in October?"

"I . . . I . . ." I trail off. The truth is, I'm caught off guard by the clear sense of betrayal in her voice. It doesn't matter that my sentence goes unfinished, because Gertie is ready to keep talking.

"It's September, Marlena! This is still high tourist season for us! And you"—she points a finger—"are the main attraction in this town! Without your audiences, our sales plummet. People don't come. Tourists don't bother." Gertie throws her right arm up and out. "We'll go broke because of you!"

Some of the other shop owners have joined her on the sidewalk. Old Mrs. Marinelli, stooped and shaky, has left her store that sells icons and other religious memorabilia. Mr. Maxwell is next to her, giving her his elbow. Mr. Almeida is here with his wife. I search the crowd for Mrs. Lewis, for a single ally, but don't find anyone.

"Gertie's right," Mr. Almeida says. "You'll ruin us with this . . . this *selfishness*."

People are nodding.

The word *selfish* is like a punch to my stomach.

I think about the party with Helen, with Finn, the changed way Fatima and José are treating me. Is it really wrong of me to enjoy life for a bit? For even a few days? Then I think of the unanswered bag of mail, all those seekers disappointed, despairing, maybe even dying. All because I wanted time off. All because I got tired of people needing me. Maybe Gertie and Mr. Almeida are right and I am being selfish.

Gertie takes a step closer. "We depend on you, Marlena. We all do."

For a split second I think something ridiculous, that I should have worn the sunglasses, put up my hair, worn a disguise like before. Stupid me. I thought I could just waltz into town as Marlena, the girl they've known for years as a healer, but with jeans on instead of a long white dress, and people would respect the change. Even be kind. But not everyone is José or Fatima.

I guess in the effort to live a normal life, I lose the respect of the townspeople, too.

What else do I lose? Who else?

I try and silence these thoughts, but they linger anyway. My face tilts toward the sky, causing the townspeople to murmur as they wait for me to say something.

When my eyes return to the crowd, a rage to match theirs fills me like plumes of smoke. I can make all the decisions in the world to change my life, but if the community around me refuses to accept them, then I am always and only Marlena the Saint. As long as I am here, in this town, I will never escape.

"Well?" Mr. Almeida's face is red with anger. "What do you have to say for yourself?"

I press my lips into a thin line, not trusting myself to speak. I don't want to lose my temper. I remind myself that Mrs. Lewis is one of the townspeople who trade off my reputation, and she has only been kind. In a way, we are all caught in the same situation— me as a healer, them as people who need me to heal for their financial survival. I start toward home, wanting to end this confrontation before it gets uglier, but Gertie shouts at my back.

"You are rich and we are not! You and your mother live in that gigantic house as though you are too good for us! You act as if you are better than all of us!"

"It's not our fault we're beholden to you!" This is from Mr. Almeida. "This place used to be different, before your mother went and built that damn church and turned this town into a circus, and now the tourists only come for the freak show on Saturdays!"

I stop walking. Their words are like darts. I can hear a few murmurs of dissent that he's gone too far, but I no longer have it in me to hold back. I turn around to shout the response that has been brewing inside me.

"It is not my responsibility to take care of this entire town! *You* are the ones who should be ashamed of yourselves! *You* should be ashamed! *You've* been making your living off a child! Don't you think it's time that you stop?" I walk closer to the crowd, left foot, right foot, as I keep speaking. "You still want to live off me? Well"—I take the fat envelope of cash I've grown used to carrying in my pocket and hold it out to them—"here!" I shake it once, then again. "Take my money! Take all of it! Apparently it's yours anyway!" Tears begin to stream down my face as I yell. No one moves to take the money, so I walk up and shove the envelope at Gertie.

She flinches. Her eyes are frightened. "I can't take this!"

I shove it at her again, and she steps back. "Why not? It's what you want!"

"I just can't!"

"Yes you can." Now I hold it out to Mr. Almeida, but his hands go up in the air, a gesture of refusal. People keep wincing each time I come near, and this makes me even angrier. "Fine! Be that way!" I take the money out of the envelope and throw it at the crowd. Bills fly into the air, then flutter to the ground. No one dares speak. I look into each of their shocked faces, and as I do, they avert their eyes. "What? This wasn't about the money?" I am screaming now, even louder than before, growing hoarse, but I don't care. "Would it be easier for you to take it if I bought something? If I bought the objects you sell to make a profit off my lonely life as the freakish saint girl?"

Before anyone can say anything, I storm into Gertie's shop, grab one of the metal baskets inside the door, and begin shoving things into it. Candles, tiny plastic statues, T-shirts, little dolls, even that stupid kite, which is on sale. When I come out, people are still frozen. They watch me silently. The money lies there, untouched, scattered all over the sidewalk and the road. I go into each shop and take things to add to the basket. Charms. Photos. Cards. Even the few remaining sweet breads in the glass case at Almeida's. After I come out of the last store on Main Street, the basket is overflowing, and things are falling out of it as I walk. When I reach the crowd again, I hold the basket out to them.

"There! Now do you feel better about taking my money?"

No one moves.

"Did you think I wasn't human?" I shout. It's as if an entire decade of rage is spilling out of me. I should be ashamed to admit how good it feels, but it feels so good I'm not ashamed at all. "Did you really think I was an angel like these stupid statues you sell of me with wings?" I grab a plaster souvenir from the basket and raise it high. Then my arm comes down in a flash and I smash it all over the blacktop of the street. The shards go everywhere and the crowd jumps. "Did you think I was too good for all of you? That I was perfect? That it was okay to exchange my life and my happiness for the money you take home at night?" One by one I start taking things from the basket and smashing them to the ground. Mugs. Key chains. Framed photographs. Candles. Those that are breakable shatter and the rest just land with a loud thump. "Well, now you know what I'm really like! That I can be just as human as you, or worse!" I tip the basket over so the rest tumbles to the ground, and then I hurl the basket as hard as I can. It lands with a great crash a few feet away.

"Marlena . . ." A soft voice, a kind voice, speaks my name.

Mrs. Lewis. To my left. Hers was the one shop I avoided. She must have heard all the shouting and come to see what was happening.

"Marlena," she says again, and I can't bear it.

I can't bear that Mrs. Lewis has seen me act this way. I can't even look at her. I burst into tears.

When I hear her steps approaching, I put my hands over my face and run away. I run from the worried-sounding Mrs. Lewis and past the crowd of shopkeepers until I've reached the end of Main Street. As I descend the hill, all I can think is that while I might have quit healing, I am still the same bratty saint girl I was a few weeks ago. Prone to temper tantrums. The kind of girl who grows enraged and throws her mother's mug across the kitchen so it splatters coffee everywhere and breaks into a million jagged pieces. That I might be a healer, but apparently I'm also a destroyer.

TWENTY-SEVEN

Hands shake me awake. "Marlena."

"Mama?" I sit up. The room is dark. No light seeps from underneath the shades. My head is groggy with sleep. It must be the middle of the night. As my eyes adjust, I can make out the shape of my mother sitting on the edge of my bed. She is fully dressed, as though it's daytime. I can't remember the last time she came to my room. "Did something happen? Are you okay?"

"We need to talk."

"Now?" All this time I've wondered if my mother and I would have a conversation, and instead we've barely seen each other aside from passing in the living room and kitchen, unspeaking, like ghosts.

"Yes, now. Come downstairs. I'll expect you in five minutes." She gets up without looking at me and leaves. Her steps are heavy and tired.

I crawl out of bed and throw on a robe. I want to know what has my mother awake in the middle of the night. Throughout all of these recent changes, I've wanted my mother to somehow change with me.

The house is dark, except for the lamps in the living room. My mother is sitting in the center of one of the couches, making it impossible for us to both sit there, or at least, highly awkward. This will obviously not be the heart-to-heart I've been waiting for. I sit across from her on the other couch, a large white coffee table between us. Tastefully decorated with a short candle and a big round silver plate.

"What, Mama?" A breeze presses against the back of my head from the open windows. It's strong enough that it feels like a hand. "What's so urgent?"

Her eyes narrow. "As if you don't know."

I swallow. Someone told her that Marlena the Saint is now Marlena the Destroyer. But I shake my head. She's not making this easy for me, so I'm not going to make it easy for her.

"Mrs. Lewis came to speak to me tonight, after you'd gone to bed."

I sink lower on the couch to avoid the breeze. This I wasn't expecting. I thought it would be Gertie or Mr. Almeida. Anyone but Mrs. Lewis.

"She told me about your little performance."

I'm absolutely sure Mrs. Lewis did not use the word *performance* to describe what I did. That is my mother's interpretation. Mrs. Lewis is too kind to speak that way.

My mother crosses her legs, getting comfortable. Now I see that these last couple of weeks my mother was just regrouping, like a shrewd soldier facing a setback but who would never consider a retreat. My mother was gathering her strength and recalibrating her methods. She shakes her head. "Poor Mrs. Lewis was worried about you. And you know she has a bad heart."

Did I not heal her?

"Has or *had?*" I am unable to stop myself from asking this.

My mother knows she's gotten to me and I can see she likes it. "Marlena, I'm not sure. That's not what she wanted to discuss."

I force myself to breathe, in, out. This conversation isn't going anywhere good.

"Well?" she presses.

"Well, what?"

My mother seems buoyed by the couch cushions, rather than sinking into them. "I've given you all you've asked for in this little experiment. This 'vacation.' And you repay my generosity by making a fool of both of us in front of the entire town?"

I stare at her. "Are you kidding?"

"No, I'm not kidding."

I don't want my mother to get the best of me, but I can't resist. "You've given me what I've asked for, for a couple of weeks! When set against, I don't know, *the rest of my eighteen years*, I'm not sure that counts as generous, Mother."

Mother.

I never call her that.

Her body goes rigid. She doesn't like it. Good. "Eighteen years spent building *your* reputation, which you squander in a few minutes of losing your temper in public." She is seething, but manages to control her voice, unlike me. "Not to mention all the other damage you're doing on this *vacation.* Going out with that *boy.*"

A little yelp of surprise escapes me.

"I'm not stupid, Marlena," my mother says. "We may not talk, you may go off on your own as though the rules no longer apply, but that doesn't mean I don't know what's going on. How you're willing to jeopardize everything because you're mooning over some idiot."

"He's not an idiot."

My mother smirks.

"He's *not,*" I repeat. "Most mothers would be happy if their daughters brought him home. Proud even."

Her *I knew it* face appears. "Don't play with your reputation, Marlena."

She makes me want to scream. "You mean *your* reputation? Isn't that what we're really talking about? And by the way, I'm *not* a thirteenth-century nun. So stop treating me like one!"

My mother gets up from the couch and leaves the room. When she returns she's dragging the mailbag. She must've taken it from my room. "Do you see this?"

"I'm not blind."

"Well. Lucky you. Some of the people who've written to you are blind. And they would like your help."

I look away. How could I ever have thought my mother might change?

My mother huffs. "You don't even have the decency to face the people who need you."

My fist closes around the edge of a blanket draped over the couch, squeezing it until my fingernails press through it into my palm. I force myself to turn back to her. I don't speak.

My mother gets a satisfied expression. "I knew it."

"You knew *what?*" I snap.

She points at the bag. "You *do* feel guilty about abandoning these people."

"I haven't abandoned anyone."

"Oh? Then how would you put it? That you've sent them in another direction, seeking their last desperate hope elsewhere? Did you refer them to a different healer, Marlena? One I didn't know about?"

"Mother." A warning loud and clear.

"Don't worry. They've all received a reply."

Breathe, breathe, breathe. "What are you talking about?"

"They've been notified that your healing powers have waned as you get older."

I jump up from the couch and stare at her. "Why would you do that? Why would you lie to them?" *But is that even a lie? Could it be the truth?* The back of my neck is hot and prickly. The blood in my veins sears through my body.

My mother is calm and poised. As though it isn't the middle of the night. "You'd rather I just tell them that you don't *feel like* healing? That you've *stopped caring* about their lives and their futures? That you've turned your back on God? On your gift?" She hesitates. "On me? And after everything . . ."

I wince. I don't need to see the self-portrait hanging behind me to remember what it looks like. To know that my mother is there on that ship, too, with the rest of the town, needing me to ferry her to safety. "You know that's not true," I say, though I'm not sure which question I'm addressing. Maybe all of them at once.

"God gave you a gift, Marlena—"

"—stop talking to me about God!" I scream, and she jumps. "I don't want to hear about God anymore!"

"Marlena! God does not—"

My hands go to my ears, pressing against them. "I hate God!" I am shouting over her, trying to drown her out. "I hate God and his stupid gifts! If God wants his gift back he can have it!"

This stops my mother's words. Her lips part in shock.

My chest is heaving. I close my eyes. This is what my "gift" brings out in me. I do not want to be this person. Why can't I stop being this person?

"I don't know you right now," my mother says.

"No, you don't," I say, determined not to lose control again. "Because I am just now getting to know who I am and what I want after eighteen years of my so-called gift defining everything I do. No more. Never again. Never ever."

My mother and I are eye to eye over the coffee table, locked in a staring contest. "You can pretend you're normal, but you aren't. You never will be. You'll see."

"I am seeing, Mother. Like I've never seen before. Like my eyes have been closed my entire life and they are just now opening."

A flicker of fear appears on her face. She thought she would win this argument. She thought I would bend and I haven't. "You must stop seeing that boy."

"No."

"You will regret it."

"I will never."

My mother's expression hardens. Her eyes harden. "There are some lines, Marlena, once you cross them there is no going back."

I stare at her for a long time, my expression just as hard. "Are we talking about sex here, Mother? Is that what this is about? The possibility that I might actually have love in my life? That someone might want me and I might want him back, for something other than a healing? Are you worried God will see and get angry and jealous that I am no longer under his thumb? That God will be disappointed that I am not his modern-day Julian of Norwich after all?"

I say this because I know how to bait my mother, too. But I also say it because deep down I am stung. It is always *God, God, God* with my mother and *what God wants* and *what God needs* and talk of my godforsaken reputation and my godforsaken gift and how it is really all about her. It is never, ever about me. It is never *Marlena, what do you need?* Or, *Marlena, what would make you happy?*

Everything about me hurts, like what she says can cause actual, physical pain to my flesh and my bones.

"I'm going back to bed." I get up from the couch. I take one step, then another, each one getting farther away from her. All I want is to go forward, forward, forward. Onward to everything she's tried to take away from me again. That she'll always try to take away.

Sometime during the night, I don't know exactly when, my mother enters my room again.

"Please don't take this from me," she whispers over me as I lie in my bed. Pain slices a deep crevasse through her words.

I hear her because since our fight I haven't been able to sleep. I guess she hasn't either.

She hovers there, maybe in the hopes that I am awake and will respond with reassurances, that I will console her with promises that of course things will go back to our version of normal. That our fight made me rethink everything, that I have a duty not only to those in need, but to her. For a split second I think I might do exactly this. My heart hurts to notice the pain in her voice, the loss piled upon loss, layered with despair. To be reminded my mother is not invincible; that she is, in fact, terribly fragile. I feel soft with her sadness, vulnerable to it, absorbing it like liquid. But it isn't long before the sadness turns back to anger.

It has always been my mother enclosed with me in my healer's cell, because she's enclosed us there together, happy to shut out the world and the loss she's endured with it.

I hear her breaths above me in the dark, short and labored.

I say nothing.

TWENTY-EIGHT

When I wake in the morning, it's late and I'm covered in sweat.

The sun is high, and I can already tell that the day will be warm. I inhale the air coming through the window. It still smells like summer even though it's September, a combination of newly cut grass with the crisp cleanness of ocean.

I sit up and the world tilts as I remember my middle-of-the-night visits from my mother. I get out of bed and rummage around in the bathroom cabinets until I find the plastic bag I stashed in the back. Inside it is a jumble of makeup I bought at the drugstore. I take out the bottles of nail polish. There must be ten. I couldn't decide which color I liked best so I bought all the ones I liked. There is a bright blue that beckons, but instead I settle on a shiny candy-apple red because I know it's the color that will most bother my mother when she sees it. And I feel like pissing her off. Because I am a terrible, unfeeling daughter. Obviously.

I sit on the toilet seat and put my foot up on the counter.

Soon it looks like someone has taken an ax to my toes.

Armed with some cotton balls and remover, I decide to start over, but this only succeeds in dying the skin around all of my ten toes a dull red. Clearly I don't know what I'm doing. My mother has always painted my nails for me, but only with clear polish. Never blue or green or pink. Especially not red. Red makes a girl look like a slut. My mother never actually said this, but it was always understood that wearing red nail polish would affect my reputation. It's all about perception, I've learned well.

"You want to appear like you have it together," my mother always said. "Like nothing can faze you. That is what people expect of you, as a healer."

I get up from the toilet seat and look down at my feet and laugh. "I look so together," I say out loud to the bathroom floor. "Like my toes have just bled out." I hear Fatima rustling around and I poke my head into the hallway. "Help?"

Fatima's eyes travel to my feet. "What did you do?" She sounds alarmed. She sets the mop in her hand against the wall.

"It's just nail polish."

She nods and pushes past me into the bathroom and picks up the bottle of remover. "This stuff is worthless," she says, then pushes past me again and disappears. When she returns she's holding a different bottle and tells me to sit back down on the toilet seat. Several more cotton balls and a lot of rubbing my toes later and they are back to their normal color. "This stuff is terrible for your nails but it's the only thing that works." She hands me the bottle she used and throws the one I bought in the trash.

The label on the one that actually removes polish says "acetone" in big warning letters, like it might be poison. "Is that yours?"

Fatima shakes her head. "It's your mother's." She whisks it out of my hands and disappears again, presumably to return it before anyone notices.

Leave it to my mother to know the difference between the good-for-you kind of remover that doesn't work and the bad-for-you kind that does. I wonder what other womanly forms of wisdom my mother knows that she's never taught me about?

When Fatima enters the bathroom again I am still sitting on the toilet seat.

"All right," she says. "I'm going to show you how to do this. Let's switch."

"What?"

"Up, up. We're switching places." Fatima kicks off one of her shoes." You're going to do my nails as practice; then you can do your own."

"You want me to give you a pedicure?"

Fatima chuckles and kicks off the other shoe. "Yes. Why not?" When I hesitate, Fatima says something else. "I know you're used to other people kneeling before you, but I'm not going to do that. And maybe it's time you kneel before someone else for a change?"

My cheeks burn. I nod, getting up but not speaking. Fatima has stolen my words. She's right. I set out the range of colors and Fatima chooses a pale pink, so pale it's almost white.

"That way it won't look like my toes are bleeding if you go outside the lines," she says. Then she plops herself down.

I get on the floor before Fatima's feet and begin to work, silently, while she offers instructions and I listen, doing my best to obey. *Start there. In the center. Then work to the edges. Go over that one again. Take your time—this isn't a race.* After a few botched toes I think I'm getting the hang of it.

"I'm sorry about what I said before," Fatima says.

I pause, not sure if I can paint nails and talk at the same time. "It's okay. I deserved it. It's true."

"Look at me," she says.

I finish the nail I'm painting, and return the brush to the bottle. Then I sit back on the bathroom tiles and meet Fatima's gaze.

"You don't *deserve* anything," she says. Her dark eyes are full of concern. "You've lived a complicated life, you're young, and you're doing the best that you can."

"Do you think I'm a bad person?" I ask.

Fatima takes a long time to answer. Too long.

I try not to feel betrayed. "You do."

"No," she says quickly. "No, no, no, Marlena. I meant what I said, that you don't deserve anything. You don't deserve to feel badly about your choices, especially since it's the first time you've had the opportunity to make choices for yourself."

I slump against the tub behind me. "Yeah, but now that I have the opportunity, am I making bad choices? All the wrong ones?"

Fatima thinks for a long time before answering this question, too. I try to be patient, and not jump to conclusions.

"Not necessarily," she says.

I curl my knees into my chest and wait for Fatima to say more. She's in her uniform skirt for work. Her shins are veined and there is a long scar up the side of one.

Fatima's eyes drift to the bathroom counter. The array of nail polish bottles lined up by the sink. "I think that your mother raised you to believe there is only one way of you being you, Marlena. And that way is very extreme, in my opinion. *Very* restrictive. Now that you have some freedom, you being you has come to mean you being the opposite of how your mother raised you. Which is also a bit extreme."

This assessment I do not like. "You think I'm being extreme?"

Fatima's eyes shift back to me. Little wisps of hair have escaped her bun and frame her face. "Honestly? In a way, I think you're being like every other teenager I know, because you're rebelling."

This perks me up. "So I'm normal?"

"Oh, Marlena." Fatima takes a peek at her unfinished toes. "I think you are *you*, which is different than most of the other girls your age—and there is nothing wrong with that," she adds quickly. "But it's like I said before, I don't think that you have to make this choice between a life as a healer, *or* a life as a 'normal' girl, as you like to say. I wish you would take a step back, maybe slow down a bit, and give yourself time to listen to whatever it is that heart of yours is telling you. The choice between healer and 'normal' might not be that stark, when you get a bit of distance."

I shift position until I am on my knees again, bent before Fatima's feet, carefully brushing the pale-pink polish across her remaining toenails. At one point, I say, "Maybe I don't have to worry about that sort of thing anymore. Maybe my gift is gone."

I hear a sharp intake of breath, but I keep my eyes on Fatima's feet. "Or maybe it's that your gift is changing," she says. "Did you ever think of that?"

"Changing to *spite* me," I say.

"Changing along *with* you," she says without hesitation. "Changing to *accommodate* the young woman you are becoming."

I bend closer to the floor, doing my best to paint Fatima's tiny pinkie nail, which requires all my attention. Then I sit back onto my feet and look up. "Done," I say. Before she can evaluate my careful work, I ask something else. "Do you think God punishes us for our mistakes? If he thinks we're being ungrateful?"

Fatima's eyes widen. "Marlena!" She leans forward. Puts her hands on my shoulders. "If you are asking me if I think God will punish you for . . . for painting your nails red and wearing a bikini on the beach and going out with a boy, the answer is *no*. I do not believe God is that way and I don't want you to either."

"My mother does."

"She may indeed, but you don't need to believe everything she does."

Fatima lets go of my shoulders.

"Do you ever wonder if there's a God at all?"

She sighs, then starts to chuckle. "*Meu Deus*, you ask difficult questions."

"You give difficult answers, Fatima."

She chuckles again. "Well, I guess that makes us a good pair."

"Thank you," I say. "For everything. For being honest."

"Oh, stop thanking me." She gets up and straightens her skirt. She looks down, wiggling her toes. "Thank you for the pedicure. It's not bad for your first time." Fatima nods at the red nail polish on the counter. "Now it's your turn. I'll supervise. But hurry up. I've got to get back to work."

I open the bottle of polish and, as Fatima stands over me, watching, pointing, barking instructions, I listen as best as I can until I have ten toes that gleam a shiny candy-apple red. The entire time Fatima's words about having to get back to work ring in my ears. That means *this*, what we are doing here, painting each other's nails, talking, she doesn't consider as work. Which means that I am not work for Fatima. When I am finished, she slips her shoes onto her feet again and walks out the bathroom door.

Within an hour I am in my new bathing suit, big Hollywood sunglasses covering my eyes, hair pulled back, bright-green towel in my bag, bright-green flip-flops thwacking a trail across the house. My red toenails clash and make my feet look like Christmas, but I don't care. I don't care if my mother sees me in this bikini and I don't care if the townspeople recognize me and do a double take at all of the skin I'm showing.

Well, I try not to care. In truth, I do feel self-conscious. But it's time I go for a swim in an actual bathing suit, and today it's warm enough. I walk to the beach, and as I breathe in the ocean air and hear the sound of the waves, the self-consciousness fades, replaced by excitement.

I'm going to the beach.

I'm going to walk in the sand. I'm going to lie in the sun and feel the burn on my skin. I'm going to put my newly red toes in the water and then the rest of myself too. Just me. Just because I want to. The second I'm on the sand a series of *what if* questions pop in and out of my head.

What if I'd always been allowed to do this? Would I be a different person? What if Fatima is right, and there are ways to be both a saint and a normal girl? What would that life look like? Would it be a life where boyfriends and long days of swimming and hanging out with friends are allowed? What if my reputation did change? Would it really erode my gift?

What if my mother's words from last night came true and just by telling people my gift was waning, it did?

What if God is really the kind of God that Fatima believes in, a God who doesn't punish?

I halt at the shoreline, my feet sinking into the dark wet sand, erasing my bright-red shiny nails from view. I kneel down, the cold of it nice in the heat. The waves are small and gentle, a child's hiccups. They thin to a pleasant sizzle as they near the place where I am, hands digging into the sand, disturbing a delicate white crab that buries itself again, disappearing into the mud. The sunshine against the water is almost blinding but I don't take the sunglasses from the top of my head. I like the glare. The heat on my bare skin. The emptiness of the beach because it's a school day and a workday and it's September, not August. I crawl closer to the water, until the edges of the waves almost reach me as they come in. I park myself there, legs extended toward the sea. I remember the little girl on the afternoon of my forbidden, rule-breaking swim. She was sitting just like I am now. *Are you an angel?* she asked. She was piling wet sand onto her legs, making a dribble castle.

I dig my hand deep into the sand, then hold it high above my right thigh, letting it seep through my fingers. When it lands on my skin it is cold and smooth and it hardens as I keep going, dig, dribble, dig, dribble. Soon a spiny tower rises up from each leg, like layers of melting frosting. The sun beats down on me and my castle, drying us both. The tide gets closer. When it seems like my dribble castle is high enough that another layer will topple it, I lie back, propping myself with my elbows, and survey my work. I am covered nearly head to toe with dark, shiny sand, like so many kids I've seen over the years at the beach. Patches of shiny red nail polish peek out from under the mess. Not exactly a sexy look, but maybe that's okay since I'm trying to make up for years of missed childhood. Besides, I practically have the whole beach to myself. The sun is high, the cool water a perfect relief. The sky is blue everywhere I look.

What if this is all there is? No God at all, but instead just this world in all its beauty and joy and horrors and pain? I dig up another handful of sand and watch as it drips through my fingers, shiny flecks of mica flashing as it falls. Could this be enough? Is it possible to love a life, to live a life, however imperfect and short it happens to be?

A wave bigger than all the others rushes into shore and bowls right over me, knocking my dribble castle to pieces, splashing sand up my body all the way to the side of my face. I start to laugh. I lie back on my elbows again as another rushes up behind it and covers me nearly to my chin. White foam swirls and bubbles around my body, the ties of my bikini bottom rising, then falling, heavy and wet as the wave recedes.

Yes, I think, as I get up, the remaining sand sliding down my legs. I think this could be enough for me. I wade into the water as another wave crests, so gentle and slow I can see right through it.

Why are we always looking upward and elsewhere when all of this is right here? If this is all I have, this day on this beach, skin salty and sandy, the promise of seeing Finn later on stretching ahead of me, then yes, I am satisfied with "just" this. This, right here, right now, is all I could ever ask for and more than I've ever dreamed.

TWENTY-NINE

"Okay, now put it in reverse."

I look over at José, then down to my hand as I shift into gear. Ever so slowly, I inch the car backward. Then I shift the gear again so I can go forward a teensy bit. Backward, forward, backward, forward. It feels like it's taking forever, but José seems pleased. *That's it,* he keeps saying. *Muy bien!*

He's teaching me to parallel park, even though we are miles from a city and the only parallel parking spots are along the seawall, and those aren't even real ones. My hair is still damp from being in the water, my legs sandy from the beach. I'm still in my bathing suit, too, but I put on a tank top and skirt over it.

I pull out of the spot that José chalked—that he actually *chalked*—onto the asphalt of the big empty lot where we are practicing my driving.

"Nice job!" he says. "Now, let's try it again."

I look at him like he must be kidding, but he is grinning. He gulps a sip of the *limonada* I brought him, then a big bite of the Twix I also brought him—payment for driving lessons. I tried to offer him more but he said that was all he wanted.

He swallows his chocolate. "Once you master this," he says, "you will be able to do anything, *cariño*. Trust me. Go ahead." He nods at the wheel. "Pull back into the space and then we'll work on getting out of it again. Just imagine there's a very expensive Mercedes in front of the car. And how about a Ferrari behind us? You don't want to scratch those things. A new paint job would cost a fortune."

"Great," I mutter under my breath.

"Hey now," he says. "Do this well and I might let you drive the car over to that boy's house."

"Really?" I asked José if he would take me to Finn's place afterward.

"He's obviously desperate to see you since your phone keeps pinging like mad in your bag." He chuckles. "*¡Ahhh, el amor!*"

I barely bring the phone anywhere, but today it's with me. "It could be someone else."

José's entire face registers his skepticism. "Who else? Helen? I bet you only have two contacts on there."

I don't say anything because he's right.

José chuckles again. "It's okay, Marlenita. It doesn't matter how many contacts you have, only that they are people who matter to you. Someday you'll have dozens of friends. You'll see."

"You think so?"

"I do." The phone pings again.

"Shouldn't I see what he wants?"

"Not while you're driving, *cariño*. You know that. After, you can ping him all you want." He taps the steering wheel. "Now let's do this one more time."

I sit up in my seat, eyes straining through the windshield in search of those chalk lines. Slow and steady, my hands placed carefully at ten o'clock and two o'clock just like José showed me, I begin the process of parking. It takes me nearly five minutes but I manage to do it. Then I breathe a sigh of relief, put the car in park, turn to José, and say, "Can I text Finn to tell him I'm on my way?"

José digs in my bag and comes up with the phone. "Now that the car is no longer in gear, *sí*."

I take it and read Finn's messages.

When are you coming over?

OMG, it's a nice day. Hurry.

What if I tempt you with culinary delights? Will that make you get here faster?

Um, if you have a phone you need to remember to USE it!

Sometimes certain people in your life want to be in touch!

If you come over now, I promise I'll let you eat all the dessert.

I'm laughing as I tap out **I'm** plus the emoji of a car plus the emoji of a house. I smile, proud of myself for this message in code that I know will make Finn laugh, too, when he receives it.

"Is he professing his undying love for you?" José asks.

"Maybe," I say with a grin.

José grins back. "Well, he should if he isn't." He waves his hand absently toward the windshield. "Marlenita, *vamos a la casa de Finn.* I'll be right here, evaluating your every move."

"*¡Sí, señor!*" I pull forward across the parking lot, trying not to be nervous. Finn's house isn't far. I've never been to it, but I know where it is. There is a neighborhood of cottages right along the ocean, just past the seawall. Finn has been living so close all this time.

I turn left out of the lot and after I am safely on the road, I speak. "Thank you, José," I say. "For teaching me. I appreciate it."

"You're welcome," he says, simply. "Just doing my job."

His words hit me like a slap. I force myself to concentrate on driving. "Your job? What do you mean?"

"It's my job to do what you ask, Marlena. You asked me to teach you to drive, so I'm teaching you to drive."

Luckily, it seems there are no other cars on the road. "But I thought you were doing this as a favor. Because I asked you to and you wanted to."

"And I *do* want to, and I'm happy to, but this is not a favor," José says, in his usual cheerful tone. "This is my job. Doing what you say. I'm on the clock right now. Did you think I wasn't?"

I swallow, the gulp of it audible in the quiet car, my eyes still fixed on the road. "This isn't in your job description. And I'm not in charge of you."

"But you are, Marlena. You're the boss," he insists.

"I am not," I protest with a shaky laugh. "My mother is."

"You and your mother are *both* my bosses. The money you make pays for my job. I have to do what you ask."

"But . . . but I thought . . . I . . . wait a minute." I put on my turn signal and glide to a stop along the seawall, where in theory I should be practicing my parallel parking but the only other car is about a quarter of a mile away.

"Nicely done," José is saying. Then, *"Mirame."*

I don't want to look at José right now. But I turn the ignition off and make myself do it.

"You thought that we were friends." José shakes his head. *"Cariño,* I am not your friend. I am your employee. I always have been."

I am speechless. My lips feel glued shut.

"But just because I work for you doesn't mean I don't care about you, *niñita.* I do. I always have. I don't know exactly what is going on, but I can see you changing and it's for the good. And because of *that"*—he gestures between us, the half-eaten Twix in his hand— "here we are, and I am teaching you to drive."

I try to nod, but instead I just drop my head and stare into my lap, at my knobby knees, the pedals on the floor, the mat, which is spotless as always. José must vacuum it every night. That just makes me sigh. José is right. I hate that he is, but he is.

"Hey," he says. "Did you hear the part about how I care about you, or did you tune out when I said that?"

I lift my eyes. "I heard it."

"Marlena, I know you are experiencing a lot all at once. But relationships take time. Changing a relationship after it's been one way for many years takes time. We'll figure it out together, eh?"

I manage to nod.

"Don't lose hope. All is not lost."

"I'm not," I say, but another great big sigh escapes me. "Fatima keeps telling me that things don't have to be all one way or all the other. But mixing everything up is so complicated. And unclear. I'm used to all the lines being *very* clear. And I'm also used to being painfully aware about what happens if I cross those lines, and what I lose if I do."

"I know," he says. "And Fatima is a smart woman."

"She is," I agree.

"But letting things be complicated doesn't have to mean loss. Do you also know that?"

"I'm not sure. Maybe? Maybe I'm getting there?"

He takes a long gulp of his *limonada* and swallows. "Marlena," he says, "sometimes when you start crossing lines, *this* is what you get." He gestures between us again, still with the Twix, which is melting between his fingers. "You get driving lessons. And I get my favorite chocolate, some soda, and a nice afternoon with my little Marlenita, who isn't so little anymore. Okay?"

"Okay," I agree.

"Patience."

"I hate patience."

José laughs. "Don't we all."

Then he taps the wheel. "Now, ten o'clock, two o'clock, *cariño.* Or that Finn is going to think you changed your mind about him."

THIRTY

"You got sun today," Finn says when he opens the door of his house.

"Show me around," I say in response. "I want the grand tour. Oh, and you promised me culinary delights!" I push past him and start looking around. Poke my head into every room, every closet. Everything is simple and everything is mismatched. Couch, two comfy chairs, lots of shelves piled with books. Books stacked one on top of the other, some horizontal, with more books wedged on those, all the way to the next shelf. The wood actually sags in the middle from the weight of them. When I poke my head in the bedroom, it is small and things are neat. The bed is made, and instead of a closet there is a metal rack where Finn has hung his clothes. On the bedside stand are more books.

"You don't need a tour, apparently." Finn is laughing as he comes up behind me. He puts his arms around my waist, but I keep walking, Finn in tow, backing up from his bedroom and heading into the little kitchen, where there is a small metal-topped table and two old wooden chairs. Several paper bags sit on the counter, one of them greasy.

I turn to him. "Are those our culinary delights?"

He lets go of my waist. "As a matter of fact, yes."

I open one of the bags and breathe deeply. "Oooh, what is it? It smells delicious."

"I went to Annie's. The shack at the end of the seawall?"

I know it, but I've never been. My mother would never eat there.

Finn grabs the bag with the grease stains. "We have clam cakes." He places it under my nose and I see fat blobs of fried dough. He returns the bag to the counter and points to the others. "We have chowder to go with the clam cakes. Also, lobster rolls, cole slaw, and corn on the cob. Maybe I overdid it?"

"It's perfect! I'm starving. Let's eat *all* of it. I've never had *any* of it."

"Well, that's a crime against humanity. And your Portuguese heritage, if I might add." Finn pulls things out and sets them onto paper plates. Then we sit and dig in.

I take a bite of clam cake and swallow it down. "Wow."

"I know, right?" Finn pops one of the smaller ones into his mouth whole. "You're supposed to dip them in the chowder," he says, in between chewing, "but there isn't a right way to do this. It tastes good no matter how you approach it."

I take Finn's advice and dip the rest of my clam cake into the broth. "Also a good idea," I concur, after I try it. We keep eating. Corn. Lobster rolls. The seemingly endless supply of clam cakes to go with the chowder. I pause in the activity of stuffing my face to ask Finn a question. "Are you ever going to tell me about your family?"

Finn picks up another clam cake like he hasn't heard me. I wait while he eats it. Finally, he says, "I'm a little afraid to."

"Why?"

"You might not like what you hear."

"I want to know everything. Whether it's good or bad."

He turns his attention to his lobster roll, then picks a kernel of corn from the cob and eats it. "Okay. Well, it's just my mother, and she and I are estranged." He picks at another kernel. "She lives in the-middle-of-nowhere Oregon, and we haven't spoken in years. I . . . I did something, and she can't forgive me."

"Oh, Finn! I'm so sorry."

"Marlena." Finn sounds strangled. "Please don't ask me what I did. I don't want to . . . I'm not ready . . ."

"Okay, okay." I say this, because what else can I say? But it doesn't change that I want to know whatever it is. "Why would you be so afraid to tell me that?"

He looks up from his plate. "Because I've worried what you will think of me, abandoning my mother."

"It sounds more like the other way around, like she abandoned you."

"That's not how she sees it."

"We really are more alike than not," I say. "It isn't as though my mother and I are the portrait of a happy family either."

This elicits a bit of a smile. "I told you."

"How old were you when you left home?"

"Sixteen."

"Wow, that's young."

He nods.

I slurp a little of my chowder. "How were you able to afford living on your own?"

"I got a special scholarship, because of my aptitude for science. School and housing paid for."

"Ah," I say. "A genius scholarship."

Finn rolls his eyes. "I'm not going to comment on that."

I down another spoonful. "Does what you just told me have anything to do with why you and Angie are so close? I've often thought that she, I don't know, treats you like you might be her son."

Finn looks away. "For the most part, yeah."

This question has him setting his lobster roll back on his plate like he can't stomach it. "Finn, what?"

He wipes his hands on one of the napkins. There are already six, crumpled and used, strewn across the table, and the pile only keeps growing. "Angie is . . . not particularly happy with me at the moment."

Something about the way he says this makes me feel implicated.

"Why?"

Finn stares at his plate. "I talked to her about us," he says. "Well, *she* talked to me about us. She figured it out. All things considered, I guess it wasn't that difficult."

I think back to Angie watching us leave through her office window. "No. I thought she might suspect. Where does that leave you?"

"I'm not sure. Angie said I was too close to you to keep working on the study—"

"But that's not fair!"

"It's totally fair, actually," he says. "I am too close. Though it is also possible that when Angie told me this, I shot back something along the lines of *look who's talking*, since Angie hasn't exactly stayed distant from you, either."

I put down my spoon. "Oh."

"Yeah. It's also the truth, though. And Angie knows it."

"Is that why she's mad at you?"

Finn leans back in the old wooden chair and it creaks. "No. It's more than that."

"So tell me more."

But he dives back into his food again, taking a huge bite of his lobster roll.

"Finn—"

"Can we change the subject? I think that's enough complicated conversation from me for the day."

I close my mouth. "Okay." I'm uneasy letting this go. "You can tell me anything, Finn. *Anything*," I repeat.

Finn stares at the messy tabletop. "I'll tell you. I promise. Just . . . later." He brightens a little. Reaches up and flicks my bathing suit ties, which are sticking out of my T-shirt at the back of my neck. "When you're done eating, let's go for a swim. We need to cross that off your list of normal, though it looks like you might have crossed it off on your own."

I laugh. "That's highly possible."

"How do you feel about crossing it off once more? Just to make sure you got it?"

"I think that's a great idea. We're on borrowed time with this beautiful day anyway. It's just warm enough to still go in the water. We should take advantage while we can."

"I agree." Finn gets up from the table and tosses his nearly empty paper plates in the trash can.

When I'm done, I clear mine, too, and after the two of us clean everything else from the table, Finn disappears into his room. When he comes out he's wearing black swim trunks and a blue T-shirt. He reaches into a closet in the hallway and comes out with two beach towels. One of them has turtles on it and the other has little smiling snakes. "Don't judge," he says, when he sees me eyeing them. "There was a point, right around when I was nine, when I was sure I'd be a veterinarian, so that was the theme of my childhood. Animals, all sorts of animals, especially of the reptile variety." He laughs, but the pain behind his eyes makes me wonder if the memory makes him miss his mother.

"Interesting new Finn tidbit" is all I say, letting the topic rest there. I take the towel with the turtles on it and drape it around my neck. We head out his front door and down the street toward the beach. "What other interesting new Finn tidbits are available for release today?"

We are so close to the water that we walk there barefoot, picking our way carefully over the hot road.

Finn sidesteps a big rock. "Let's see. That you should be glad that I no longer keep a pet tarantula?"

"Ew, a tarantula? Really?"

"Yup, really."

A rickety brown fence, tall thin slats of wood held together by chicken wire, marks the entrance to the beach. We climb up and over the dune. "You're right, I think I am grateful for that."

When we reach the high tide line we drop our towels. Finn pulls off his shirt and sets it on top of his towel. I try not to look at his skin, his bare chest. Try to act like it isn't a big deal that I am essentially disrobing in front of the boy I can't stop thinking about. "Any other Finn tidbits you want to share?" I croak as I pull off my top and slide my skirt down my thighs and off.

Finn's eyes flicker over me from head to toe. Then he grins. "Wait, sorry, were you saying something I was supposed to answer? I got distracted by the sight of Marlena the Saint in a string bikini. You don't look so saintly right now."

I cover my eyes with my hands. "Shut up. You're going to make me blush."

He moves my hands away and plants a kiss on my lips. "I think I already did."

"You were going to tell me about yourself," I remind him. "Maybe something more recent?"

His eyes linger another moment on my neck, my stomach, then along my legs. "Right. Recent." We walk toward the water. "How about the fact that I finally have a girlfriend?"

"I'm your girlfriend?" I yelp when my toes touch the water. It's colder than it was this morning.

Finn bends down to kiss me again. "Yes." We wade farther in. The water is up to my chest and Finn's waist. Both of us duck under.

I know it will warm up the longer we stay in. I am up to my neck, then over my head, treading water. The ocean is nearly flat. Finn swims to where I am bobbing up and down. My hand brushes across his skin under the water. He pulls me close.

"Hi," he says.

"Hi."

"You're smiling."

I smile harder. Finn wraps his arms around me and I wrap my legs around his waist. I try not to think too much about what I'm doing. I lean in and kiss him. Then I unwrap my legs from his body and dart away, closer to the shallows.

"Hey, where are you going?"

I dive under, my hands reaching for the ocean floor. I plant them there and kick my feet up until they feel air, before I right myself again. "I've always wanted to try and do a handstand."

Finn laughs. "Another thing on your list?"

"No. But I'm adding it now."

We stay in the water until my teeth are chattering. Finn still has to drag me back to shore, because I could stay in the water all evening. He wraps me up in the towel with the turtles. We grab our clothes and walk back to his house, our bathing suits soaked and dripping. When we get there Finn points to the bathroom so I can change, but of course, it didn't occur to me to bring a spare set of clothes. I dry off as best I can, leaving on my bathing suit bottom and pulling my skirt over it, but taking off my bathing suit top so it doesn't leave two damp marks on my shirt. I decide this would be worse than going without a bra. I drape my bikini top on the towel rack and head into the hall. Finn's door is open and I see him standing there, shirt off, searching for another one. I knock, then push and walk up to him, running my hand across all that bare skin.

"Well, come on in, Marlena." He laughs, but there is also a catch in his voice.

I'm too busy studying the heart on Finn's arm to answer, brushing my fingers across it. When I look up into his eyes, his mouth is suddenly on mine and we are kissing. These kisses are hungry and wild and dizzying, our bodies pressed up against each other. Before I'm aware of what I am doing, I'm pushing Finn backward toward the bed and climbing onto him, my legs around his waist like when we were in the water. I'm wearing more clothes this time, but somehow it feels like I'm wearing less. My skirt rides up to the tops of my thighs. Our breaths come quickly as we kiss. I press harder and harder against him, as if I want to move through him. Even though we are as close as we possibly can get I want to be closer. I grab the hem of my shirt, ready to pull it off.

"Marlena? What are you doing?" Finn's hand shoots out, stopping me. There is a dazed expression on his face.

"Getting undressed?"

His hand is firm, preventing me from moving my top any higher. "Wait a minute."

"Why?" I demand. "Why wait another second?"

"Well, let's see." Finn lifts me up and sets me to the side on the bed. Then he lies down facing me. "Oh, let me count the ways."

"I want to *do* this," I tell him.

"Do *what* exactly?"

I tap my hand on the bed between us. "This?"

Finn gives me a look. "If you can't say it out loud, then we're not doing it."

"Sex, sex, *sex*," I burst out, staring straight into Finn's face.

And he laughs. "You certainly said it, there."

I stare down at my hands.

Finn leans down and kisses each one of my fingers. "Marlena, please don't think that I don't want to be with you."

I look up again. "See. You can't say it either."

Finn is smiling. "Do I want to have sex with you? Yessssssss." He draws out the word with such agony that it brings a smile back to my face. "Of course I do. But we can take things slow. It doesn't have to be all or nothing."

I groan and flop onto my back. "Everyone keeps telling me that!"

Finn laughs. "Maybe because it's true?"

"All or nothing. All or nothing! Why can't it be all? What's so wrong with *all*? Why is everyone always warning me against it? Are extremes really that bad?" I let my eyes slide back to Finn, down his face and over his chest, so much beautiful skin. "All looks pretty good to me right now."

This makes Finn laugh again.

"I'm serious. I'm eighteen. I'm ready. Haven't most girls my age already done this?"

"Plenty, sure, but not everyone. And none of them have the history you do, since there's that part about being a healer your entire life."

I glare. "A few minutes ago, you were loving the saint girl in a bikini."

It's Finn's turn to groan and flop back onto the bed. "Oh no. I haven't forgotten a single bit of that image."

"Then what's the problem?"

"There isn't one, not technically," Finn says. "But there are *lots* of things we can do other than kissing, Marlena. And there are *many* kinds of sex." Gently, Finn reaches out to grasp the hem of my top and raises it a little. His hand sears a trail across my skin, a trail that would be a dark-pink riot of peonies if I could paint it. I close my eyes, the light touch of his fingertips along my ribs ticklish.

"What's so funny?" he asks. When I open my eyes he is grinning.

I bite my lip. "I don't know. I guess maybe I'm a little nervous."

"Good. I am, too."

"But *you* know what you're doing. You're the one who's talking about all the things we can do and all the different kinds of sex. You've done all of this before."

"Not with someone like you."

I sigh. "I know, I know, sheltered miracle-healer-saint."

Finn's face loses the grin, his eyes growing serious. "Not with someone I love." He kisses my stomach, just above the waistband of my skirt. His breath falls across me in soft bursts, petals falling from a tree.

My breathing has stopped. "I'm someone you love?"

Finn lifts his head to look me in the eyes. "Yes, you are," he says. Then, "I love you, Marlena. I knew it from the first moment I saw you."

I hold his stare, like a beautiful but fleeting treasure. "I love you, too, Finn."

Then, in the fading light of the day, Finn gets up on his knees and leans over me. I sit up so he can slip my top the rest of the way up and over my head. "Look how beautiful you are," he says, eyes on my body.

The body, *my* body, as a source of miracles, has also been a source of shame. I remember when I turned thirteen and my breasts began to poke through my long white sheaths, two points I could no longer hide, how my mother looked at me, horrified, how she mourned the changes of my body. She immediately went to the store and came back with these tight, stretchy half shirts. They were bras that pressed my breasts so hard against me they nearly disappeared, which was the point. Any curves on my silhouette have always been regarded as embarrassing, shameful, something to make disappear. Evidence of the profane on this sacred body of mine. This sense of needing to hide myself has even carried over into moments when I'm changing clothes, or getting out of the shower. A girl like me is not only never to be touched, but never to be naked, at least not for long. A big part of that girl knows she should feel shame right now, being so exposed in front of a boy. But the thing is, I don't.

"You have a dreamy look on your face," Finn says.

"I'm happy," I tell him.

Finn lies down next to me on his side, propping his head with his hand. "Good. Because I am too. And I'm so many other things I won't say out loud."

A thought occurs to me. "Hey, how does, um, *this* affect your photographic memory? Do you remember, ah, pretty much everything?"

He grins. "Oh yes, I do, Marlena. This is one of the moments when my photographic memory is truly useful. In the best of ways." He presses a kiss against my mouth, his tongue searching, parting my lips until it slides against my own. When I pull him closer, pull him on top of me, he shakes his head and pulls back. "Mm-mm. We have all the time in the world, remember?" His stare slides down my neck and over my chest and stomach. Starting at my collarbone, his fingertips move across my skin, down the curve of my left breast, then over the right one. There is a tightening in my belly, between my thighs, a tingling along the skin of my chest. When I close my eyes and a sigh escapes, Finn whispers in my ear. "I think it's time someone else is in charge of healing all the lost and lonely parts of you, Marlena. I want it to be me."

As his fingertips continue their journey over my body, I open my eyes long enough to say, "I want it to be you, too."

The warm feeling between my thighs keeps building while Finn's hands explore every inch of my torso. He leans over me for another kiss, and when I open my eyes there is a lustful but tender expression on Finn's face, Finn, whose entire being is forever a contradiction. Young but intelligent beyond his years. Serious but fun. Skeptical but full of faith. Fierce but tender. Full of restraint yet willing to abandon himself completely. To me, at least.

"What are you smiling about?" I manage to ask.

"I feel like an explorer," he says, "discovering all of Marlena's hidden secrets."

"I didn't know I had any hidden," I tell him.

"Let's see what else I can find out." His hand makes its way down my stomach, sliding softly over the skin of my belly until it slips past the band of my skirt and dips underneath the edge of my bathing suit. He stops a moment, and looks at me.

I nod, unable to speak, and the tips of his fingers reach the place between my legs, gliding slowly over this part of my body that I've never touched, not like this, that I'm never supposed to allow anyone else to touch. Certainly not like this. It isn't long before a feeling so intense, so unlike anything I've ever known yet somehow similar to that sheer, blinding ecstasy that accompanies a vision, grows up my back and down my thighs and over my stomach to my breasts and my neck until it is all that I am, one great streak of fire and burning that cannot contain my breath.

If pleasure was a vision, it would start out deep and dark and blue, the color of the ocean, cold and sharp. It would become an arrow of stars, streaming through the body on a crash course with the heart. If pleasure was a song composed by a mystic, it would begin with a chorus of soft voices that rise to a startling tangle of bells. If it had a taste, it would be of the sharp salty sea and the bright tang of ripe berries. I had no idea that love, human love, could permeate every one of the bodily senses, that it could take shape in so many different forms. I cannot believe I've lived a life that would have me deprived of this until my death in the name of God, of a so-called gift, with a mother who colluded to do just this. If loving Finn has profaned me, then I wish with all my heart that every ounce of sacredness in me is washed away forever.

But somewhere inside me, too, I know for the first time in my life that I am finally discovering what is truly sacred in this world. No God can ever take that from me. This is Finn's gift to me, a boy so real I can feel his hands on my body and his breath on my lips, which is so unlike the gift that has hidden in my healing hands for so long and kept me from so much of what is truly good and beautiful.

"Marlena," Finn whispers in my ear, as my lungs slow their effort to gulp the air. "Are you okay?"

"Hm-hmm," I murmur back, eyes fluttering open.

I look up at Finn, his face hovering over mine, his beauty a wonder, a vision. I trace the curve of his cheek.

"What are you thinking?" he asks.

I hook one of my legs over his and pull him closer. "That all my life I've been taught to feel ashamed of this, but now that we are here, I don't feel ashamed at all."

"Oh Marlena, shame is the last thing you should feel." He buries a kiss in my hair. "You are beautiful and I love you and there is no shame in this. Not a bit."

THIRTY-ONE

There are days when you wake up and the whole world feels good. Like everything you see is beautiful and in its place. The way the sun filters through a break in the clouds, a single ray of light raining down to the ocean below. The strawberries piled in a basket on the kitchen table, plump and red. A stack of books waiting for you to read them. Even the sound of the coffee percolating on the stove gives you a sense of peace and harmony. Sometimes there are entire weeks like this. And when they happen, they seem like a miracle.

Before, I didn't know that being in the world could feel so good. But now, as the days slide into weeks, I live like I have never lived. Like I've always wanted to. I let myself change, I let my life change, I let my relationships change. Most of all, I let myself love and be loved by Finn. We walk the beach, even when it rains. We go through the things on my list, one by one, and things that weren't on my list, too. Finn takes me to his university campus, where there aren't any lockers but there are people everywhere, sitting on the grassy quad, carrying their books, heading to classes, and I imagine myself here one day. I think about what I might study. I go to the mall and eat in the food court. Helen and I have sleepovers, and we talk into the woozy hours of morning. I stay out all night, more than once. I learn to ride a bicycle. I get better and better at driving. Then one day, Finn and I go on a road trip.

Before we leave, Helen takes me shopping in the city. We go from store to store on a pretty street with clothes that seem ridiculously expensive, but today I don't care.

"I need to find the perfect outfit," I tell her. "For . . ."

Helen and I have just emerged from a dress boutique with price tags the same as her monthly rent. She gives me an exaggerated surprise-face. "For *whaaaaat*, Marlena?"

"You know what," I tell her.

Finn has devoted himself to proving exactly how much there is to do other than kissing, and I am enjoying this proving. Before, I'd thought that pleasure just happened. I didn't know that girls were different from boys, that their boyfriends or girlfriends would have to spend time learning their bodies. Finn has made himself into an excellent student of the body that is mine, and I've done my best to do this in return for him. But while there may be many kinds of sex, there is still one kind Finn and I have refrained from having. And I'm glad that we've waited.

But I don't want to wait anymore.

Helen yanks my arm and pulls me into a fancy lingerie store. "Well, if *that's* what we're preparing for, what you wear underneath the outfit is just as important!"

"Helen!" I plant my feet firmly just inside the door. We are surrounded by lace, by things it would never occur to me to put on my body. "It's not like he hasn't seen me!"

She pulls harder, dragging me to a rack of pale-pink, flimsy— what are they called, teddies? "It's not like that matters!"

"There is *no way* I'm wearing something like that."

Helen bats her eyelashes with exaggerated innocence. "And why not?"

"I can see through it!"

"Exactly!"

"No, Helen. No way!"

"Oh, Marlena," Helen sighs. "If you are going to end up naked anyway, then what does it matter if Finn can see through what you're wearing before you take it off?"

"I don't know?" I cover my mouth and start to laugh. "I guess maybe it doesn't?"

Helen drags me to another rack. "Finally, you are talking sense!"

I look at all the complicated black lace, and try to figure out how a person is supposed wear whatever is dangling from the hangers. "That looks so uncomfortable."

Helen is admiring something satin and shiny. "You aren't

supposed to wear it all day."

"Do you put on this stuff for Sonia?" Ever since the party Helen and Sonia have been dating.

"Sonia loves me in lingerie."

"Does Sonia wear it for you?"

She shakes her head. "No. I'm the lingerie girl in the relationship."

"Well, what does Sonia like then?"

Helen tears her eyes from the rack to look at me. "The better question is: what does *Finn* like?"

"Me?"

"Of course, *you*. You're not exactly helping me help you, here."

I think of the colors I see when I'm with Finn. "What about pink? Just not that pale washed-out color you showed me before."

"Finally." She leads me over to another rack.

At some point, while I'm trying things on, I text Finn, in my still very slow and labored tapping of the screen.

Me: You will never guess what I am doing.
Finn: Tell me.
Me: I'd rather show you when we go away.
Finn: Gulp. Stop killing me, Marlena.

I smile at this and put the phone away.

In the end, I get something simple, but pretty, and I am grateful when we return to dress shopping. After hours of looking, I find the perfect one. It is a bright, silvery green, with a halter that ties around my neck and a skirt that reaches to my knees.

"What do you think?" I ask Helen, when I emerge from the dressing room.

She looks up from her phone and smiles. "I think that's the one."

"Me too."

"Well, then, buy it, so we can go to dinner. My feet are killing me!"

Later, when we are seated in a booth, waiting for our pizza, Helen asks me about my decision to be with Finn, and I ask her what it's like to have sex with Sonia, and what made her decide she was ready.

Helen takes a sip of her Coke. "It was easy. I knew I wanted to, and she wanted to, so we did."

"No regrets?"

"No way."

Our pizza arrives, and we each pull a piece from the steaming pie.

Helen waits for hers to cool so she can take a bite. "Promise me I'll get the full report, Marlena."

I pick up a fork and knife to avoid getting burned and cut a piece, blowing on it a little. "I promise," I tell her, and our attention turns to eating.

❖ ❖ ❖

My road trip with Finn turns out to also involve a boat trip. We drive to a ferry, then drive the car onto the ferry so it can take us to an island disconnected from the mainland. There are no bridges or causeways. It makes it seem like Finn and I are heading across the ocean to be in a completely new world that is all ours.

The inn where we are staying is across the street from the beach, near a little downtown with shops and restaurants. It is so much like the town where I live, but so unlike it. This town, for instance, has never sold souvenirs with my image, and I can walk down its Main Street without fear of being recognized. And I can do it with Finn and not worry about being judged.

We head into the foyer of the big old house. "What do you think?" Finn asks.

There are little couches and nooks to sit and read, and a pretty porch visible through the windows. "I love it."

When we get to our room, I feel shy. I've spent so much time with Finn, just Finn, but there's something different about going away with a boy. It feels grown-up, in a way I've never been. In my bag, I've packed my perfect dress, and the underwear I plan to wear underneath it. When Finn runs out to the car for something he forgot, I put everything away in the closet and drawers. I don't want him to see what I've brought just yet.

Finn and I go for lunch at a takeout place on the docks. We buy sandwiches and eat them sitting in the sun, our legs dangling over the water. Afterward, we drive all over the island, looking at the old houses, trying to decide which one is our favorite. Which one we would buy. *If we got married someday*, I think. All afternoon there is a flutter in my stomach about our dinner ahead, and about what will happen *after* dinner.

In the end, when it does happen, I'm not wearing the special dress or the lingerie Helen made me buy. It isn't even at night after we've eaten, and gone back to our room, as I'd imagined.

When we return from our drive, the two of us go upstairs so I can put away the souvenir I bought in one of the shops. A little framed postcard of the exact spot where Finn and I ate lunch. I set the bag on the floor and begin digging through my suitcase for a hair tie. Finn is sitting on a chair next to one of the windows, flipping through the novel he bought at a bookstore where a cat was sleeping on one of the table displays, which made us laugh. I find the tie for my hair and put it up in a knot. Then I go to Finn and sit on his lap. He closes the book and sets it on the table. Finn turns me so I am facing him, my legs on either side of his waist. He leans in for a lingering kiss.

"This isn't fair," I say, when I can't seem to pull away. "You know all my secrets."

"And I've loved finding out every one of them." His fingertips run up my back underneath my shirt and my cardigan.

"I was just going to sit here for a minute."

"Well, I think you should stay longer."

I kiss Finn's neck, once, then again. "I know all your secrets, too."

I expect him to laugh, but he doesn't. When I look up at him, his eyes are far away. "Where did you go?"

Instead of answering, he starts unbuttoning my shirt.

"I thought we were going to the beach for a walk before dinner," I say, as Finn is sliding my shirt and sweater open, over my shoulders and down my arms. He undoes the clasp on my plain cotton bra and suddenly I don't want to leave the room for anything.

"You really think we should go for a walk? Right *now?*" he asks as I lift his shirt up. He raises his arms so I can slip it off and toss it to the floor.

"No."

I press myself against him. I love the feeling of my bare skin against his bare skin. We've been so careful not to be completely naked together—Finn's rule. One of us has been, but not both of us. Not at the same time. Finn seems to have decided it's my turn today.

He lifts me off him and I let him undress the rest of me, my jeans, then my underwear. "This *really* isn't fair," I tell him.

"I was naked last time," he says, kissing my shoulder.

"Is this another one of your rules? We have to switch back and forth?"

"Maybe."

He kisses my mouth and there is no more talking. Our kisses are like waves, swelling slowly, then rising more forcefully until we are a tumble of hands and limbs and mouths. His fingers on my skin, my back, my hips, my thighs, are a beautiful torment, his lips on my shoulders, my neck, my breasts, make it impossible to breathe. Like always, I want to be closer, closer to Finn, like I can never be close enough, pressing myself against him like I really could find a way to press through him.

When we slow down again, Finn laughs, soft and low. "We were going for a walk?"

"What walk?"

He leads me to the bed and pulls me down on top of it. He trails a finger from my knee to my thigh and over the curve of my hip and the swell of my breast. Finn replaces his finger with his lips and it is dizzying. I shift onto my back and close my eyes. "I can't believe I might have lived my whole life without this," I whisper.

"I can't believe it either, Marlena," he whispers back.

I reach for the buttons on Finn's jeans.

"It's too tempting if both of us are naked," he says. "You know that."

"But what if I need it to be both of us?"

He pulls back. "Is that what you want?"

"Yes," I say, undoing his top button as I say it. "It's what I've always wanted." I undo another one, and Finn's breathing speeds up. "Are you going to tell me no?"

"No," he says. "I mean yes. Yes, I want to."

"I think it's time."

"Me too," he says.

The two of us look at each other for a long time, taking this in. I stare at this boy I love, who loves me back, in every way, at his beautiful eyes that are all for me, that are full of me, the bright-red and pink hues of love that color my vision. They are all that I see. Finn is all that I can see. It is the most beautiful vision of my life.

"I love you so much." These words are the glorious petals of a peony flower in bloom.

"I love you just as much," Finn says, as he lets me undress him.

When we are both naked, I study the tattoo on his arm, something I have done a dozen times at this point, but this time seems different. I brush my fingers across the lines of it, and the shadows. "I could never forget this part of you, Finn. You are my heart. And I am yours."

THIRTY-TWO

I stare up at the wall of my room on this first day that feels like fall. There is a new painting hanging there. The entire canvas is a bright, beautiful red, touched with a glaring, swirling pink. Slopes of white curl through it. It is abstract, but if you stare at it long enough you might make out that the swirls of red and pink come together to make peonies. A trail of them. My vision, a portrait of what it is like to love and be loved by Finn. I am brimming with love, carrying it all around like a pail of overflowing water at the beach. Like with my healing visions, I wanted to make it tangible.

I reach up and touch the rough edges of the canvas, glide my fingers over the paint, now dry and brightened by the light of the sun coming through the windows. Evidence that what I have with Finn is real.

Maybe someday I will give this to him.

I turn away from the painting and head downstairs for some

coffee. The heat of the mug warms my hands. It's strange how the chill of fall came so fast; from one day to the next the temperature must have dropped twenty degrees.

Through the kitchen window I see a car I recognize parked in the white pebble driveway. Angie is walking up to the door.

What is she doing here? Did she come to see the artwork of my visions?

I race to greet her before she can ring the bell, but I'm too late. The door swings wide, my mother blocking the view. My mother is wearing heels, dressed up, even though she's been in the house and it's morning.

"So you are the woman who's taken my daughter away" is the first thing she says. "Poisoned her mind."

"Mother," I hiss from behind her. I wish I could say I'm surprised she would speak this way to Angie when they haven't even been introduced, and while Angie is still standing outside on the front steps. But I'm not.

"I have taken no one's daughter," Angie says, sounding offended.

I push past my mother and stare at Angie, wanting to tell her, *Run, run while you can!* But after barely a nod to me, Angie's eyes are stuck on my mother.

"I am the one who made the decision to speak to Angie," I say, cutting into their staring match. "I am the person who decided to take this break from healing. Angie had nothing to do with it."

My mother is shaking her head, the purple bruises of

sleeplessness under her eyes darker than ever. They make me wonder if my mother has slept at all. She points to me and looks at
Angie again. "This girl here"—my mother's gaze swipes from my
head to my toes, from my bright-green top to my jeans and my loud,
obnoxious flip-flops—"is no longer mine."

For the first time, I see anger on Angie's face, a tightness in her
jaw, a clench in her teeth. "Mrs. Oliveira, that is a choice you've
made about your daughter that has nothing to do with me, to the
detriment of yourself, I might add." Angie reaches an arm out to
me. I see the quiver of protection in it. But the devastation on my
mother's face stops me short from leaning into the crook of Angie's
elbow.

"It is not just me who is suffering," my mother goes on, as if
Angie hasn't spoken. "You've taken everything from my daughter,
her gift, her purpose, her sacred touch, even her virginity—"

"Mother!"

My mother is far from done, ignoring my protest. "From the
moment you entered Marlena's life you started her down a path
from which there is no turning back. The entire town has seen her
prancing around with that boy and knows she is ruined." My mother's eyes flicker upward, one might think toward the beautiful fall
sky, but she is looking toward God. "God knows she is ruined and
that is the worst of it. Lives will be lost because of you."

Angie is trembling. "Mrs. Oliveira." She keeps her voice slow and
steady. "I did not come to speak with you, though it is obvious you

have things you'd like to say to me. I'm happy to come back another time for that conversation. I'm here because I have important issues to discuss with your daughter." Angie glances at me finally. The way she looks at me, her normally bright laughing eyes so grave, a frown on her lips, nearly makes my knees want to buckle. What could be wrong?

My mother huffs. "What could you need to tell Marlena that you can't say in front of me? That you've officially proved her a fraud?" Her eyes finally shift to me. "Oh, Marlena, do you think me stupid? This town is full of gossips and I've heard about the inquiries your scientist has been making about your gift." Her gaze slides back to Angie. "What then? Tell us both why you're here."

The tremble in Angie's body subsides. "Marlena, do you have somewhere we can talk in private?"

My mother is unmoving in the doorway, but I beckon Angie past her. "Follow me."

As Angie and I go upstairs, my heartbeat seems to have slowed, like it is resisting my moving forward. I usher her inside my room. It is still mostly bare, apart from my bed, my reading chair, and a stack of books on the table beside it. The only thing that brightens it is the new painting on the wall.

Angie goes straight up to inspect it. I sit down on the edge of the bed and put my hand to my chest to feel the pulse of my heart and make sure it's still there.

"You told me you painted your visions," Angie says finally. She is still studying the canvas.

"I do."

"But there's only one painting here. Where are the others?"

I can't tell if Angie is genuinely curious or if she is stalling. Maybe the scientist in her wants to see my art as evidence, additional resources, for her study. But the person in her is using them to distract from the real reason she is here. "All the paintings from my visions are stored away."

She turns to me. Her blue eyes are worried. "You said *all*. And this one? It's not about a vision?"

"It's about Finn," I say. "It's about how I feel when I'm with him." I pause for a breath. "I know you know about us. He told me."

Angie comes over to the bed and sits down. "What did he tell you, exactly?"

"That you didn't approve of us."

Angie's eyes drop into her lap. "I see."

"I know he works for you and that a relationship with me might be inappropriate—"

"Marlena, no. That's not the issue. Well, it is *an* issue, but not the one that has me disagreeing with Finn."

"Then what is it?"

She sighs heavily. "Tell me something first. And be honest."

"Okay," I say slowly.

Angie is watching me with a strange look on her face. "Do you love him?"

I glance at the painting and smile the tiniest bit. I can't help it. When I think of Finn my happiness overflows.

"Oh, Marlena," she exclaims. "You do love him."

I nod. My smile fades because Angie takes my hand and her eyes are sad. No, they are panicked. She doesn't even hesitate when she touches me. I swallow. "What?" The word gets caught in my throat. "You think it's a bad thing that I'm in love with Finn?"

Angie's fingers squeeze harder. She doesn't shake her head yes or no. She just keeps saying, "Marlena." Then, "I told Finn that he *has* to tell you. That if he didn't that *I* would tell you."

I search her eyes while she is searching mine. "What?"

"You really don't know? Not anything?"

What don't I know? I race through everything I do know, every thought and feeling related to Finn. About his photographic memory and his estrangement from his mother and his desire to be a veterinarian when he was small. Then my brain sharpens to a single point. On it is a half-formed vision from before my healing break, its colors pale and faded, Finn walking away from me at some later date, walking toward a place I will never reach. "Say it now, Angie. I can't take this."

Angie breathes deeply. Then she starts. "Finn is sick."

I shake my head. I feel my hair brushing along my bare shoulders. "No, that can't be." The words seem like they are from someone else. An image, bright and clear, appears to me. The tattoo on Finn's arm. The way it's always seemed like there was something else to it, something he wasn't telling me. That he wasn't quite ready to share. "It's his heart," I state.

"Yes." Angie leans forward. "I would never lie to you about this." There is a shuffle of feet outside my bedroom door but I tune them out, straining toward whatever Angie says next. "I'm so sorry, Marlena. Finn is dying."

THIRTY-THREE

Angie and I haven't said a word since we got in her car. We passed my mother in the hall on the way out of my room. I know she heard every word of what Angie told me. It was her feet I heard outside the door.

The seawall appears with the ocean beyond it, usually a comfort, but I stare at it as though I'm suddenly blind. I know it is there but I can't take it in. I am ever the anchorite, but the heart in my chest is an anchor dragging my soul to the ground, one forged of crystal and glass that will shatter when it hits bottom. I don't even know if it's still beating. My senses have stopped working, everything numb. Perhaps I'm the one who is dying.

"Angie." A great hard lump has lodged in my throat. I can barely swallow around it.

She is shaking her head. She turns down the road that leads to Finn's neighborhood. "The rest is for Finn to tell you." When she pulls up in front of his house and turns off the car, she says, "I'll wait here. I'm not going anywhere. Take as long as you need. All day if you want."

I get out of the car and walk up to the house, but it's like I am underwater, that anchor pinning me to the ocean floor. My legs carry me forward up the porch stairs and my hand is reaching for the door to knock. When Finn answers and sees that it is me, his eyes light up. "Marlena," he says with a smile. Then his eyes land on Angie, standing there by her car, and every bit of happiness fades, just like those colors in my vision paled as though draining away Finn's life. *I should have known.* "What did you—" he calls out, but Angie gets in the driver's side without a word. Slams the door.

"Finn," I whisper. "How could you keep this from me?"

He stares down at me. I stare up at him. For a moment, a beautiful fleeting instant, I forget why I'm here. *This is love, this is love* is racing through my brain.

Finn's hand twitches. His fingers cross the distance to mine, wrapping around them. My heart pounds all of a sudden, like someone has pulled up that anchor and is readying to cross the sea. Finn bends forward. At first I think he's going to kiss me but instead he presses his forehead to mine. I close my eyes, soaking up the proximity of his face, his strong body, the smell of his skin, a dizzying feeling traveling over my limbs to the tips of my fingers and toes. I wonder if we are both angels with wings that will carry us away. I wish for this, despite all my wishing against just this for so long.

"Marlena." He grasps my other hand, presses my palm into his chest, firmly against his heart. The pulse and pound of it reaches into me. "What did Angie say?"

"Just tell me it isn't true." I stare up at him and wait.

He says nothing.

"No, Finn, no." My eyes cloud, everything turning the color of rust. I crumple forward, still pressing my palm into the center of his body. I yank my hand away and point to the heart tattoo peeking out from under Finn's sleeve. A tinge of anger spreads through my voice, like a drop of stormy color. "I want the real story, because the one you told me is a lie."

Finn's eyes seek the porch floor. "Not entirely." He raises his head, slumps against the wall of the porch. "I was born with a heart defect," he says, and stops, as though this is the whole story.

I shake my head. Remember Finn's body, his every inch of perfect skin, unmarred by scars. "But you've never had any surgeries."

"The doctors didn't discover it until I was older. There was nothing they could do, short of a heart transplant, which I will likely never live to see. The waiting list is too long." He sighs. "It's why I moved so far from home. Why my mother and I aren't speaking. I was tired of hospitals and doctors, because believe me, every avenue has been explored. There is no fixing me. She wanted to keep trying to fix me and I needed her to stop."

My breaths come in short, quick bursts, like I am running. "Every avenue but, say, a miracle saint girl."

Finn fixes his stare on me. "Marlena."

Tears pool in my eyes. "Is that why . . . ?"

"No, *no.*" He reaches out, maybe to put his arms around me, but I step backward. "Me and you," he says. "My caring about you, my loving you, has *nothing* to do with you being a healer."

A shiver rolls across my body, the shudder dislodging the tears in my eyes. "Why should I believe you?"

"Because it's true."

"You've tried everything else, so why not a healer? Is that why you work for Angie? Mr. I-don't-believe-it-unless-I-can-knock-on-it Finn was hoping that one of Angie's freak subjects might turn out not to be a fraud? Me, particularly?"

"I told you to stop saying that about yourself."

I wish there was something I could hit hard enough to break a bone. "Like that matters. Like anything matters right now." Finn tries to catch my hand but I don't let him. "Look at me," I demand. "You didn't once think that maybe, just maybe, I could be the answer? That I could be the one to fix"—my eyes slide to the edge of his tattoo—"your heart? Not even on the day you came to my audience?"

"Of course it crossed my mind. Of course it did, and it still does. I'm not going to lie and say that I haven't thought about it. I have. I've wondered."

"Finn, you *told* me to stop healing. It was *your* idea that I take this . . . this vacation. You gave me the idea to quit!" My voice is rising and rising. "Why would you tell me to do something that goes against everything you need? How could you *do* that? How could you do that to *yourself*? What were you thinking?"

"It wasn't about me," he says quietly. "It's what you needed."

"No! What I needed—what I *need*—is for you to live a long and happy life! What I *need* is to keep on loving you and for you to keep on loving me! How could you do this to *me*, Finn? How could you allow me to love you in exchange for my not saving you?"

Finn's lips part but nothing comes out. A single tear rolls down his cheek.

"Is it true what Angie said, that you're dying? *Dying?*" There is a hysterical edge to that word the second time I say it.

He is still. But then he nods.

"When? How long?"

"I don't know. Months at least."

My knees start to buckle. "Months?"

He nods again.

"Give me your hand," I demand. It comes out a bark. Finn doesn't, so I say it again. "Give. Me. Your. Hand."

He holds it out.

I do something I thought I might never do again. I get down on my knees. I inhale a long, hoarse breath, and I close my eyes tight. I reach up and take Finn's hand. Press my forehead to the back of it. Feel his skin against me, inhale the dizzying scent of him.

And I wait.

I wait for that familiar tug in my body that signals the start of a vision. My heart and mind and soul together search for that familiar charm, wait for the reassurance of its presence, imagine it popping up to me from the floorboards where it's lain hidden, hoping for me to call it back. I wait for the colors to start, to flood my being, followed by the scenes and that great surge of energy that passes through me into the person I touch. I wait for the healing process to begin, any part of it. I pray for it. As I hold Finn's hand, press my cheek into his palm like my entire life depends on it, because his entire life depends on it. I silently call out to God, and as I beg and I plead, I realize something I have never before been able to say for sure.

I do believe in God.

But the God I know is a punishing God, a God using Finn to castigate me for forsaking my gift. My mother was right. She's been right all along. This is what I get for wanting a life, for trying to have a life and love for even a few weeks. God is a being who is punishing both of us because of my hubris.

I sob into Finn's hand.

There is nothing in me. No sign of my gift. The well of healing inside me is dry.

Finn's arms are around me, pulling me up.

A jumble of words spills from my lips. "Maybe if I change my clothes, maybe the tank top, the jeans . . . maybe if I take my hair down . . . maybe . . . maybe . . ." I am face-to-face with Finn. Tears are streaming from his eyes. I jump back from him like his arms are made of red-hot iron. "Don't touch me. You can't . . . not like this . . . not anymore . . . I felt nothing, Finn, don't you understand?" The full realization of the situation dawns like a monster rising, hulking and terrible between us. "There is nothing left in me. So we can't . . . we have to stop."

His face drains of color, and then I am gone, turning around and heading back the way I came toward Angie, running down the steps and across the yard as fast as I can. "Take me home," I choke out when I get inside the car.

When I enter the house my mother is the first person I see. She is waiting, maybe since I left. "I overheard your conversation with that scientist," she informs me. "I heard every bit of it."

Before she can say anything else, I tell her the decision I made in the silence of Angie's car. But I stop short of telling her the bargain I made with the punishing God.

I stare over my mother's head at the self-portrait hanging on the wall, and I think of the shipwrecked girl I am once again. "Make the announcement. My audiences will resume next Saturday. I will heal again on the anniversary of the Day of Many Miracles." My words are like a last, desperate prayer to Saint Jude, to Julian, to Hildegard, to all the women mystics who lived before me. I see the satisfaction on my mother's face. "You have won. *Mama*," I force myself to add. My eyes flicker toward heaven. Maybe my return to healing, to my life as it was before, *exactly* as it was before, will be enough to appease the angry God above me. Above all of us.

PART THREE

The In-Between

THIRTY-FOUR

All night I work.

I climb into the attic and take down the boxes marked "Marlena," bring them to my room, and return my bedroom to its former appearance. I take everything out of my closet, remove every bit of color. I take the novels I will never have the chance to read, the bright-green thwacking flip-flops I love so much, the platform sandals, the teeny flowered bikini Fatima helped me pick out, the phone with the texts from Finn that keep lighting up its screen nonstop, and heap them onto the chairs and the shelves and the floor of the gift room. The only thing I can't bear to part with is my Finn painting. That I bring to the attic and shut it away there tight.

I unpack the boxes with my books by mystics, about mystics, about healers like me. I set them on the table by my reading chair just so, line them up on the shelves as they were before. I try to remember their exact order. *The Dark Night of the Soul*, by Saint

John of the Cross, on the bottom, followed by *Revelations of Divine Love*, by Julian of Norwich, *The Interior Castle*, by Teresa of Ávila, Hadewijch's slim volume of poems, *The Book of Margery Kempe*, by Margery Kempe. Finally, the thickest among them, *The Showings*, by Hildegard of Bingen. I return the paintings and collages of my visions to the wall. I put them in the same places they hung for years.

Will being so precise, so exact and so careful, help to restore my gift?

The last thing I do is the thing I loathe most. I unpack those horrible white shifts, the filmy long-sleeved dresses I thought I would never touch again. One by one I unfold them and hang them in my closet until my closet is full. The last one I put on, pulling it over my head and letting it slide down my body.

I go into the bathroom and look in the mirror, stare into the face of the girl who looks back. Once again she wears the uniform of Marlena the Healer. This Marlena looks exactly the same as before on the outside, dark hair falling around her shoulders, long-sleeved cotton dress, demure and tentlike, concealing all the curves of her body.

My body, the shape of it, is unchanged, my skin may be unmarked, but inside I am different.

A body that has been loved by another is somehow different from the body of someone who's never felt love.

But maybe if I can go back to that other girl, then Finn will live.

There are some lines, Marlena, once you cross them there is no going back.

Those words from my mother have been ringing within me all night. Was my mother right? Did I cross too many lines? Have I ruined my gift?

But loving Finn didn't feel like ruining myself.

It felt like finally making myself whole.

Helen's words keep plaguing me, too, Helen the unassuming prophet. "But what if someone is sick?" she asked me the night of the party. "What if I came to you now in that chair? Would you turn me away?"

My answer had been a nonanswer, a sidestepping of the question to avoid staring the unthinkable in the face, the possibility that someday I would want those healing powers again because I would need them to save someone I love. I was naïve to think it wouldn't happen because it had never happened before. It hadn't happened, I guess, because before I never really had anyone to lose.

I see myself shudder in the mirror.

I turn away from my reflection, return to my room, and get in my chair without attempting to sleep, curling my legs up underneath me and pulling my cotton sheath over them to my toes. I look out over the sea, waiting. Waiting some more. Waiting for that feeling to come back to me, the feeling of healing. I wait for it to return to my body, for it to take me over again, to possess me like a demon.

How does a person who knows love unknow it? Can I unweave it from my being? The phrase *steeling oneself* crawls to the surface of my mind. Is that how I must do it? Become steel, a hard and cold unfeeling metal, in the face of Finn? Would hardening myself against Finn make me stop loving him? Would it help me forget what I've lost?

I hope so.

The thought of never being with Finn, never having him to myself, never feeling his eyes on me or his lips on my lips, makes me want to die. But isn't that why I'm doing this? My life for Finn's? Because if I don't at least try, then Finn will surely die, because he is dying already. This is the bargain. I would rather be in a world where I know Finn is alive, even if I can't have him. Even if that.

It is the middle of the night, but I find myself leaving the house.

I head down the stairs and onto the beach. My feet slip and slide in the dry sand as I walk toward the water. The sea is rough, the waves churning like a storm might be coming. I stop when I get to the high tide line and stare into the black ocean. I concentrate, prodding every corner of my body and soul for the hint of a vision, but I am blank. A vast white space of nothingness.

My gift has disappeared and I know it, as intimately as the lines on my own hand.

How do I get it back? What do I do?

God, God, if you are listening, I will do anything. Anything!

I've heard of artists getting blocked, of writers who can't find words, painters who've lost their inspiration. But healers? Do we go through periods where the gift won't come to us? I am inching my toes across the wet packed sand and toward the cold churning sea when it comes to me.

The dark night of the soul.

The mystics always talk about this. These long periods when they feel their connection to God—their ability to see God, to talk to God, to receive words and images and visions of God—has left them entirely. They write of total abandonment, being banished into silence and isolation, a despair beyond any consolation. For them, the dark night is torture. It is the loss of the will to believe, to have faith in anything.

I feel this darkness in me now, spreading through my veins.

A tiny wave crashes over my ankles, splashing my knees and shins with icy, salty droplets, soaking the bottom of my shift.

Maybe my mother knew something I didn't. Maybe she always has known. Maybe that's why she's kept me in long white gowns and thin, fragile slippers, a girl from another era, a ghost from centuries long past. My gift belongs in another time, when people believed in such things. When religion was all the science they'd ever known. Maybe my mother has tried to keep me living not quite in this world because she knew that once I stepped foot into the world as it is today, the gift would die with me, an ancient object that can no longer withstand the air and the elements and gives way to nothing. For Finn's sake, I should've stayed in that liminal place between then and now, between there and here. Maybe then he would be okay. Maybe then I could save him.

The black water rushes around my ankles and up to my knees. For the mystics, the dark night was a test from God, after which their visions returned with even more force, more glory, than ever before.

This is my test.

I must take the shipwrecked pieces that I am, hold them together with all my might, and weather whatever comes.

By the time I go downstairs in the morning, the sun is high. My mother is busy, Fatima is busy. Papers are everywhere. There is the feeling of anticipation, of urgency. Fatima keeps glancing at me from the kitchen, like she wants to say something. But she doesn't.

"Oh good," my mother says. "You're up."

"I've always been up. I never slept."

My mother pushes a sheet of paper across the table. "We need to do this as soon as possible. To quell the rumors."

I peer at the paper in front of me. On it in big capital letters above and below the photo it says, "The Anniversary of the Day of Many Miracles, a Special Audience with Marlena." The photo is of me on that day last year. I am surrounded by seekers, everyone reaching out to me. My eyes are closed and my arms are extended. My forearms, my elbows, all the way to my shoulders, are covered with the hands of others.

My mother doesn't ask if I like the announcement or if I approve. She just goes about the business of restoring things to their former state, goes about the business of me, like there has been no break or vacation. She snatches the paper back and studies it.

"This will appear in all the papers and online," she is saying, more to herself than to me. "And José has already talked to the print shop about the posters for the town. It will go out as an email to the local merchants and on your mailing list of people waiting for an audience, past attendees, tourists, etc." She looks up.

"That is great, Mama," I say quietly. "Thank you."

In a way, I do have to thank her. My mother is nothing if not efficient with managing my life as a healer. Soon the trappings of it will be in place again and all I have to do is slip back into them. Like I never stepped away from them at all.

"Where is the bag of mail?" I ask Fatima the next time she looks at me.

Her expression is worried. "I can call José to have it brought in."

I tear my eyes from her. "I would appreciate it."

"What are you going to do with the mail?" my mother asks, sounding distracted.

"I'm going to answer it."

"It will take you weeks to go through it."

I clasp my hands. Try to seem like I am at peace. "I will work as long as it takes."

"Whatever has gotten into you, Marlena, it is a very good thing," my mother says.

"I'm glad you feel like Finn dying is a very good thing, Mama," I reply.

"That is not what I meant," she snaps.

"Isn't it?"

"I meant that what you are doing now, coming back to your senses, is what needed to happen regardless of that boy."

I turn, ready to leave, because I can't take standing here any longer. "What I am doing now, Mama, is penance."

The rest of the day I go through the mail, letter by letter. I respond at length by hand to each one. There is so much mail. My mother was right. It will take me weeks to get through it.

It's not like I'll be out doing other things.

It's not like I'll be with Finn.

The hours pass and my hand aches from holding the pen.

Dear Amy . . .

Dear Gero . . .

Dear Lupe . . .

Please forgive me . . .

I'm so sorry . . .

Please, please, please.

I beg for understanding, for forgiveness, I apologize again and again. I do this until my fingers are callused and bleeding. I keep going. I used to think that people who crawled to my audiences were crazy, but now I understand them in a way I never could before. When someone you love is sick, when they might die, you will do anything for any little bit of hope. Nothing is beyond you. You would give your life for theirs.

Dear Mario, I apologize . . .

Dear Tamika, It is unacceptable that I took so long to respond . . .

Will all of this begging and repentance make up for what I have done? Will it transform me back to the healer-saint I was? In writing these letters, I am begging God to hear me, forgive me, to allow the gift I never asked for to flourish again inside me.

Please. Please. Please.

Letter by letter, I do my best to pay for what I have done. It is true, what I said to my mother, that this is my penance. Penance is a form of payment, like currency exchanged between humanity and God for one's sins. How much payment might God require to make my gift work again? How much payment does God want from me to help Finn? Does helping Finn require more penance because I fell in love with him?

At four o'clock in the afternoon I hear voices downstairs.

I set down my pen and wipe the blood from my knuckles. Then I go into the hallway and listen.

"I need to see her—"

"She doesn't want to see you!"

My knees give way and I slide down the wall. Finn has come to my house and is fighting to see me. Fighting *for* me.

"You ruined my daughter!"

"Mrs. Oliveira, I am in love with your daughter!"

Finn is in love with me.

I should go to him, I should . . .

They yell back and forth. There is desperation in Finn's voice and a clear tone of satisfaction in my mother's.

"My daughter never wants to lay eyes on you again!"

"I won't believe that until Marlena tells it to my face!"

I can barely swallow.

Steel. I must steel myself. Harden my heart so that it is cold metal, impervious to dents and marks. Impervious to Finn. Loving him isn't going to appease God. I made a bargain and must keep it. Still, I strain to hear each and every word between Finn and my mother. Soon they become too muffled to understand. My mother must have pushed Finn outside, hoping I don't realize Finn is here.

There are footsteps on the stairs. I look up.

Fatima is crouching down to my level, a few steps from where I sit, curled into myself. "Marlena, *querida*, your boy needs you to come and see him."

I drop my head back to my knees and pull my arms tighter around my legs.

She sits down and keeps talking. "*Querida*, I don't know everything that has happened, but I know at least some from what I've overheard. I think I understand what you are trying to do, but *querida*, please, it does not have to be this way."

"Yes it does," I say into my knees.

Fatima sighs. "Marlena, I have worked for your mother a long time, and I am grateful to her for many things. She has been loyal, and pays me more than anyone else would ever pay for this job. But it is like I have said, I do not agree with her about the way you've been raised and treated because of this gift. It does not have to be all or nothing—I beg you to hear me on this, *querida*. I have watched you become a different person these last weeks. I've watched you light up and laugh and live. You do not have to give that up. This boy loves you, so you should go to him. The God I believe in celebrates love and wants love for us."

"The God I believe in forbids it," I say. "At least for me."

"Marlena." Another long sigh from Fatima. "Do not do this to yourself. Do not do this to that boy who is standing there, taking on your mother."

The front door slams, the house shaking with the force of it.

"Marlena," Fatima says again, her tone urgent.

Finn must be leaving. He is probably walking away right now. What if he never comes back? What if he believes the things my mother said to him?

Steel, steel. I tell myself this over and over. The tears pour from my eyes regardless. My body shakes with them.

"Oh *querida*." There is a hand on my back—Fatima's hand.

Quickly, as quickly as I can, I shift out of reach, as though Fatima's hand is burning. "Don't touch me," I snap, looking up. Fatima's lips part, this time her words lost. I stare at her. "I am not to be touched. You know this. Everyone does."

THIRTY-FIVE

I take a deep breath.

Gertie's shop is in front of me. The posters about the anniversary for the Day of Many Miracles are going up, but I wonder if the townspeople already know from the messages my mother has sent out. From the look of things on Main Street, maybe not. The town seems deserted, and Gertie is not in her usual spot in the doorway, gossiping with people walking by and just generally keeping an eye on things. I can see her behind the counter, though. The doll of me is gone from the window, leaving a gaping hole among the candles and T-shirts.

A handwritten letter is clutched between my fingers and a stack of other letters is folded neatly inside my bag.

A huge puff of air bursts from my chest. I keep forgetting to breathe. I tug the edges of my sleeves down to my wrists. I force myself inside Gertie's shop.

She looks up. "Marlena?" Her gaze sweeps over me.

I make my way to the counter, past an aisle of sale items. Is it my fault so many things are reduced price? I hold out the letter. "I wanted to apologize for the other day."

Gertie doesn't take it. She stares at it; then her eyes slide back to me. "What is this?"

What do I say? Do I tell her the truth?

"My vacation is over."

"Yes. I got your mother's messages. I was surprised. You seemed to have . . . moved on."

I nod. "I . . . I . . . realized that . . ." My eyes flicker upward, as though God is sitting there in heaven, looking down, arms crossed and judging. "I realized that everyone was right and that it was terribly selfish of me to have done what I've been doing. Healing is my true calling. People depend on me, people like you, and I have failed you. I'm sorry. I really am. I regret everything that's happened. The letter says this more eloquently. I hope." Tears fill my eyes, but they aren't tears of apology or repentance. Everything I am saying to Gertie is one big lie. The only reason I'm here is because I don't know how else to get my gift back. In truth, I regret nothing. Those were the best weeks of my life. My only regret is how they ended, that somehow I may have squandered Finn's future.

"Now that my audiences are resuming," I go on, with a catch in my voice that I try to swallow away, "the tourists will return and your shop can go back to normal."

"Marlena." Gertie sounds hesitant. Or maybe worried. It takes me back to that day when she didn't recognize me and was concerned about my well-being.

Is she concerned about it now? Even though she knows it's me this time?

"What?"

"This shop isn't going 'back to normal,' as you put it. I've decided to stop selling souvenirs related to you."

"But I need you to keep selling things! You have to."

She studies me. "That doesn't make any sense. The other day you . . . you were enraged, Marlena, that we've been taking advantage of you for years." Her eyes lower to the counter. A sign is taped there that reads "Cash Only." "You were right."

Stars flare across my vision, and a rushing sound fills my ears. I grab the edge of the counter. "No," I whisper. "No, I wasn't. Please. Gertie, *please*."

"Please what?"

"Please make things go back to the way they were."

She tilts her head. "They can't, Marlena. I decided I would do my best to sell the rest of what's left in the shop until the day of the anniversary audience, and then I'd be making changes about what I sell. It's about time." She leans forward. "This town can't survive on you forever. You made that clear, and it was good you did. We needed to hear it."

As Gertie is speaking, it's like she has one of those plastic beach shovels and is scooping my heart from my body and tossing it aside until there is nothing left of it.

She eyes my bag and the stack of envelopes sticking out of it. "If your plan is to go to the other store owners, I wouldn't bother."

"Why?" I croak.

"It's up to you if you want to apologize, but if it's your hope that we go back to the way things were, you're too late."

I try to swallow but I feel like I'm choking.

"We had a town meeting. We decided that it's time for us to get out of the Marlena business."

I don't even remember taking the stack of letters out of my bag but I must do this, I must leave them with Gertie, drop them on the counter of her store, because when I get home later on they are gone.

For a long time, I sit, staring out the window.

Staring into space. Thinking.

This is all my fault.

I brought this on myself.

I brought this on Finn.

But then I am up, crossing the room like some robot, grabbing more of the mail I haven't yet responded to, and getting down to work again.

Maybe things can't go back exactly as they were, but maybe if they go back enough . . .

I bargain and bargain some more as I plead with my pen and paper. I bargain with myself, with these people I am writing to, with the world, the universe, the galaxy, and all the stars and planets within it. Most of all I bargain with God, this being, this divinity, whatever God is, that has chosen to reveal himself only when he wants to punish me.

I bargain about my gift.

I bargain about my future, the possibility that I will never get married and have children and my own family.

I bargain about sex and my body and all those things I was supposed to guard as though my entire gift depends on them.

In my bargaining I promise God to give everything up that has ever meant anything, I promise that I will never allow myself to be touched again, that I will be a good healer-saint for all the rest of my seconds on this earth, that I will live like those women mystics of the past, cloistered and obedient and utterly devoted to the service of God, a good anchorite even if I drown in the process. I promise God that if he will just spare Finn I will never ask for anything else again. I promise God everything, all that I am and ever will be, in exchange for Finn. I promise God my own life, because what is the point of a life if Finn is not there to live it with me?

Are you listening, God?

Are you?

Is this enough?

Send me a sign, God!

Send me a fucking sign!

My breath catches after this last thought echoes through my room and I realize I've actually said it out loud.

"I'm sorry, God," I whisper. "I didn't mean that last part."

Yes I did.

I press my pen harder to the paper, blood trickling down my fingers and onto the clean white sheet. I wonder if the recipient will realize what those dark splotches are. I think about all the relics of saints I've read about, the tiny swatches of fabric claimed to hold the sacred drops of blood of one famous apostle or another, how worshippers have encased them in glass and exquisitely wrought jeweled containers in order to showcase them. I wonder how much a letter with my blood on it might fetch in one of the souvenir shops downtown. If anyone would try and sell it.

They certainly would have before.

My eyes sting as I write.

My fingers sting even more.

THIRTY-SIX

The anniversary of the Day of Many Miracles arrives. I've spent all my time preparing. Every letter has been answered. Main Street has gone back to something like normal, even if it's only temporary. I have settled into the familiar routine of the life I used to know. Once again, my mother sticks to me like sand after a swim. She goes everywhere with me, does everything with me, setting things right, helping me make up for my crimes.

"Marlena," my mother says. "Turn to the left. And suck in your stomach."

I do as she asks as she buttons me into a wedding gown. It is fit for a ball, with a skirt that bells out wide and metal boning throughout.

"Suck in your stomach more. And your chest."

I close my eyes as she tugs and tightens, careful not to brush my skin.

"You ate too much candy."

The top of the dress is like a cage around my torso, imprisoning my ribs and my lungs, all the way up my neck to my chin. It is elaborate and conservative. I think of Catherine of Siena, who starved her body, and other women like her who purposely made their bodies uncomfortable, who harmed themselves, as penance for having bodies at all. Denial of the body and its physical needs is classic among these women. I try and imagine that my imprisonment in this dress, my inability to expand my lungs fully, is the same thing.

"There." My mother finally sounds satisfied.

I open my eyes. There I am in the mirror. The dress, I admit, is beautiful, with its hand-sewn lace. But I swore to myself that I wouldn't wear another wedding gown again. Not unless I decided marriage was for me and I was going to my own wedding. And maybe not even then.

"You look like a queen. Regal. As you should."

I look sad. Lost.

A memory flashes of that giggly afternoon with Fatima, when she took me to try on bathing suits. How nervous I was to see my reflection in a bikini. How excited I was to finally pick one out. Fatima didn't seem to think there was anything wrong with showing off my body at the beach. She thought it was normal and fun. How is it that what is normal for so many people is forbidden for me? A threat to my gift? Why did people make it this way? Why did God make it this way?

"You could at least smile," my mother says. "People have come from far and wide to see you on this day."

I plaster a smile on my face.

The car is silent as José drives us to the church.

He is in the front, my mother and I are in the back. I can barely fit inside wearing this dress. My mother is in one of her signature white outfits. The scenery goes by in the window, and I see it, but also I don't. I know there is ocean and seawall and eventually the church up ahead. The closer we get, the more I wonder if I might pass out. Not because of the tight-fitting gown, but because I am terrified.

What will happen today?

Will I feel my gift returning to my body?

Will it finally be there when I need it? When others do, too?

"José, please pull around back," my mother directs.

He does as she asks silently.

Don't we all?

The parking lot is full. Cars spill onto the street. A crowd of people has gathered on the lawn and snakes up to the doors, which are not yet open.

"People are here so early," I say.

"I'm not surprised," my mother says. "This is a very special day." I feel her eyes on me. "And of course, this is your first audience in weeks."

José pulls up to the private entrance and opens my mother's door. Then he runs around and opens mine. He doesn't extend his hand to help me out, even though I'm struggling in this gown. We are back to the way things were. I am Marlena the Untouchable. I don't even meet José's eyes as he waits for me to get both feet on the ground. I focus on the task of arranging my skirt and righting myself so I can walk inside. I am halfway to the door when I stop.

What am I doing? Why am I really here? What do I truly think is going to happen when I walk out there onto the stage? That all will be fixed?

"Marlena, hurry. You don't want people to see you before the audience starts." My mother acts like I really am a bride and the crowd gathered in front is my groom.

"Marlena?"

I hear José behind me. The way he says my name is an invitation to turn around and go, it informs me that he is willing to drive the getaway car and whisk me to safety. My eyes lower to the ground, to the sand that covers the asphalt in a thin layer, swept here from the beaches. I pick up my skirts and follow my mother inside, the door clicking shut behind us.

There are so many flowers. Their scent is everywhere.

My mother hasn't let me go out into the church for fear that I will be seen, which will ruin everything and because I am always on the verge of ruin. Isn't that how I got here in the first place?

She walks through the door to where I wait backstage. "Let's go over the list of special guests."

I nod, and listen as my mother explains where the people are sitting, how things are supposed to go. I stop myself from asking how much money each one paid in exchange for my touch.

"What sort of surprises do you have planned today, Marlena?" she wants to know. "I'd rather you clue me in ahead of time."

The truth is, I've avoided thinking about what might happen when I go out there. Or what might *not* happen.

"Marlena?" My mother's tone is impatient and a warning.

I shake my head. "Nothing, Mama. I don't have any plans other than what you tell me I should be doing."

She studies me. "Of all days, Marlena, this would be the one when you go off script. Give the crowd a little something extra. Something unexpected."

"Okay, Mama. I'll see what happens then."

She eyes me suspiciously. She still doesn't know what to make of my newfound obedience. "All right then." My mother glances at the clock. "It's almost showtime."

Showtime? Is that what we're calling it now?

With her heels clicking, my mother comes over to primp and puff my gown. "I'm going to go out and open the audience, Marlena."

I nod.

My mother is still staring. "Marlena?"

"Yes, Mama. I'm ready."

I barely hear her heels clicking as she heads out the door again.

So much is riding on this audience.

Everything that matters.

Finn. His life.

I pray to Hildegard, I pray to Julian. I pray to Teresa, with her little sword, and Margery, with her endless tears, and Hadewijch, with her poetry. I beg every one of the mystics and visionaries and healers I have ever read about, known about, studied, because they seem closer to me than God ever has. They seem so much realer than God. Like they might understand where I am coming from because they were human once, too. Women and girls who wanted and hoped and yearned for things like me. Maybe even who loved, once upon a time.

When I walk out onto the stage, all I feel is shame. Shame that I left and came back. Shame for the reasons I did. Shame for what happened while I was gone from this life and shame at the thought that people have heard rumors about me. Shame at the size of the crowd, so many people I abandoned without warning. Shame that they've come back as though I never stepped away, as though all is forgiven, just like that. Like maybe I didn't even need to apologize in the first place.

If they can forgive me, will God?

A tiny flower of hope blooms. This is the moment I've been waiting for, the moment when I might find out that everything is going to be okay, if I might give Finn back his life, his dreams, his future. Even if it's a future I won't be in.

I bite my lip hard, so hard I taste blood.

I take one step, then another, until I am standing at the center of the stage, shoulders back. Chin lifted. Watching. Waiting.

The church looks both familiar and different. My mother went all out on the flower arrangements. It could be Easter, with so many lilies and big white blooms. There is a banner to commemorate the day, and even more people than usual packed in the back. But the seating is the same, the placement of the altar is the same, the platform where I walk out into the crowd is the way it's been ever since my mother had it installed.

So why does it feel so strange to be here? What am I not noticing or seeing?

I do my best not to focus on any one particular person in the church. I don't want to have to look anyone I know in the eyes. Not Gertie, not Mrs. Lewis if she is here, not Mr. Almeida, and especially not Fatima or José or Helen. I know Helen is here somewhere, because my mother told me she was coming. I make my eyes go blurry, so I see only colors and movement, until it's like I'm watching the world from under the ocean.

People start to whisper.

I close my eyes tight.

I search for that familiar feeling, for the physical tug of my gift within me. I wait and I wait and I hope.

Then I hear rustling nearby on the stage.

"Marlena," my mother hisses. "What is taking you so long?"

I don't look at her.

Her sigh is worried. Or maybe it's angry.

The clock ticks by the seconds and minutes.

The whispering from the crowd gets louder.

My shoulders curl forward. My breaths strain against the cage of this dress. Sweat pours down the sides of my face and mixes with the tears streaming from my eyes. Before I even realize what I'm doing I'm shaking my head.

No, no, no, no, no.

The murmurs turn into talk. Words that I can make out clearly.

"What's wrong?"

"Is she okay?"

"Is this normal?"

"Maybe we should leave."

"Maybe that vacation . . ."

"Maybe the rumors . . ."

"Maybe . . ."

"Maybe . . ."

"Maybe . . ."

As the crowd speculates and fills with doubt, their doubt courses through me. They are only confirming what I've feared. I've hoped that it would happen today, that if I just showed up, my gift would show up with me. But it hasn't. And maybe it's not going to.

Maybe, *maybe, maybe.*

Maybe my gift is gone for good.

THIRTY-SEVEN

I am shaking, fingers curled tight, nails biting into the skin of my palms. I wish I could tear the lace at my neck. There is a rushing sound in my ears. Stars fill my vision and turn the world around me shiny.

The crowd is in an uproar. Some people are standing. Others are shouting for them to sit. A line of people begins to file out. I should just run backstage and end this.

But then, my eyes focus and I see an island of calm at the center of the crowd. Helen. Fatima. José. Mrs. Lewis. They watch me with hope, with steadiness, without doubt. They hold hands, lifting their wrists in a chain. Then I notice the others. Children with their families, people I don't know, who are watching me, waiting and hoping. Some of them are kneeling in the aisle. Their patience in the face of this angry crowd helps to slow my breathing. I wipe the tears from my face. Lift my chin like before.

I should at least try, shouldn't I?

I take one step forward. Then another. The crowd quiets. People settle into their seats again.

"Marlena!"

"Marlena!"

"Over here, Marlena!"

I start down from the platform and into the crowd. I lay hands on those who gather around me, the special guests my mother told me about. I kneel, I offer my blessings, I press my forehead to the backs of people's hands. I walk among the people, allowing some of them to touch my arms, even the side of my face. I go through the motions of healing, which I know by heart. I know exactly how to hold myself, the right tilt of my head, the stretch of my fingers, when to close my eyes, when to murmur, when to reach my hands to heaven.

It's just like before.

But also not like it at all. There are no visions to accompany my laying on of hands, no bursts of color, no physical tug in the parts of my body that correspond with those I am meant to heal. I am an actress acting a part, doing my best to get it right.

"Marlena, please!"

"Take my hand!"

People believe I am still Marlena the Healer. They walk away happy, relieved. Seemingly cured. Convinced that whatever I have done has helped them.

How is this possible?

Did my mother pay them to do this? Did all of us agree to participate in theater today? Or . . . is it possible that my gift is back and I just don't feel it? That it has changed so drastically I don't recognize it? That I am healing people in a new way?

"Marlena?"

A small child kneels before me. She might be four, or maybe five. Her hair is black and wiry and long. Her mother looks at me, eyes brimming with tears. So I do what I know she wants me to do. I place my hand on the little girl's head, firm and sure, and close my eyes. I wait for something, anything to happen. The shine of pink or blue or green to color my vision, the scene of some future moment. But there is nothing.

I open my eyes again.

"*Gracias*," the mother says, crying. "*¡Gracias!*"

I nod like I have actually done something, when I am just a girl laying hands on a child. It's almost worse that everyone around me believes. But belief is powerful, isn't it? Pain and grief make us desperate.

"Marlena! Over here!"

"Marlena!"

People everywhere clamor for my touch, but my eyes search the crowd for someone I'm not used to seeking out. I find my mother, and give her a look. I need her to close this down. She heads to the microphone and as she speaks, people recede and I am able to make my retreat. As I head across the platform and onto the stage, disappearing into the back room, a feeling of gratitude toward my mother spreads through me for her readiness to take control. It is not a feeling I'm used to.

"You did well," my mother says when she sees me backstage.

I lift my head from the table. The metal boning of the gown digs into my ribs. "I did?"

The smile on her face is pleased. "Yes." Her hands smooth out her expensive white skirt. "You don't agree?"

"I don't know." I shift in the chair, trying to get comfortable. This wedding dress was not made for sitting. "Were the people . . . the special guests . . . happy?"

My mother goes to the mirror and fixes her hair. A hair pin that was escaping her bun gets put in its place again. "Oh yes. Very."

"Are you sure?"

"Of course." She tames another errant hair pin. "Why would I lie?"

I go about the business of standing up. "I can think of a number of reasons why you would, Mama."

She turns away from the mirror. "Marlena!"

"Appearances are everything. Isn't it you who tells me this all the time?"

A flicker of guilt crosses her face. "What is this really about?"

"I just . . . I just didn't feel anything. But people acted like I healed them."

"And you don't think you did."

I hesitate. Then I shake my head.

She walks toward me, stops, inches away. She peers into my face. "Sometimes all people need for healing is hope." Her voice is gentle, surprising me. "You provide that hope. That is enough."

"But if I don't *really* heal them, why do they act the way they do?"

"But you do heal them, Marlena."

"I don't. I *didn't*. Not today. I know that I didn't. Before, healing felt real. Today, my gift . . . it just wasn't there."

My mother does something unexpected. She reaches out a finger to lift my chin. "Some things are best left a mystery. Some knowledge is best left to God. That's what faith is. It doesn't matter if you know for sure. You just have to believe despite this."

"But it does matter," I whisper, looking into her eyes. "It matters *a lot*."

"You're thinking of that boy who came to the house."

I don't answer.

"Oh, Marlenita." She says my name so softly. For a moment I think she might pull me into a hug. "I'm sorry about that. I really am." Her hand drops from my chin, and she straightens. "It's time to do the receiving line. People are waiting."

Again, I act my part and the crowd acts theirs. I am tempted to question each one of them, to interview them like Angie might, about what they saw me do, what they believe happened today, if anything happened, but I refrain.

Suddenly, Angie is in front of me. Just like the first time we met, which seems like a hundred years ago. "Hi," I say.

She hesitates. "Marlena, I came because . . . I didn't know how else to talk to you. I haven't been able to get in touch with you. Why won't you see me or answer my calls?"

I force myself to hold her gaze. "I'm sorry, but I just . . . can't. I made a promise not to." I don't mention that the promise is to God.

"Okay," she says. It doesn't sound like she believes me. "But . . . how can you refuse to see Finn? If I'd known, I never would have involved myself. Marlena, he's—"

I put up my hand. "Angie, don't. Please." I glance at the man behind her in the line, waiting less and less patiently. "It's more than I can explain right now."

"Come by the center and explain it to me there," Angie says, a little defiant.

I shake my head. "No."

"This is not you, Marlena." She sounds angry. No, worse. She sounds disappointed. "The you I've gotten to know would not act like this. She would not refuse her friends and the people she loves. And who love her," she adds quietly.

I grip the skirt of the gown and hold on tight. "But it is me. This is how things have always been. You just knew me in a strange time." My voice catches. "And that time is over."

Angie stands there, words brimming on her lips. I wait for more admonishment. But just before she walks away, she says, "I am here for you, no matter what. If there is anything you need, or even anything you still want to know about yourself. I haven't given up on you, Marlena." She hesitates. "And neither has Finn."

THIRTY-EIGHT

The days turn into weeks that turn into months.

Every morning I get up out of bed, empty and tired. I look around my room, searching, as though God may have left me a note during the night. But nothing is ever different. No lightning strikes in the remaining hours of the morning. It's always just me, alone, in my uncertainty. In my regret.

The air gets cold with the onset of winter. On the first day of December snowflakes hover in the air.

Every Saturday I perform for my audience. Every Saturday I go through the motions. The offerings come into the house and are stored in the gift room. At the end of the month they are donated to Goodwill. Gertie was true to her word about changing her wares, though the shift downtown is gradual. Tourists come looking for souvenirs and snatch up whatever remains at the stores that still sell them.

People act as though my touch still heals. Has it come back, even if I don't feel it? Why would people behave this way if nothing really happened? Or is my mother right, that it doesn't matter whether I feel proof of healing like I used to? Maybe God needs me to take a leap of faith, to trust that though my gift remains invisible to me, it is still there.

But that sort of test just seems cruel.

Until I can *feel* my gift, until I *know* it's there, I can't go to Finn. I can't do that to him. It wouldn't be fair.

"Thank you for coming to get me, José," I say, when I walk out of the house and see him standing there by the car.

"Ten a.m. sharp, just like always, Marlenita."

I slip into the back seat. Alone. My mother has stopped accompanying me everywhere. I try not to notice José glancing at me in the rearview mirror as he drives me where we are going and parks in front.

He hands me an umbrella when I get out of the car. "I'll be here, waiting."

I can feel his eyes on my back, watching as I head inside the visitors' entrance of the hospital. The antiseptic smell of the air is familiar to me now, the fluorescent lighting, the shiny tiled floors and long hallways.

The Healer has started doing house calls.

It started because of a letter I received from a mother whose six-year-old son, Jacob, was in the hospital with leukemia. The hospital was close, only a twenty-minute drive. One day I just got in the car and went. Found his room and his mother, sitting there next to him. She was so happy I came, I talked to her, to Jacob, held their hands. I don't know if my touch healed or not, but I know it mattered to them that I showed up. So I kept going.

Keep going.

First was Jacob, then there were Aurora, Sarena, Dante, Ethan, Diego, Gabby, and Laurel. The list goes on. In the beginning it was penance, it was practice for Finn, it was the hope of the feeling of healing returning. But now, I'm not so sure what compels me. I see the people who've written me, and I see their doctors. I watch the medics and nurses come and go, study the things they do, the pills offered, the machines and bags of fluid adjusted. The kind words, the brusque manners, the hope they bring, the way they are needed by the sick and the suffering.

Are we somehow the same? Is there any connection between what the nurses and doctors do and what I do? These questions grow louder with each visit. Hildegard was a visionary and a doctor, a medicine woman in her day. Could I be another kind of healer, too?

"Can you tell me how to find room 302?" I ask the nurse at the reception desk.

She stands and points. "Down the hall to the left, take the bank of elevators to the third floor, turn right, and go all the way to the end."

"Thank you," I tell her, and try to remember the directions.

When I get to the room, I'm nervous.

Today's visit is special.

I knock.

"Come in," calls a voice.

I go inside.

A short woman who is all soft edges gets up to greet me. "Marlena! I'm Valeria." Valeria's face is round and friendly. Her voice is reverent. "I can't believe you're here. After all this waiting. Thank you."

"I'm glad I could come, but you need to know, I can't make any promises."

"But I have faith that you will save my daughter!"

"Mama! Stop!"

My eyes go to the bed. I see a girl with dark wavy hair and big brown eyes. A thick metal-and-plastic brace is like a box around her torso. Her arms are thin, and from the outline of her legs underneath the blanket, they are thinner. "Hi, Alma," I say. "It's good to finally meet you."

"I can't believe you're here, either." Alma glances at her mother. "Though not for the same reasons as Mama's."

"*Alma, ¡no seas así!*"

Alma gives her mother a pleading look. "*¿Nos dejas un minuto a solas? ¿Mama?*"

Valeria inhales. I can tell she's about to protest her daughter's request to give us time alone. "I work better that way," I say, before Valeria can speak.

"I'll be in the hall then," she says, grabbing her sweater and hurrying out.

When the door shuts I sit down in the chair next to Alma's bed. "I've appreciated your letters."

Alma's eyes drop to my hands, which rest on the railing of the bed. "So you decided you wanted to come fix me?"

"I meant what I said to your mother, that I'm not sure if I can."

"Don't you want to try?"

The brace Alma wears looks so uncomfortable. It's difficult not to wish for her to be free of it. "Do you want me to?"

Alma blinks her long lashes, breathing labored. She reaches out and places her hands on top of mine. "It's what my mother needs."

"Okay." I close my eyes, draw Alma's hand to my cheek. Wait, as I always do, for that feeling in me to stir. Sometimes I think it might be there, just waking up after a long sleep, yawning its way back into my veins. Plenty of gifts of gratitude have arrived at the house, alongside claims of miracles.

So why do I continue to feel nothing?

"Marlena?"

I lift my head. Alma is watching me, eyes curious. *Like Finn.* I draw in a breath. "Yes?"

"Are you okay?"

Alma's concern reaches around my heart. Suddenly my arms are around her boxy brace and I am hugging her. "I don't know," I find myself saying. I pull back. "Not really."

"You seem sad."

"I am sad."

"Why?"

Alma's statements, her questions, are straightforward. Spoken so simply and honestly. I can't help but answer. "Someone I love is sick. His name is Finn."

"I'm sorry. I know that it's hard to love someone who is sick."

I study Alma. We are nearly the same age. I am grateful she didn't ask me why I don't heal Finn and make things better. "It is the hardest thing I've ever known."

Alma sighs the sigh of someone far older than her years. "It's so hard on my mother."

"Did I . . . did I help?"

"I don't know. I don't really feel any different." Alma adjusts her blanket. The hospital air is thick with a stifling heat. "Do you think you helped?"

I shrug. "I'm not a doctor, Alma. I don't know the answer. I wish I did."

"You don't know how your gift works?"

This is the question, right? How *does* it work? How did it, if it's gone?

"I used to think I understood it, but lately, I don't know anymore. Maybe it's real. But maybe it never was."

"Maybe it all depends on the person you're healing," she says.

"What do you mean?"

"Maybe it takes two people to make a miracle. You might be the one to initiate it, but maybe the other person has to meet you halfway and finish it. Maybe you didn't heal me because I don't need you to."

This theory swirls in the heavy air. I try to take it in. "But why wouldn't you want to be healed, Alma?"

Alma takes a labored breath. "Because I'm tired of people trying to fix me. I've accepted my death and I'm ready for it."

It is true—even with all the tubes and the beeping machines, Alma radiates a sense of peace. "But your mother . . ."

Now her eyes become sad. "I wish she could accept this reality, and accept my life, and its end, for what it is. I don't mean to hurt her. And I know she doesn't mean to hurt me. Love is complicated that way."

"It is," I tell her. "Alma, thank you."

This makes her laugh. "For what?"

"For your wisdom."

"You're funny," she says. "I'm glad you came to see me."

I stand up, memorizing everything I can about Alma's face, her open expression, the swoop of her hair and the shape of her body beneath the brace and the blanket. "I'm glad I did, too. Twice now, you've been there for me when I needed understanding."

Alma's smile is weak. "It's nice to know that you are real."

"It's nice to know you are, too." My last words come out hoarse. I turn to go. The reality that Alma will not be there for us to meet again goes unspoken between us.

José drops me off at the seawall instead of taking me home. I want to walk. I stare out at the ocean, the beach, at the way the dark gray clouds collide with the horizon. No one is around except for a few surfers, straddling their boards, bobbing up and down over the swells.

It's been nearly three months since I said good-bye to Finn.

Months.

Finn only has months left to live.

Months. Not years. *Months, months, months.*

Three have passed.

What are you doing, Marlena?

This voice, the voice of doubt, is suddenly contradicting all that I've done, the constant bargaining with the God who never stops punishing. The God I don't even like.

The God I don't even believe in.

Why should I?

Why would I give such a terrible God so much power?

Why would anyone?

All this time, I have been drowning in darkness, waiting for God to turn the lights on again, to return my gift and make me whole again. Turning to some divine asshole for forgiveness I don't even want, because maybe I didn't do anything wrong in the first place. Maybe it's God that's wrong. Maybe that's been the problem this whole time.

My whole, sheltered life.

I wonder if Hildegard, or Julian, or any of them ever felt any relief that in those dark nights of the soul they were finally free of God's grasp, of the responsibility their visions brought to their lives. If they did, they kept it to themselves.

Snow starts to fall. Flakes of it cling to my eyelashes and melt against my cheeks. I walk through it, veer right. At first I don't realize where I'm going, my feet taking over.

But I walk and walk for miles until I am tired and sore, and then I am there and I know.

I stop in front of the house. Study it in a way I couldn't when I was a child.

The snow is falling heavier now.

Why haven't I returned here before? Why hasn't my mother taken me?

The little cottage has white siding, some of it eaten away with age. Forest-green metal shades arc outward from the windows. A big wooden swing hangs on the porch, tilted and in need of repair. The gray shingles on the roof are blackened with age and neglect. The grass has been regularly cut, but the bushes along the front are so wide and tall they nearly cover the windows. There is nothing remarkable to distinguish this place from the other houses around it, save the disrepair. And the fact that my grandfather built it with his own hands when my family came here from the Azores, when my mother was still just a girl, her whole life ahead of her, unknown and still unfolding.

My feet take me forward again, this time up to the windows. I wedge myself between the overgrown bushes and wipe a hand across the glass. It comes away smeared with dirt. I peer inside.

Everything is there, just as I remember it. My grandmother's figurines. The shelves my grandfather built. The chairs and the furniture he shaped and sanded and pieced together in an effort to make this modest cottage a home for their new life in America. It's just that the carpet is caked with mildew and the figurines are covered in a thick coat of dust. From here I can see into the kitchen in the back. The plates stacked on the shelves above the sink. Pots and pans hanging from the ceiling.

How would life have been different if I'd grown up here? If my grandparents had never died? If my father hadn't either? If my mother had never had to mourn them? Would I have grown up a healer, or something else entirely? Would I be happier if I had?

THIRTY-NINE

"You have to be totally still, Marlena," Angie warns. "No touching the insides."

My heart is hammering. "But—"

"Do not move a muscle. I mean it."

"Okay." The ceiling of Angie's center is far above, the light around us a strange, bright gray from the snow and the pale white sky. She's wearing a thick cable-knit sweater and jeans, her hair in a messy knot.

I am in a wedding dress.

"Are you ready?" Angie asks.

"Yes," I tell her.

Soon the machine is on and whirring and Angie is blocked from view as the platform where I lie moves. For the second time I enter the hulking, curved chamber, this human-made cave. I am as unmoving as I can be while still breathing, and while I listen to all the loud banging and knocking and whirring of the machine. The seconds tick by, tick toward the hour of my Saturday audience. I am supposed to be there right now. José and I didn't talk in the car, he didn't ask why we were headed to Angie's center instead of the church where my mother is waiting for me to appear right now. But when I got out of the car in front of Angie's big glass box of a building for the first time in ages, doing my best not to step on the lavish white gown billowing around my legs, he spoke to me.

"Marlenita, take as long as you need" was all he said. "I'll be right here, waiting for you. I'm not going anywhere. No matter what."

It was like he was telling me to consider not showing up for my audience. That he would be fine helping to facilitate just this. I bet my mother is going crazy, wondering where I am. People will be arriving. What will she do? Will she cancel? Will she wait until the last minute, hoping I'll show up?

Will I show up?

There's still time.

The machine shuts off and I am sliding into the lab again. I blink, trying to adjust to the light, and sit up. The skirt of my gown is wrinkled from lying down. Angie is already walking away.

"Give me a few minutes to read the results," she calls over her shoulder, then disappears down the hall and into the room with the screens that light up the brain scans.

Angie has been all business since I arrived. Like she's afraid if she says something too intimate, too pushy, I'll flee and never come back. She didn't even comment on my attire, or make a joke about how I am overdressed for an MRI. The skirt of the gown rustles as I swing my legs over the side of the platform. Carefully, I climb down. I pad off barefoot to wait in Angie's office. The light is different in wintertime, with the sun gone and the snow covering the ground to the sea.

I sit down on the couch. Ten minutes pass. Then fifteen.

When I can't stand it any longer, I get up and knock on the door of the lab. Angie opens it. "What's taking so long? Can I see my scan?" She moves aside so I can enter. On the big screen in the middle are several brain images, lit up bright. "Are all of these me?"

Angie nods.

I walk up to the one in the center. It is drenched in purple and I am struck, even more than before, by how similar it is to one of my visions. I point at it. "What does this color tell you about me?"

"That you're terribly sad, Marlena."

I drop my arm. "Well, that's true." I try not to be disappointed that the color's significance is so ordinary. That it doesn't somehow confirm my brain is unusual, the brain only a healer could claim. I gesture at another scan with a big round image in black and white. If I could paint it, it would be an oak tree, its trunk nearly obscured by its leafy branches. I wish I could read the scan like a scientist would. Or a doctor. "And that one?"

The knot in Angie's hair is sliding to the side, coming undone. "Why don't we go back to my office and talk about it there?"

She is stalling. "What aren't you telling me, Angie?" I ask as I follow her.

Angie takes her usual position, cross-legged on the rug. When I am once again sitting on the couch, she starts talking.

"Marlena," she begins. "Your brain, it's . . . ," she goes on, then stops. Her mouth opens again. Nothing comes out.

I hold my breath. I want to know if Angie has found something in my brain, some mark she can point to that distinguishes my brain from others. For the first time in my life I want scientific proof that I am different. Or scientific proof that I am not. "What?"

Angie shakes her head, slowly. "Your brain is totally normal," she says. "I didn't see one thing that was unusual. Your brain is perfect. Healthy."

I stand up again, then I sit.

I'm not sure how to process this. Angie has informed me of the very thing I'd longed to hear—until I found out about Finn. That I am normal. "Really."

Angie crosses and recrosses her legs. "You're upset."

I shake my head. "No. I don't know." I wonder if the machine would have showed something different about my brain if I'd done this in August. Would we have before and after pictures for comparison? *Before Marlena Quit Healing* and *After Marlena Quit Healing*? Could we literally see the difference, scientifically document it? Or is it that my brain has always been this way, and healing is more like what Alma suggested, a union of two people, of two matching desires? Or even what my mother suggested, a simple passing of hope from my body into the body of the person who needs it?

I guess I'll never know.

"You're surprised," I tell Angie.

"I am," Angie says.

"Why? What did you imagine you'd see?"

"Honestly?" Angie pulls apart the knot in her hair, then starts fixing it up all over again. Soon the knot is neat on the top of her head once more. She gets up and comes to the couch to sit next to me. "Marlena, I thought I'd find a tumor."

I nod. "Are you disappointed you didn't?"

"No! How can you even think that? I would never wish a brain tumor on you! Or anyone." She is studying me. "But are *you* disappointed I didn't find one?"

"I don't know. It would have explained a lot, right? The visions, the colors. The fainting spells. That's why you suspected one."

"Yes," she admits.

"It's not like I haven't wondered," I admit back. "My mother never allowed anyone to check. I've never been to a doctor."

Angie gets up and cracks a window. The icy air feels good amid the heat of the building. "I know. I remember you telling me that one of the first times we met in this office. I've been worried ever since. It's a relief, Marlena, to find out that you have a perfectly healthy brain. Tell me how you feel about hearing this."

I pull my knees to my chest and wrap my arms tight around

my shins. "Well, brain tumors, epilepsy, migraines, are what some people believe explains the visions of mystics. Any sort of brain abnormality that might cause hallucinations. Today we don't think of what happens to me, what *used to* happen to me, as real. We only think of visions as delusions. Or girls who perform miracles as crazy people."

Angie is still studying me. What is she hoping to see? To figure out?

"Did you think I'm delusional, Angie? Or do you think it even more now that you've seen my brain?"

She doesn't answer this question. Instead, she says, "You wanted a reason to believe in yourself, didn't you—a concrete, scientific explanation for your visions?"

I shake my head, then I shrug. "I don't know what's true anymore. People act like I can still heal, you know . . . after . . . these last months . . . but I don't feel my gift. It's gone. Poof." I snap my fingers. "Like it was never there. I've been going to see people in the hospital. I've been watching these doctors and nurses and trying to understand what they do, and seeing how different it is from my healings, but how similar too. Tell me the truth, Angie. After all your research, what did you conclude? Am I a healer or not? Or was it always just one big wish?" I stare out through the window at the falling snow and the ocean behind it.

I feel Angie's arm slide around me.

"I know this is about Finn," she says. "It's not your fault that he's sick and it's not your responsibility to heal him. It never was, and he never thought that it was. He doesn't think that now either. Neither do I. No one does."

Her mention of Finn makes my eyes fill. "I keep thinking . . . this whole time I keep thinking . . . if I'd just . . . if I'd just . . ."

"If you'd just what, Marlena? Never come to my office and met him? Never cared for him at all? Never tried to live a little?" She sighs. "There's no way to prove beyond a shadow of a doubt whether your gift is 'real,' as you put it, or was. Not scientifically. Not in the way you wish for. I can do all the interviews in the world with every single person who believes to be healed by you, before Finn, after Finn, but that still doesn't mean you will be able to heal him. And if you can't, I would never be able to pinpoint why that is."

"What I can't do," I whisper, tears starting to spill down my cheeks, "is accept that he might die. That he *will* die. I don't know how."

Angie takes my hand. "Oh, honey. You have to. This is life, the hardest part of it, but it is life. Your life. His life. You can't turn away from it."

I stare at her fingers on mine. I try to breathe. "I need to go find the bathroom. I need . . . I need a minute."

"I'll be right here," Angie says. "Take your time."

I get up and leave her office, her words swirling through me like the snow outside. I head down the hall and round the corner. Then I come to a halt.

Finn.

There he is. After all this time.

His face pales as he takes me in, dressed in a wedding gown. "Marlena, what are you doing here—" and "—I didn't expect you to be here today," the two of us blurt at the same time.

We stand there, looking at each other. I know I can't accept a world without Finn, and I know that I have to try to heal him again, to keep trying. How can I not? What do I have to lose? What does Finn? I go to him and take his hand, grab it, because he resists.

"Marlena, no."

I refuse to let it go, pull it to my cheek and press it there. Close my eyes and wait. I pray and I hope and I pray some more. But just like before, I am dry inside. Colorless. When I open my eyes, tears are streaming down my face and down Finn's as well. "Did anything happen?" I ask him. "Did you feel anything change?" I hear how pathetic I sound. "Because maybe, the people at my audiences . . . they seem to think that . . . that I can still heal. . . ." I think of what Alma said. "Maybe it's not working because of *you*. You need to try, too. Maybe I can only heal if you want to be healed. Finn, Finn?"

He is shaking his head.

I can feel him pulling back his hand.

This only makes me hold on harder.

"Please?" My eyes are raised toward the windows of the center, toward the cold gray sky above. "Just one more time. I will do anything. Give anything. *Everything*."

"Marlena." Finn's tone is decisive. "You have to stop."

"I can't," I sob. "I can't, I can't, I *can't*."

He peers into my tear-filled eyes. "Yes, you can. I need you to."

I shake my head. My nose is running. I don't even care. What does it matter? What does anything matter if I can't save Finn?

"I'm okay with this," he says.

I stare up at him, sniffling. Wiping at my cheeks. "You're okay with *what*?"

"With . . . my situation."

"With *dying*?"

There. The word is out. Between us. Gleaming.

"Yes, with dying," Finn says quietly.

"But, but *how*? Why? You can't be! You're too young!" I choke out words between sobs. "You're so smart! You're supposed to change the world! You're a genius!"

You're mine, I think, and sob harder.

He takes my hands and holds them lightly in his. "But this is my life. It's the only life I have. The doctors can't do anything else. I have to accept this. So do you."

"No." I am shaking my head back and forth. He sounds just like Alma.

"Yes."

"It's not enough."

"Marlena," he says. His hands tighten around mine. "It has to be."

"But what if—"

"No more what-ifs, no more begging God to help you save me. No more trading with God, your life for mine. No more promising God you'll never sleep with me again so that you may be able to heal me. No more regretting our time together because maybe God is punishing you for it. *No more.*" Emotion thunders across his face. "I do not *give a shit* what you told God you'd do in order to save me or whatever it is you promised that good-for-nothing deity people are always promising things to. What I care about is what you promise *me*. Right now, during my last days on this planet."

I've nearly stopped breathing. "What do you want me to promise you?"

"I want you to promise to love me until the very end. Like you did before all this—" He sweeps a hand across my white dress.

"You want me to love you," I whisper. "That's all you want?"

Finn nods. "That, to me, is plenty. More than enough."

"And in loving you, you also want me to give up on you? While you give up on you, too?"

"It's not giving up," he says. "It's a choice to live."

"No," I say forcefully. "It's a choice to *die*."

"If you want to look at it that way, that's your decision. But in my mind, it's choosing to live every one of the last days I have with the person I love the most in the world. Which is you. What more could I ask for in life?"

More days. More years.

Finn takes my hands again. "Promise me, Marlena," he says. "Please? I need you to stop trying to heal me. I want you to accept me the way that I am. I want you to accept that the best thing for me to do right now is to enjoy the time I have left."

"I don't know if I can." I close my eyes. The press of Finn's fingers on my skin causes my heart to skip and stutter.

A vision starts right then. I haven't had one in so long that I nearly don't recognize it. It reaches out to me like the hand of an old friend and I take it, eagerly, letting it spread through my body and my heart and my mind like a salve, wondering if maybe this is it, the moment when I am going to heal Finn. But then it's not like the visions from before all of this started, from my audiences during a healing. This vision is more of a memory.

In it, I see the beach and the wet sand, smell the warm air and the bright-blue sky. I see the gentle, crystal waves of the sea swelling toward me. There I am in my bathing suit, alone, the remnants of a toppled dribble castle on my legs, asking so many questions— what-ifs about God and the world and God versus the world. And then, as I get up and wade into the water, one foot in front of the other, I am making a decision that the world is enough for me, that this one glorious day is enough for me, that the promise of seeing Finn is enough for me. I am deciding I don't need anything more than that, *this*. Me. Finn. What is right in front of me, here and now.

I open my eyes and find myself deciding this once again. I want what is right in front of me now, for however long it is mine to have.

And that is enough. It has to be. Finn is not just enough, he is *more* than enough.

Finn blinks back at me, waiting for my answer.

"Finn," I begin, slowly, carefully, knowing that each word, each syllable matters. "You are right. Every day I have with you is more than I've ever hoped for." He steps forward and curls into my chest, pulls my arms around his body, and we stay there, holding each other. I whisper one more thing, as though it's a prayer, a holy vow, the most loving of promises, because Finn deserves to hear this truth from my lips. "I promise to never let you go. Not for another second that you have on this earth. For all of those I will be with you, until the very last one."

And I am.

Four months later

PART FOUR

Now & Then

FORTY

The day of the funeral is sunny and warm. One of the first nice days of spring. The snow is gone; the air smells like grass and flowers. The ocean sparkles with light.

We gather at the beach to remember him. Angie, of course. Helen. Fatima and José. Friends of Finn's from graduate school. Finn's mother, who I had the fortune of meeting during his last months alive—estrangement makes no sense at the end, I guess. Finn was loved, this much is clear. But there are other people here, people I didn't expect. People who came for me. Mrs. Lewis. Gertie. The Almeidas and some of the other shop owners from Main Street. A lot can change in a few months.

Everything, really.

We stand there on the rocks as the sun rises in the sky. We laugh and we cry, and after everyone has said what they need to say, Angie, Finn's mother, and I spread Finn's ashes into the sea.

When it is my turn to let Finn go, I stare out onto the water for a while. And I talk to him. I don't care if I seem crazy or strange. Finn is with me still, and I don't need to see him to know this, to take that leap of faith. I feel it in my heart and soul and mind and all throughout my body. I still don't know what I believe, exactly, with regard to miracles and gods, but I know that I believe in this world and the people in it. I believe that love and loving others is the most important part, the one command we must obey if we are going to think in those terms. I know that the people here on this beautiful morning have taught me this. Flesh-and-blood people who are ready with a hand, a hug, a soothing touch, to reassure me that this much is real. Finn, most of all, taught me this. How to love and how to give myself over to a life of love. I will be forever grateful for this lesson.

"I love you, Finn," I say out loud. "Thank you for every minute." I let the last of Finn's ashes be taken by the breeze, and I watch as they float out toward the sea.

Angie glances at me as we walk toward the cars parked on the side of the road. "I've never known anyone like Finn," she says, with a sad smile. "He was exceptional. So smart."

I smile a little. "I know."

We grow silent. Our arms brush as we walk. My days of no touching are over. I welcome the reassurance of so much humanity.

Something catches my eye.

At first I think I am seeing things.

Then I realize that no, it's definitely her. My mother came to the funeral. Her back is to me and she is about to vanish around the curve of the road. But before she turns I catch her gaze.

Tears sting my eyes. I've spent a lot of angry tears because of my mother, but these are strangely hopeful. In her expression I see something I've longed to see but never have. Or maybe I've never let myself. There is an understanding there on her face that can only come from having known the pain of grief herself. If there is anything my mother knows, it is loss.

Maybe there is hope for my mother and me.

"Bye, Marlena," Angie says when she reaches the car. "Don't be a stranger."

I nod. Then watch as she drives away.

The end came fast for Finn, but it was also slow.

It's difficult to explain what it's like, to be with someone so constantly during the last days of their life, until they take their last breath, especially when that person is someone you love. I used to think that describing my visions was hard, talking about what it was like to heal, but even that doesn't compare. How could mere words capture the extraordinary beauty that is, *was*, the life of Finn? His last days? The two of us together?

We moved into my grandparents' house.

The two of us worked fixing it up. We dusted and polished my grandmother's things, cleaned the kitchen, the shelves, the workshop where my grandfather had his carpentry business in the basement, still full of his old tools. We found his sign for it there, the letters hand stenciled with a pencil, his name *Manuel Oliveira* painted tall and proud at the top, the word CARPENTRY in all caps underneath it. Finn set the sign on one of the shelves in the living room.

All during that winter, we lit fires in the fireplace, and we cooked dinner as the snow fell during a blizzard. He told me about his life growing up in Oregon, how he discovered his love of the brain and decided to become a scientist. I told Finn about my mother's stories of my grandparents, about growing up on São Miguel in the middle of the Atlantic, and then immigrating to America, and trying to make a life here.

"I wish I could get to know your mother," Finn said once.

"I wish I could get to know yours," I said to him back.

Finn looked away. He and I were so similar in so many ways. Even the painful ones.

We had visitors. Fatima and José. Helen and Sonia. Angie, of course. One afternoon, José came over with something I asked him to retrieve from my mother's house. It took some effort to get it through the door.

"Okay, Marlenita." José offered me a quick kiss on the cheek and gave a wave to Finn. "I hope I got the right one," he called out as he shut the door behind him.

I took the thin rectangular package and brought it to the couch where Finn was sitting. "I made this for you. Because of us," I told him.

Finn peeled back the brown paper wrapping.

"Marlena," he breathed. "What is this?"

The two of us held it there, looking at it together. Thick swirls of red and pink and white danced across the canvas, abstract peonies bursting in their bright and dizzy glory.

I got up and propped the painting against the wall. "You know how I've always painted my visions." I let my eyes settle on his. "I painted this because of us. It's my vision of loving you, of being with you, of us together."

"It's beautiful," Finn said.

That night, he took the tools from my grandfather's workshop and hung the painting on the wall of the living room so we would always see it.

It's still hanging there today.

I live alone now, in my grandparents' house. When the weather is warm I sit on the porch swing that Finn fixed for me. Remembering him, and us together.

"We make an ironic pair," I told him once.

It was mid-February, just after Valentine's Day. I'd filled the cottage walls with paper collage hearts. I'd never had a valentine before.

"How so?" he asked me.

"I'm a washed-up healer dating a dying boy." I tried for a laugh. It came out a sob.

Finn didn't laugh either. "Don't think like that."

"But it's true," I said, then changed the subject.

I learned a lot of things about Finn while we lived together. Like the fact that when Finn was still alive, he slept like the dead. Not funny, I know, but also true. Every night we spent in this house, I would wait for Finn to fall asleep. Then, quietly and ever so slowly, I would place my hand on his chest, right over the smooth skin that covered his ribs, slightly to the right, until I felt the pulse of his heart underneath my palm.

And then, I would call upon my gift.

I called and I waited. Called and waited.

Again and again, I tried to heal Finn, even though he made me promise I wouldn't. I couldn't help myself. How could I not at least try? What Finn didn't know wouldn't hurt him, I decided. But my knowing that I gave up would hurt me.

Eventually, I would retract my hand.

I still don't know why I couldn't heal Finn. Maybe I never will. Maybe that is just life. Normal life.

It's what I always wanted, isn't it?

Then one night, late in March, I had a vision. That charm of mine, the charm that is my gift, was suddenly, magically, back in my pocket. One palm closed around it, tight, while the other pressed into Finn, seeking the heart within his chest.

First came the pain that filled up my body, and the exhaustion that forced my eyes closed. But soon I was awash in colors, so many colors.

At first they were only shades of gray, but I fought beyond this darkness to the brighter shades, the reds and the pinks and the vibrant roses. I settled into this vision like the comfiest of chairs, like going home after the longest of absences. That's when the scenes came to me, came for me, and I was content to see all that was there, to watch as hope bloomed under my fingertips. One after the other I saw them, scenes of Finn and me on the beach, of Finn and me with friends, of Finn cooking dinner while I watched over his shoulder, of Finn and me walking through the snow, through the rain, through the neighborhood where my grandparents and mother once lived and where I live now, of Finn and me talking late into the night as we lay in bed. It was a moment of true ecstasy, of union between our souls. I don't know how many scenes I experienced before I realized what every single one of them had in common.

I retracted my hand.

They were all scenes from the past.

I swallowed around the thick lump in my throat. Watched the labored breathing of the boy I loved, the rise and fall of his chest.

I should feel consoled, I suppose.

Even after everything, I am still a visionary.

❖ ❖ ❖

Sometimes I wonder what would happen if the girl I used to be knelt down to take the hand of the girl I am today. The one who walks the beach on this evening, looking out at the sea.

What would that girl see and feel if she pressed her forehead to my skin, against the back of my hand? Would the vision start in the heart like so many others? Or might it begin in the chambers of the soul, darkened by grief? Would there be colors, and if so, which ones? Would the scenes she saw be an endless stretch of emptiness, or would they be laced with a love that carries a person forward, like an endless swell across the ocean?

There are some people who will never forgive me for letting the healer that I was go. They send bags of letters saying I shouldn't have given her up, that I owed the world more miracles and that I turned away from the responsibility that comes with being a living saint. There are people who believe I was rightly punished by God by having to face the loss of someone I love. By not being able to save him. That being unable to save Finn is a fitting payment for the lives I have taken.

But there is one thing I know, and that is that I do not regret Finn.

I could never.

"I thought I was protecting you," my mother said the other day, nearly at this very same spot on the beach where I stand now.

She and I are speaking again. Or trying to.

"I knew that I wouldn't be around forever, but the church, your gift, the house, the money, your legacy as a healer, they would still be there for you after I was gone."

I nodded. I've been doing my best to understand my mother's logic, because she's been doing her best to explain it to me.

"But you're still here," I said.

"And your Finn isn't," she said back. "I'm sorry for that."

"I know, Mama."

"Remember what you promised, Marlena," Finn said to me during one of the last days we shared together. He took my hand into his across the table.

His was shaking.

Not long before, I'd told Finn a secret.

"I've been thinking that maybe I'll become a doctor," I said.

We were tangled together on the porch swing, under a blanket. It creaked as it moved.

"A doctor like Angie? A doctor like . . ." Finn trailed off.

Like me. That's what he was going to say but didn't.

"Not like Angie," I told him. "Like, in a hospital."

Finn tightened his arms around me. "So the healing kind."

"Yes," I said. "You know, Hildegard was a medicine woman. She studied herbs and plants. She cared about healing the bodies of her fellow nuns."

"I did not know that."

I laughed. "I've always admired her. I used to kind of wish I was more like her than like Julian." I thought about my self-portrait on the wall of the living room in my mother's house, wondering what new one I might paint if I was to try again. "And then, I keep dreaming about those brain scans, the way they remind me of my visions. Maybe they were . . . are . . . a sign of sorts."

"Look at me," Finn said.

I shook my head.

"Marlena, come on."

Slowly, I shifted so I could meet Finn's eyes.

"You shouldn't be embarrassed," he said. "I think it's perfect."

The next day when Finn came home, he had a present for me. "You have to promise me you'll use this someday."

I looked at the gift he'd placed on the table. It was wrapped in bright pink paper, the same pink of the peonies in the painting on the wall of the living room. "What is it?"

"Just open it."

I removed the paper carefully, and opened the box inside. Took out what was waiting for me.

"Do you like it?" he wanted to know.

I nodded. Held it up in my hands. Finn helped to put it around my neck. I picked up the round metal circle that dangled like a heavy charm down the front of my chest and pressed it against Finn's. And I listened.

I looked into his eyes, heard the thump of his heart quicken.

"It's perfect," I told him.

Finn gave me a stethoscope.

❖ ❖ ❖

I am twenty. It's October. The trees are a fiery red and orange and yellow. It's drizzling outside, the leaves wet and sticking to my shoes. I don't care.

Big thick textbooks are hugged to my chest.

I am a college student.

The campus is buzzing with people hurrying to the cafeteria. To class. To the library. To their residence halls.

"Hi, Professor Carse," I say when I enter the biology lab.

"Marlena," she says, nodding.

Professor Carse doesn't smile much. She's all business, so unlike Angie. But she's also all brilliance, so very like Angie.

I take my seat on the stool by the tall black table I share with Kelsey, another first-year student. She is my lab partner. My books land with a loud thump. "They should give us carts to carry these things around."

Kelsey laughs. "Speak for yourself. The late nights and lack of partying are enough to distinguish us premed people, I think."

"Probably," I say, laughing along with her.

Kelsey and I are becoming friends.

My first friend at college.

My mother was wrong about so many things, but she was right about this:

I was born to heal.

Knitting together the bones of the body, the muscles, the flesh, ridding a person of what ails them, soothing the pain in people's hearts and minds, is what I am called to do, what I have always been called to do.

But Fatima was right, too. It's possible to be both things, to both have a life and use one's gifts, to be a person of faith and a person of science. If there is anything I've learned over this last, complicated year of love and of loss, it is this:

There are many ways to be a healer.